"Hold your noise!" cried a terrible voice.

"Keep still, you little devil, or I'll cut your throat!" . . .

"O! Don't cut my throat, sir," I pleaded in terror. "Pray don't do it, sir."

"Tell us your name!" said the man. "Quick!"

"Pip, sir."

"Once more," said the man, staring at me. "Say it clear!"

"Pip. Pip, sir."

"Show us where you live," said the man. "Point out the place!"

I pointed to where our village lay, a mile or more from the church.

The man, after looking at me for a moment, turned me upside down, and emptied my pockets. There was nothing in them but a piece of bread. Roughly, he placed me on a high tombstone, trembling, while he ate the bread ravenously.

"You young dog," said the man, licking his lips, "what fat cheeks you ha' got. Darn me if I couldn't eat 'em," said the man, with a threatening shake of his head.

A Background Note about *Great Expectations*

Charles Dickens wrote *Great Expectations* in 1860–1861. At that time, young men (and some young women) did not go to school to learn a trade. Instead, like Pip at the beginning of the story, they apprenticed themselves to master craftsmen. The apprentice would sign a contract legally binding him to work for a specific length of time, usually seven years. In return, the master would teach him; provide food, shelter, and clothing; and care for him if he became sick. After the time was up, he could either become a journeyman, working for a master for wages, or try his luck as a master. Today's interns are the modern equivalent of apprentices.

Later in *Great Expectations*, we learn that one of the characters has spent many years in New South Wales, Australia. In nineteenth-century Great Britain, some individuals convicted of crimes were sent—or "transported"—to the British possession of Australia. Depending on the sentence handed down by the British courts, some of these convicts served their time and were then released from jail. They were then free to earn their living in any lawful manner of their own choosing. Some of these former convicts, in fact, accumulated considerable fortunes, and many well-to-do Australians today can trace their ancestry back to them. However, British law prohibited, upon pain of death, any convict transported to Australia from ever returning to Great Britain. This prohibition applied even to those convicts who had served their sentences. They could live as they chose in Australia, but they could not return to Great Britain. If they did return—and if they were captured—they would pay with their lives.

Great Expectations

CHARLES DICKENS

Edited, and with an Afterword,
by Martin E. Goldstein

TP THE TOWNSEND LIBRARY

GREAT EXPECTATIONS

TP THE TOWNSEND LIBRARY

For more titles in the Townsend Library,
visit our website: **www.townsendpress.com**

Printed in the United States of America

0 9 8 7 6 5 4 3

Townsend Press, Inc.
439 Kelley Drive
West Berlin, New Jersey 08091
cs@townsendpress.com

ISBN-13: 978-1-59194-060-9
ISBN-10: 1-59194-060-5

Library of Congress Control Number:
2005936325

CONTENTS

VOLUME 1

VOLUME 2

VOLUME 3

AFTERWORD

VOLUME I

I was born Philip Pirrip. As a small child, I found it impossible to pronounce my name correctly. My name always came out Pip. And so I became known as Pip.

I never saw my mother or my father or the five little brothers that preceded me. What I know about them I learned from my sister, Mrs. Joe Gargery, who married the blacksmith. I did visit them regularly, however, for they were buried in a nearby churchyard.

We lived in the marsh country, by the river, twenty miles from the sea. One raw afternoon toward evening, I was standing in the churchyard where my parents and brothers were buried. Beyond lay the marshes, a dark flat wilderness criss-crossed by ditches and mounds. Some cattle were feeding there. Far past the marshes was the river, which looked like a low leaden line in the gray light. I was quite frightened, and I began to cry.

"Hold your noise!" cried a terrible voice. "Keep still, you little devil, or I'll cut your throat!"

A fearful man, in ragged gray clothes, with a great iron on his leg. A man with no hat, and with broken shoes, and with an old rag tied round his head. A man who had been soaked in water, and smothered in mud, and lamed by stones, and torn by briars. A man who limped, and shivered, and glared and growled, and whose teeth chattered as he seized me by the chin.

"O! Don't cut my throat, sir," I pleaded in terror. "Pray don't do it, sir."

"Tell us your name!" said the man. "Quick!"

"Pip, sir."

"Once more," said the man, staring at me. "Say it clear!"

"Pip. Pip, sir."

"Show us where you live," said the man. "Point out the place!"

I pointed to where our village lay, a mile or more from the church.

The man, after looking at me for a moment, turned me upside down, and emptied my pockets. There was nothing in them but a piece of bread. Roughly, he placed me on a high tombstone, trembling, while he ate the bread ravenously.

"You young dog," said the man, licking his lips, "what fat cheeks you ha' got. Darn me if I couldn't eat 'em," said the man, with a threatening shake of his head.

I earnestly expressed my hope that he wouldn't, and held tighter to the tombstone to keep myself from crying.

"Now lookee here!" said the man. "Where's your mother?"

"There, sir!" said I, pointing.

He started and began to run. Suddenly he stopped and looked over his shoulder.

"There, sir!" I timidly explained, extending my finger toward her grave.

"Oh!" said he, coming back. "And is that your father beside your mother?"

"Yes, sir," said I.

"Ha!" he muttered then, considering. "Who d'ye live with—supposin' I let you live, which I han't made up my mind about?"

"My sister, sir—Mrs. Joe Gargery—wife of Joe Gargery, the blacksmith, sir."

"Blacksmith, eh?" He looked down at his leg with the iron ring around it.

The fearful man came closer to me, grabbed me by both arms, and tilted me back as far as he could. His eyes looked most powerfully down into mine, and mine looked most helplessly up into his.

"Now lookee here," he said, "the question being whether you're to be let to live. You know what a file is?"

"Yes, sir."

"And you know what food is?"

"Yes, sir."

"You get me a file." He tilted me again. "And you get me food." He tilted me again. "You bring 'em both to me." He tilted me again. "Or I'll have your heart and liver out." He tilted me again. "You bring me, tomorrow morning early, that file and that food. You do it, and you never tell anyone that you met me, and I'll let you live. You fail, and your heart and your liver shall be tore out, roasted and ate. Now, I ain't alone. There's a young man hid with me. Compared to him, I am an Angel. That young man has a secret way of getting at a boy, and at his heart, and at his liver. It is impossible for a boy to attempt to hide himself from that young man. A boy may lock his door, may be warm in bed, may tuck himself up, may draw the clothes over his head, may think himself comfortable and safe, but that young man will softly creep and creep his way to him and tear him open. I am keeping that young man from harming you at the present moment, with great difficulty. Now, what do you say?"

I said that I would get him the file and whatever food I could. And I would come to him early in the morning.

"Say Lord strike you dead if you don't!" said the man.

I said so, and he put me down on the ground.

"Now," he pursued, "you remember what you've promised, and you remember that young man, and you get home!"

"Goo-good night, sir," I faltered.

At the same time, he hugged his shuddering body in both his arms—as if to hold himself together—and limped toward the low church wall. He looked as if he were avoiding the hands of the dead people, stretching up out of their graves, to clasp his ankle and pull him in.

He came to the low church wall and got over it. Then he turned around to look at me. When I saw him turning, I ran toward home. I stopped for a moment to look over my shoulder, and saw him going on again toward the river. He seemed to be making his way toward an ancient scaffold, one of the few structures that rose above the flat misty marsh. Dangling from the scaffold were some chains that had once held a pirate. The man was limping on toward this grisly object, as if he were the pirate come to life and was going back to hook himself up again. I looked all round for the horrible young man and could see no signs of him. But now I was frightened again. I ran home without stopping.

My sister, Mrs. Joe Gargery, was more than twenty years older than I. She had established a great reputation because she had brought me up "by hand." I did not know what that expression meant. However, I knew she had a hard and heavy hand. I was also aware that she often laid her hand upon her husband as well as me. I supposed, therefore, that Joe Gargery and I were both brought up by hand.

My sister was not a good-looking woman. I had a general impression that she must have made Joe Gargery marry her by hand. Joe was a fair man, with curls of hair on each side of his smooth face. He was a mild, good-natured, sweet-tempered, easy-going fellow.

My sister had black hair and eyes. She was tall and bony, and almost always wore a coarse apron.

Joe's blacksmith forge adjoined our house. When I ran home from the churchyard, the forge was shut up, and Joe was sitting alone in the kitchen. "Mrs. Joe has been out looking for you, Pip. She's furious. She's a-coming! Get behind the door, old chap."

I took the advice. My sister glared at me. "Where have you been, you young monkey?" said Mrs. Joe, stamping her foot. "Tell me directly what you've been doing."

"I have only been to the churchyard," said I.

"Churchyard!" repeated my sister. "If it warn't for me you'd have been buried in the churchyard long ago."

My sister turned her attention to preparing tea and bread-and-butter. Though I was hungry, I dared not eat my slice. I felt that I must have food for my dreadful acquaintance and the still more dreadful young man. Therefore, I slid my hunk of bread-and-butter down the leg of my trousers.

It was Christmas Eve, and I had to stir the pudding for the next day. As I finished, I heard a loud muffled bang from the direction of the marsh.

"Ah!" said Joe. "There's another conwict off."

"What does that mean, Joe?" said I.

Mrs. Joe, who always took it upon herself to provide explanations, said, snappishly, "Escaped. Escaped."

"There was a conwict off last night," said Joe, "after sunset-gun. And they fired warning of him. And now, it appears they're firing warning of another."

"Who's firing?" said I.

"Lord bless the boy!" exclaimed my sister, as if she didn't quite mean that, but rather the contrary. "From the Hulks!"

"And please, what's the Hulks?" said I.

"That's the way with this boy!" exclaimed my sister. "Answer him one question, and he'll ask you a dozen. Hulks are prison-ships."

"Who's put into prison-ships, and why are they put there?" said I.

It was too much for Mrs. Joe. "People are put in the Hulks because they murder, and rob, and do all sorts of bad things. And they always begin by asking questions. Now, you get along to bed!"

I went to bed in mortal terror—of the young man who wanted my heart and liver and the dreadful man with the ironed leg. I was afraid to sleep. I knew that at the first faint dawn of morning I must rob the pantry.

As soon as light appeared in the sky, I got up and went downstairs. I stole some bread, some cheese, about half a jar of mincemeat, some brandy, a meat bone with very little on it, and a pork pie. Then I seized a file from among Joe's tools, and I ran for the misty marshes.

It was an unusually damp morning. On every rail and gate, clammy wetness lay. The marsh-mist shrouded every object.

The mist was heavier yet when I reached the marshes. Objects I could barely make out seemed to call, "A boy who stole a pork pie! Stop him!" One black ox stared at me in such an accusatory manner that I blubbered out to him, "I couldn't help it, sir! It wasn't for myself I took it!"

With great difficulty, I managed to creep my way to the meeting place. I saw the man sitting before me. His back was toward me, and he had his arms folded. He was nodding forward, heavy with sleep. I went forward softly and touched him on the shoulder. He instantly jumped up. To my great surprise, it was not the same man, but another man!

This man too was dressed in coarse gray. He also had a great iron on his leg. Indeed, he was everything that the other man was, except that he had a different face. Startled, the man took a wild swing at me but missed. Then he ran into the mist, and I lost him.

"It's the young man!" I thought, feeling my heart jump.

Soon after I met the right man—hugging himself and limping to and fro. He seemed awfully cold and looked very hungry too. I set the file and my bundle on the damp ground before him.

"What's in the bottle, boy?" said he.

"Brandy," said I.

He wolfed down the food and brandy, shivering violently all the while. Every so often he paused between bites of pork pie and bread and cheese and brandy to listen. Some real or fancied sound startled him, and he said, suddenly, "You're not a deceiving rascal? You brought no one with you?"

"No, sir! No!"

Pitying this starving creature soaked through to the skin, I said, "I am glad you enjoy it."

"Thankee, my boy. I do."

I had often watched a large dog of ours eating his food. I noticed a decided similarity between the dog's way of eating and the man's. The man took strong, sharp, sudden bites, just like the dog. He swallowed, or rather snapped up, every mouthful, too soon and too fast. And he looked sideways here and there while he ate, as if he thought there was danger in every direction.

"I am afraid you won't leave any of it for him," said I timidly.

"Leave any for him? Who's him?" said the man.

"The young man. That you spoke of. That was hid with you."

"Oh!" he returned, with something like a gruff laugh. "Him? Yes, yes! He don't want nothing to eat."

"I thought he looked as if he did," said I.

The man stopped eating and turned in my direction. He had a most surprised look on his face.

"Looked? When?"

"Just now."

"Where?"

"Over there," said I, pointing. "I found him nodding asleep and thought it was you."

He held me by the collar and stared at me so, that I began to think his first idea about cutting my throat had revived.

"Did you notice anything particular about him?" he asked.

"He had a badly bruised face," said I.

"Not here?" exclaimed the man, striking his left cheek.

"Yes, there!"

"Where is he?" He crammed what little food was left into the breast of his gray jacket. "Show me the way he went. I'll pull him down like a bloodhound. Curse this iron on my sore leg! Give us hold of the file, boy."

He was down on the rank wet grass, filing at his iron like a madman. I was very much afraid of him again. I was also very much afraid of staying away from home any longer. I told him I must go, but he took no notice. I thought the best thing I could do was to slip off. The last I saw of him, his head was bent over his knee and he was working hard at his iron fetter.

I fully expected to find a policeman in the kitchen waiting to arrest me on this Christmas day. But not only was there no policeman there, but no discovery had yet been made of the robbery. Mrs. Joe was busying herself in getting the house ready for the festivities of the day.

Mr. Wopsle, the clerk at church, was to dine with us. Other guests included Mr. Hubble the wheelwright and Mrs. Hubble, and Joe's Uncle Pumblechook. Mr. Pumblechook was a well-to-do corn merchant in the nearest town, who drove his own carriage. The dinner hour was half-past one. When Joe and I got home, we found the table set, and Mrs. Joe dressed. Still, not a word of the robbery.

At length the company sat down to the festive meal. Inevitably, the conversation turned to me.

"He is a world of trouble to you, ma'am," said Mrs. Hubble, pointing to me.

"Trouble?" echoed my sister, "trouble?" And then she entered on a catalogue of all the illnesses I had been guilty of, and all the acts of sleeplessness I had committed, and all the high places I had fallen from, and all the low places I had tumbled into, and all the injuries I had done myself, and all the times she had wished me in my grave, where I stubbornly refused to go.

"Have a little brandy, Uncle," said my sister.

It had come at last! He would find it was weak, he would say it was weak, and I was lost! I held tight to the leg of the table under the cloth, with both hands, and awaited my fate.

My sister poured his brandy out. No one else took any. The wretched man trifled with his glass, prolonging my misery. All this time, Mrs. Joe and Joe were briskly clearing the table for the pie and pudding.

Uncle Pumblechook threw his head back and drank the brandy in one gulp. Instantly afterward, he sprang to his feet, coughed violently, and ran out the door.

I was certain that I had murdered him. Obeying the marsh-man's order, I had poured out the brandy for him. Then I filled up the bottle from the tar-water jug. Thanks be to God, Uncle Pumblechook staggered back into the house, fully alive. For the time at least, I was saved. I began to think I should get over the day, when my sister said to the guests, "You must taste, to finish with, the delicious present of Uncle Pumblechook's!"

I clutched the leg of the table again immediately. I knew what was coming, and I felt that this time I really was gone.

My sister went out to get it. I heard Mr. Hubble remark that "a bit of savory pork pie would make a wonderful end to a Christmas meal." I felt that I could bear no more, and that I must run away. I released the leg of the table and ran for my life.

But I ran no further than the house door, for there I ran into a party of soldiers with their muskets. One of them held out a pair of handcuffs to me, saying, "Here you are, look sharp, come on!"

The arrival of soldiers on our doorstep caused the dinner party to rise from the table in confusion.

"Excuse me, ladies and gentlemen," said the sergeant. "I am on a chase in the name of the king, and I want the blacksmith."

"And what do you want with him?" retorted my sister, quick to resent his being wanted at all.

"I have a little job for him. The lock on one of these pairs of handcuffs isn't workin' right. I expect we'll need 'em tonight. Could they be repaired?"

Joe replied that he could fix them, but it would take two hours, for he would have to light the forge.

"That's not so bad," said the sergeant, reflecting. "Even if I was forced to halt here two hours, that'll do. How far might you call yourselves from the marshes? Not above a mile, I reckon?"

"Just a mile," said Mrs. Joe.

"That'll do. We'll begin to close in upon 'em about dusk."

"Convicts, sergeant?" asked Mr. Wopsle.

"Ay!" returned the sergeant, "two. They're pretty well known to be out on the marshes still, and they won't try to get clear of 'em before dusk. Anybody here seen anyone who looks like a convict?"

Everybody, myself excepted, said no. Nobody thought to ask me.

"Well!" said the sergeant, "they'll find themselves trapped in a circle, I expect, sooner than they count on."

Joe got his coat off, and his leather apron on, and passed into the forge. Then Joe began to hammer and clink, hammer and clink, and we all looked on.

At last, Joe's job was done, and the ringing and roaring stopped. As Joe got on his coat, he summoned courage to propose that some of us should go with the soldiers and see what came of the hunt. The sergeant agreed, and Mr. Wopsle, Joe, and I followed the soldiers out the door. When we were all out in the raw air and were steadily moving, I treasonably whispered to Joe, "I hope, Joe, we shan't find them."

The weather was cold and threatening, the way dreary, the footing bad, and darkness coming on. A bitter sleet assaulted us, and Joe took me on his back. As we marched, the sheep stopped in their eating and looked timidly at us. The cattle, their heads turned from the wind and sleet, stared angrily as if they held us responsible for both annoyances.

All of a sudden there reached us, on the wings of the wind and rain, a long shout. It was repeated. It was at a distance toward the east, but it was long and loud. The sergeant ordered that his men should make toward it "at the double." So we slanted to the right (where the East was), and Joe pounded away so wonderfully, that I had to hold on tight to keep my seat.

As we came nearer to the shouting, we realized that it was made by more than one voice. Sometimes, it seemed to stop altogether, and then the soldiers stopped. When it broke out again, the soldiers made for it at a greater rate than ever, and we after them. After a while, we had so run it down, that we could hear one voice calling "Murder!" and another voice, "Convicts! Runaways! Guard! This way for the runaway convicts!" Then both voices would seem to be stifled in a struggle, and then would break out again.

The sergeant ran in first, when we had run the noise quite down, and two of his men ran in close upon him. Their guns were cocked and leveled when we all ran in.

"Here are both men!" panted the sergeant, struggling at the bottom of a ditch. "Surrender, you two wild beasts! Come apart!"

Water was splashing, and mud was flying, and oaths were being sworn, and blows were being struck. Some more men went down into the ditch to help the sergeant, and dragged out, separately, my convict and the other one. Both were bleeding and panting and cursing and struggling.

"Mind!" said my convict, wiping blood from his face with his ragged sleeves, and shaking torn hair from his fingers: "I took him! I give him up to you! Mind that!"

"It's not much to be particular about," said the sergeant. "It'll do you small good, my man, being in the same plight yourself. Handcuffs there!"

"I don't expect it to do me any good. I don't want it to do me more good than it does now," said my convict, with a greedy laugh. "I took him. He knows it. That's enough for me."

The other convict seemed to be bruised and torn all over. He could not get his breath to speak, until they were both separately handcuffed. He leaned upon a soldier to keep himself from falling.

"Take notice, guard—he tried to murder me," were his first words.

"Lookee here!" said my convict to the sergeant. "I escaped from the prison-ship. I could ha' got clear of these death-cold marshes likewise. But then I discovered that he was here. Let him go free? Let him make a tool of me afresh and again? Once more? No, no, no."

The other fugitive, who was evidently in extreme horror of his companion, repeated, "He tried to murder me. I should have been a dead man if you had not come up."

"He lies!" said my convict, with fierce energy. "He's a liar born, and he'll die a liar. Look at his face. That's how he looked when we were tried together."

"Enough of this talk," said the sergeant. "Light those torches."

A soldier lighted three or four torches. He took one himself and distributed the others. It had grown very dark.

"All right," said the sergeant. "March."

Our lights warmed the air about us with their pitchy blaze. The two prisoners seemed rather to like that, as they limped along in the midst of the muskets. We could not go fast, because of their lameness. And they were so exhausted that we had to halt two or three times while they rested.

After an hour or so of this traveling, we came to a rough wooden hut and a boat landing-place. There were three or four soldiers already in the hut. The sergeant made some kind of report and some entry in a book. Then the other convict was marched off with his guard, to go on board first.

My convict then declared, "I wish to say something about this escape. It may prevent some persons from falling under suspicion."

"You can say what you like," returned the sergeant, standing coolly looking at him with his arms folded.

"A man can't starve. I took some wittles, up at the willage over yonder—where the church stands."

"You mean stole," said the sergeant.

"And I'll tell you where from. From the blacksmith's."

"Halloa!" said the sergeant, staring at Joe.

"Halloa, Pip!" said Joe, staring at me.

"It was some wittles and a pitcher of liquor, and a pie."

"Have you happened to miss such an article as a pie, blacksmith?" asked the sergeant, confidentially.

"My wife did, at the very moment when you came in."

"So," said my convict, turning his eyes on Joe in a moody manner, and without the least glance at me. "So you're the blacksmith, are you? Then I'm sorry to say, I ate your pie."

The convict turned his back to us, just as the boat returned. We saw him put into the boat, which was rowed by a crew of convicts like himself. No one seemed surprised to see him, or interested in seeing him, or glad to see him, or sorry to see him. No one spoke a word, except that somebody in the boat growled as if to dogs, "Give way, you!" which was the signal for the dip of the oars. By the light of the torches, we saw the black Hulk lying out a little way from the mud of the shore, like a wicked Noah's ark. Cribbed and barred and moored by massive rusty chains, the prison-ship seemed in my young eyes to be ironed like the prisoners. We saw the little boat go alongside, and we saw him taken up into the prison-ship. Then, the ends of the torches were flung hissing into the water, and went out, as if it were all over with him.

As I was sleepy before we were far away from the prison-ship, Joe took me on his back again and carried me home.

By that time, I was staggering on the kitchen floor like a little drunkard. As I came to myself (with the aid of a heavy thump between the shoulders, and the restorative exclamation "Yah! Was there ever such a boy as this!" from my sister), I found Joe telling them about the convict's confession. All the visitors suggested different ways by which he had got into the pantry. Before they had gotten very far, however, my sister escorted me up to bed. Soon I was fast asleep.

At the time when I stood in the churchyard, reading the family tombstones, I had just enough learning to be able to spell them out. When I was old enough, I was to be apprenticed to Joe. Until that time, I became a pupil of Mr. Wopsle's great-aunt, who kept an evening school in the village.

More by my own efforts than any assistance from Mr. Wopsle's great aunt, I struggled through the alphabet as if it had been a bramble-bush. In other words, I got myself scratched by every letter. After that, I struggled with numbers and learned some mathematics. At last I began to read, write, and calculate on the very smallest scale.

One night, I was sitting in the chimney corner with my slate, expending great efforts on the production of a letter to Joe. I think it must have been a full year after our hunt upon the marshes. My sister was out with Mr. Pumblechook.

Mrs. Joe made occasional trips with Uncle Pumblechook on market days, to assist him in buying such household items as required a woman's judgment. Uncle Pumblechook was a bachelor and knew little about such things.

Joe made the fire and swept the hearth, and then we went to the door to listen for Pumblechook's carriage. It was a dry, cold night, and the wind blew keenly. The frost was white and hard. A man would die tonight lying out on the marshes, I thought. And then I looked at the stars. I considered how awful it would be for a man to turn his face up to them as he froze to death, and see no help or pity in all the glittering multitude.

"Here comes the carriage," said Joe. Soon they drove up, wrapped to the eyes. Mrs. Joe and Uncle Pumblechook hurried into the house and placed themselves before the fire.

"Now," said Mrs. Joe, unwrapping herself with haste and excitement, "if this boy an't grateful this night, he never will be!"

I looked as grateful as any boy possibly could, who was wholly uninformed why he ought to feel that way.

"It's only to be hoped," said my sister, "that he won't be pampered. But I have my fears."

"She an't in that line, Mum," said Mr. Pumblechook. "She knows better."

She? I looked at Joe in a questioning manner. "She?" Joe looked at me, returning my puzzled look.

"Miss Havisham, who lives uptown, wants this boy to go and play there," asserted my sister. "And of course he's going. And he had better play there," said my sister, "or I'll work him."

I had heard of Miss Havisham. Everybody for miles round had heard of Miss Havisham. She was an immensely rich and grim lady who lived in a large and dismal house. She rarely went out, preferring to be alone most of the time.

"Well, to be sure!" said Joe, astounded. "I wonder how she come to know Pip!"

"Idiot!" cried my sister. "Who said she knew him?"

"—Which some individual," Joe again politely hinted, "mentioned that she wanted him to go and play there."

"Uncle Pumblechook is a tenant of hers. And she asked Uncle Pumblechook if he knew of a boy to go and play there. Uncle Pumblechook realized that this boy's fortune may be made by his going to Miss Havisham's. He has even offered to take him into town tonight in his own carriage, and to keep him tonight, and to take him to Miss Havisham's tomorrow morning. And Lor-a-mussy me!" cried my sister, casting off her bonnet in sudden desperation. "Here I stand talking to mere Mooncalfs, with Uncle Pumblechook waiting, and the mare catching cold at the door, and the boy coated with dirt from the hair of his head to the sole of his foot!"

With that, she pounced upon me, like an eagle on a lamb. My face was squeezed into wooden bowls in sinks, and my head was put under a water-spout. I was soaped, and kneaded, and toweled, and thumped, until I was most uncomfortable.

When my washings were completed, I was put into clean linen of the stiffest character. Then I was trussed up in my tightest suit. I was then delivered over to Mr. Pumblechook.

"Goodbye, Joe!"

"God bless you, Pip, old chap!"

I had never parted from him before. Between my feelings and the soapsuds, I could at first see no stars from the carriage. But then they twinkled out one by one, as the carriage proceeded on.

That night, I had been sent straight to bed in an attic with a sloping roof. The roof was so low in the corner where the bedstead was, that the tiles were only a foot above my eyebrows.

At ten o'clock next morning, we started for Miss Havisham's. The lady's house, known as Satis House, was of old brick, and dismal, and had a great many iron bars to it. Some of the windows had been walled up. Of those that remained, all the lower were rustily barred. There was a courtyard in front, and that was barred. While we waited at the gate, I peeped in and saw that at the side of the house, there was a large brewery. No brewing was going on in it, and none seemed to have gone on for a long time.

At length a young lady came across the courtyard with keys in her hand.

"This," said Mr. Pumblechook, "is Pip."

"This is Pip, is it?" returned the young lady,

who was very pretty and seemed very proud. "Come in, Pip."

Mr. Pumblechook was coming in also, when she stopped him with the gate.

"Oh!" she said. "Did you wish to see Miss Havisham?"

"If Miss Havisham wished to see me," returned Mr. Pumblechook, a little surprised.

"Ah!" said the girl; "but, you see, she doesn't."

She said it so absolutely that Mr. Pumblechook found himself unable to protest. But he eyed me severely and proclaimed, "Boy! Let your behavior here be a credit unto them which brought you up by hand!"

My young guide locked the gate, and we went across the courtyard. It was paved and clean, but grass was growing in every crevice. The brewery buildings were all empty and disused. The cold wind seemed to blow colder there than outside the gate. It made a shrill howling noise, like the noise of wind in the rigging of a ship at sea.

She saw me looking at it, and she said, "You could drink without hurt all the strong beer that's brewed there now, boy."

Though she called me "boy" often, she was about my own age. She seemed much older than I, of course, being a girl, and beautiful and self-possessed. She was as scornful of me as if she had been twenty-one, and a queen.

We went into the house by a side door, because the great front entrance had two chains across it.

The first thing I noticed was that the hallways were all dark. The girl lighted a candle. We went through more passages and up a staircase, and still it was all dark, and only the candle lighted us.

At last we came to the door of a room, and she said, "Go in."

I answered, more in shyness than politeness, "After you, miss."

To this, she returned, "Don't be ridiculous, boy. I am not going in." And she walked scornfully away.

The only thing to be done being to knock at the door, I knocked, and was told from within to enter. I entered, therefore, and found myself in a large pretty room, well lighted with wax candles. No glimpse of daylight was to be seen in it. It was a dressing room, as I supposed from a draped table with a gilded mirror. Sitting by the table in an armchair was the strangest lady I have ever seen.

She was dressed in rich materials—satins, and lace, and silks—all white. Her shoes were white. She had a long white veil hanging from her hair, and she had bridal flowers in her hair, but her hair was white. Some bright jewels sparkled on her neck and on her hands, and some other jewels lay sparkling on the table. Dresses, less splendid than the dress she wore, and half-packed trunks, were scattered about. She had not quite finished dressing, for she had only one shoe on. The other was on the table near her hand. Her veil was half arranged. Her watch and chain were not put on, and some lace for her dress lay with those trinkets. Her handkerchief, and gloves, and some flowers, and a prayer-book, were all haphazardly heaped about the looking-glass.

Everything within my view which ought to be white, had been white long ago, and was faded and yellow. The bride within the bridal dress had withered like the dress, and like the flowers, and had no brightness left but the brightness of her sunken eyes. The dress had been put upon the rounded figure of a young woman. But now the figure upon which it hung loose had shrunk to skin and bone.

"Who is it?" said the lady at the table.

"Pip, ma'am."

"Pip?"

"Mr. Pumblechook's boy, ma'am. Come—to play."

"Come nearer. Let me look at you. Come close."

It was when I stood before her, avoiding her eyes, that I saw that her watch had stopped at twenty minutes to nine, and that a clock in the room had also stopped at twenty minutes to nine.

"Look at me," said Miss Havisham. "You are not afraid of a woman who has never seen the sun since you were born?"

I told an enormous lie. "No."

"Do you know what I touch here?" she said, laying her hands, one upon the other, on her left side.

"Yes, ma'am."

"What do I touch?"

"Your heart."

"Broken!"

She uttered the word with strong emphasis and a weird smile.

"I am tired," said Miss Havisham. "I want diversion, and I have done with men and women. Play."

I could think of nothing more difficult to do under the circumstances. Helpless, I stood absolutely still.

"I sometimes have sick fancies," she went on, "and I have a sick fancy that I want to see some play. She motioned impatiently and ordered, "Play, play, play!"

Still I could not move.

"Call Estella," she barked.

I opened the door and did as I was told. Shortly, the girl answered, and her light came along the dark passage like a star.

Miss Havisham beckoned her to come close. The faded woman took up a jewel from the table, and tried its effect upon the girl's dress and against her pretty brown hair. "Your own, one day, my dear, and you will use it well. Let me see you play cards with this boy."

"With this boy! Why, he is a common working-class boy!"

I thought I overheard Miss Havisham answer—only it seemed so unlikely—"Well? You can break his heart."

"What do you play, boy?" asked Estella of me, with the greatest disdain.

"Nothing but beggar my neighbor, miss."

"Beggar him," said Miss Havisham to Estella. So we sat down to cards.

It was then I began to understand that everything in the room had stopped, like the watch and the clock, a long time ago. I noticed that Miss Havisham put down the jewel exactly on the spot from which she had taken it up. As Estella dealt the cards, I glanced at the dressing table again. I saw that the shoe upon it, once white, now yellow, had never been worn. I glanced down at the foot from which the shoe was absent. I saw that the silk stocking on it, once white, now yellow, had been worn ragged.

So she sat, corpse-like, as we played at cards.

"He calls the knaves Jacks, this boy!" said Estella with disdain, before our first game was out. "And what coarse hands he has! And what thick boots!"

I played the game to an end with Estella. She beggared me. She threw the cards down on the table when she had won them all.

"When shall I have you here again?" said Miss Havisham. "Let me think. Come again after six days. You hear?"

"Yes, ma'am."

"Estella, take him down. Let him have something to eat, and let him look about him while he eats. Go, Pip."

I followed the candle down, as I had followed the candle up. She led me out to the courtyard and ordered, "You are to wait here, you boy." Then she went back inside.

She came back with some bread and meat and a little mug of beer. She put the mug down on the stones of the yard. She then gave me the bread and meat without looking at me, as if I were a dog in disgrace. I was so humiliated, hurt, and angry, that tears came to my eyes. The moment they sprang there, the girl looked at me with a quick delight in having been the cause of them. Then she left me, without a word.

When she was gone, I looked for a place where I could be alone. In a corner of the yard, I allowed my injured feelings to come out by crying so deeply that my whole body shook. Then I smoothed my face with my sleeve and sat down to eat. The bread and meat were acceptable, and the beer was warming and tingling. I began to feel better and proceeded to look about me.

It was a deserted place. The grounds included a brewery, which at one time had produced a steady output. But now there were no malt in the storehouse, no smells of grains and beer in the copper or the vat. In a side yard, there was a wilderness of empty casks. Behind the brewery was an untended garden, overgrown with tangled weeds.

I saw Estella approaching with the keys to let me out. When she saw me, she unceremoniously pushed me out and locked the gate behind me. I went straight to Mr. Pumblechook's, and was immensely relieved to find him not at home. So I set off on the four-mile walk to our house.

When I reached home, my sister was very curious to know all about Miss Havisham's. She asked a number of questions. I soon found myself getting slapped in the nape of the neck and the small of the back, and having my face shoved against the kitchen wall, because I did not answer those questions at sufficient length.

To make matters worse, bullying old Pumblechook paid us a visit that afternoon. He seemed afflicted by a bottomless curiosity to learn of all I had seen and heard.

"Well, boy," Uncle Pumblechook began, as soon as he was seated by the fire. "How did you get on up town?"

I answered, "Pretty well, sir," and my sister shook her fist at me.

"Pretty well?" Mr. Pumblechook repeated. "Pretty well is no answer. Tell us what you mean by pretty well, boy?"

I reflected for some time, and then answered, as if I had discovered a new idea, "I mean pretty well."

My sister made an exclamation of impatience and was ready to hit me again. However, Mr. Pumblechook stopped her. "No! Don't lose your temper. Leave this lad to me, ma'am."

"Boy! What is Miss Havisham like?" Mr. Pumblechook asked.

"Very tall and dark," I told him.

"Is she, Uncle?" asked my sister.

Mr. Pumblechook nodded his agreement. From this I concluded that he had never seen Miss Havisham, for she was nothing of the kind.

"Good!" said Mr. Pumblechook.

"Now, boy! What was she doing when you went in today?" asked Mr. Pumblechook.

"She was sitting," I answered, "in a black velvet coach."

Mr. Pumblechook and Mrs. Joe stared at one another—as they well might—and both repeated, "In a black velvet coach?"

"Yes," said I. "And Miss Estella—that's her niece, I think—handed her in cake and wine at the coach-window, on a gold plate. And we all had cake and wine on gold plates. And I got up behind the coach to eat mine, because she told me to." Frightened by the threat of torture, I would have told them anything.

"Was anybody else there?" asked Mr. Pumblechook.

"Four dogs," said I.

"Large or small?"

"Immense," said I. "And they fought for veal cutlets out of a silver basket."

Mr. Pumblechook and Mrs. Joe stared at one another again, in utter amazement.

Mr. Pumblechook then reminded us that I had been sent there to play. "What did you play at, boy?"

"We played with flags," I said.

"Flags!" echoed my sister.

"Yes," said I. "Estella waved a blue flag, and I waved a red one, and Miss Havisham waved one sprinkled all over with little gold stars, out at the coach-window. And then we all waved our swords and cheered."

"Swords!" repeated my sister. "Where did you get swords from?"

"Out of a cupboard," said I. "And I saw pistols in it—and jam—and pills. And there was no daylight in the room, but it was all lighted up with candles."

"That's true, Mum," said Mr. Pumblechook, with a grave nod. "That much I've seen myself."

Not long after, Joe came in from his work to have a cup of tea. My sister related to him my pretended experiences.

While Joe digested this tale with wide-eyed wonder, my sister and Mr. Pumblechook sat debating what benefits would come to me from Miss Havisham's acquaintance. They had no doubt that Miss Havisham would "do something" for me. Joe fell into the deepest disgrace with both, for offering the bright suggestion that I might only be presented with one of the dogs who had fought for the veal cutlets.

After Mr. Pumblechook had driven off, and when my sister was washing up, I stole into the forge to Joe. I remained by him until he had done for the night. Then I said, "Before the fire goes out, Joe, I should like to tell you something."

"Should you, Pip?" said Joe, drawing his shoeing-stool near the forge. "Then tell us. What is it, Pip?"

"Joe, you remember all those stories I told about Miss Havisham and the young lady? That's what they were, Joe, stories. None of it is true."

"What are you saying, Pip?" cried Joe, falling back in the greatest amazement. "You don't mean to say it's—"

"Yes I do; it's lies, Joe."

And then I told Joe that I felt very miserable. And that there had been a beautiful young lady at Miss Havisham's who was dreadfully proud. And that she had said I was common, and that I knew I was common, and that I wished I was not common. That's how the lies came out, though I didn't know how.

"There's one thing you may be sure of, Pip," said Joe, after some reflection, "namely, that lies is lies. However they come, they didn't ought to come. Don't you tell no more of 'em, Pip. That ain't the way to get out of being common, old chap. And as to being common, I don't see it so clear. You are uncommon in some things. You're uncommon small. Likewise you're a uncommon scholar."

"No, I am ignorant and backward, Joe."

"Why, see what a letter you wrote last night! Wrote in print even! You must be a common scholar afore you can be a uncommon one, I should hope! The king upon his throne, with his crown upon his 'ed, can't sit and write his acts of Parliament in print, without having begun, when he were a unpromoted Prince, with the alphabet."

There was some hope in this piece of wisdom, and it rather encouraged me.

When I got up to my little room and said my prayers, I thought how common Estella would consider Joe, a mere blacksmith. She would laugh at his thick boots and coarse hands.

That was a memorable day to me, for it made great changes in me. But it is the same with any life. Imagine one selected day struck out of it, and think how different its course would have been. Pause you who read this, and think for a moment of the long chain of iron or gold, of thorns or flowers, that would never have bound you, but for the formation of the first link on one memorable day.

There was a pub in the village called the Three Jolly Bargemen. Joe liked sometimes to smoke his pipe there. I had received strict orders from my sister to call for him Saturday evening and bring him home. To the Three Jolly Bargemen, therefore, I directed my steps.

I found Joe smoking his pipe in company with Mr. Wopsle and a stranger. Joe greeted me as usual with "Halloa, Pip, old chap!" The moment he said that, the stranger turned his head and looked at me.

He was a secret-looking man whom I had never seen before. One of his eyes was half shut up, as if he were taking aim at something with an invisible gun. He withdrew a pipe from his mouth and blew all his smoke away. He looked intently at me all the time and nodded. So I nodded back, and then he nodded again.

I took a seat beside Joe. The strange man glanced at Joe and saw that his attention was otherwise engaged. He nodded to me again when I had taken my seat. Then he rubbed his leg in a very odd way, as though he were trying to send me a signal.

"You was saying," said the strange man, turning to Joe, "that you was a blacksmith."

"Yes. I said it," said Joe.

"What'll you drink, Mr.—? You didn't mention your name, by the way."

Joe mentioned it now, and the strange man called him by it. "What'll you drink, Mr. Gargery? At my expense."

"Rum," said Joe.

"Rum," repeated the stranger. "And what will the other gentleman have?"

"Rum," said Mr. Wopsle.

"Three Rums!" cried the stranger, calling to the landlord. "Glasses round!"

"This other gentleman," observed Joe, by way of introducing Mr. Wopsle, "is a gentleman that you would like to hear speak out at church."

"Aha!" said the stranger, quickly, and cocking his eye at me. "The lonely church, right out on the marshes, with the graves round it!"

"That's it," said Joe.

The stranger, with a comfortable kind of grunt over his pipe, put his legs up on the bench that he had to himself. He wore a flapping broad-brimmed traveler's hat, and under it a handkerchief tied over his head, so that he showed no hair. As he looked at the fire, I thought I saw a cunning expression, followed by a half-laugh, come into his face.

"I am not acquainted with this country, gentlemen, but it seems a solitary country toward the river."

"Most marshes is solitary," said Joe.

"No doubt, no doubt. Do you find any gypsies now or tramps or vagrants of any sort, out there?"

"No," said Joe; "none but a runaway convict now and then. And we don't find them, easy. Eh, Mr. Wopsle?"

Mr. Wopsle agreed.

"Seems you have been out after such?" asked the stranger.

"Once," returned Joe. "Not that we wanted to take them, you understand. We went out as lookers-on—me, and Mr. Wopsle, and Pip. Didn't us, Pip?"

"Yes, Joe."

The stranger looked at me again and said, "He's a likely young parcel of bones, that. What is it you call him?"

"Pip," said Joe.

All this while, the strange man looked at nobody but me. He stirred his rum-and-water pointedly at me, and he tasted his rum-and-water pointedly at me. And he stirred it, and he tasted it, not with a spoon, but with a file!

He did this so that nobody but I saw the file. When he had done it, he wiped the file and put it in a breast-pocket. I knew it to be Joe's file. I sat gazing at him, spellbound. But he now reclined in his chair, taking very little notice of me, and talking principally about turnips. Finally, it was time to go.

"Stop half a moment, Mr. Gargery," said the strange man. "I think I've got a bright new shilling somewhere in my pocket, and if I have, the boy shall have it."

He brought it out from a handful of small change, folded it in some crumpled paper, and gave it to me. "Yours!" said he. "Mind! Your own."

I thanked him, staring at him far beyond the bounds of good manners, and holding tight to Joe. He wished us all good night, and we departed.

On the way home, I found myself amazed by this turning up of my old misdeed and old acquaintance, and could think of nothing else.

My sister was not in a very bad temper when we presented ourselves in the kitchen. Joe was encouraged by that unusual circumstance to tell her about the bright shilling. "A fake un, I'll be bound," said Mrs. Joe triumphantly, "or he wouldn't have given it to the boy! Let's look at it."

I took it out of the paper, and it proved to be a good one. "But what's this?" said Mrs. Joe, throwing down the shilling and catching up the paper. "Two one-pound notes?"

Two one-pound notes they were—a sizeable sum of money. Then my sister sealed them up in a piece of paper, and put them under some dried rose leaves in an ornamental teapot. There they remained, a nightmare to me, many and many a night and day.

In my bed that night, I thought constantly of the strange man and how coarse and common it was to be on secret terms with convicts. I was haunted by the file, too. A dread possessed me that when I least expected it, the file would reappear. I coaxed myself to sleep by thinking of Miss Havisham's, where I was to go next Wednesday. And in my sleep I saw the file coming at me out of a door, without seeing who held it, and I screamed myself awake.

At the appointed time, I returned to Miss Havisham's. Estella admitted me, as she had done before. When she had her candle in her hand, she said to me, in a very off-hand manner, "You are to come this way today."

We passed through a long corridor that led to another outside courtyard. Beyond that stood a dwelling that looked as if it had once belonged to the manager of the extinct brewery. There was a clock in the outer wall of this house. Like the clock in Miss Havisham's room, and like Miss Havisham's watch, it had stopped at twenty minutes to nine.

We entered and found ourselves in a gloomy room with a low ceiling. Estella directed me to turn facing one of the windows. In the room were three ladies and one gentleman. They all had a listless and dreary air as if they had been waiting for a long time.

The ringing of a distant bell interrupted the conversation and caused Estella to say to me, "Now, boy!" On my turning round, they all looked at me with the utmost contempt. Estella led me out of the chamber. As I took my leave, I heard one of the ladies, named Sarah Pocket, say, "Well I am sure! What next!" Another lady, named Camilla, added, with indignation, "Was there ever such a fancy! The i-de-a!"

We went with our candle along a dark passage. Estella stopped all of a sudden and turned around to face me.

"Am I pretty?" she asked.

"Yes; I think you are very pretty."

"Am I insulting?"

"Not so much so as you were last time," said I.

"Not so much so?"

"No." My reply must have angered her, for she slapped my face with surprising force.

"Now?" said she. "You little coarse monster, what do you think of me now?"

"I shall not tell you."

"Why don't you cry again, you little wretch?"

"Because I'll never cry for you again," said I.

We went upstairs after this episode. As we were going up, we met a gentleman groping his way down.

"Whom have we here?" asked the gentleman, stopping and looking at me.

"A boy," said Estella.

He was a burly man of an exceedingly dark complexion, with an exceedingly large head and a corresponding large hand. He meant nothing to me at the time.

"Boy of the neighborhood?" said he.

"Yes, sir," said I.

"How do you come here?"

"Miss Havisham sent for me, sir," I explained.

"Well! Behave yourself. I have a pretty large experience of boys, and you're a bad set of fellows. Now mind!" said he, biting the side of his great forefinger as he frowned at me, "you behave yourself!" With those words, he released me and went his way downstairs.

I was happy to be rid of this presence. There was no way I could know that in the future he would occupy a role in my life.

Soon we were in Miss Havisham's room. She and everything else were just as I had left them. Estella left me standing near the door. I stood there until Miss Havisham cast her eyes upon me from the dressing table.

"So!" she said, without being startled or surprised. "The days have worn away, have they?"

"Yes, ma'am. To-day is—"

"There, there, there!" with the impatient movement of her fingers. "I don't want to know. Are you ready to play?"

"I don't think I am, ma'am."

"Not at cards again?" she demanded, with a searching look.

"Yes, ma'am. I could do that, if I was wanted."

"Since this house strikes you as old and grave, boy," said Miss Havisham, impatiently, "and you are unwilling to play, are you willing to work?"

I said I was quite willing.

"Then go into that opposite room," said she, pointing at the door behind me with her withered hand, "and wait there till I come."

I crossed the staircase landing, and entered the room she indicated. From that room, too, the daylight was completely excluded, and it had an airless smell that was oppressive. A fire had been lately kindled in the damp, old-fashioned grate. A few candles faintly lighted the chamber. It was spacious, and I dare say had once been handsome. But now every object in it was covered with dust and mold. The most prominent object was a long table with a tablecloth spread on it, as if a feast had been in preparation when the house and the clocks all stopped together. A centerpiece of some kind was set in the middle of this cloth. It was so heavily overhung with cobwebs that its actual shape could not be seen. I saw speckled-legged spiders with blotchy bodies running home to it, and running out from it, as if some circumstance of the greatest public importance had just transpired in the spider community.

I heard the mice too, rattling behind the panels. A host of black beetles groped about the hearth in a ponderous elderly way.

While I was observing these comings and goings, Miss Havisham laid a hand upon my shoulder. In her other hand she had a crutch-headed stick on which she leaned.

"This," said she, pointing to the long table with her stick, "is where I will be laid when I am dead.

They shall come and look at me here."

With some apprehension that she might get upon the table then and there and die at once, I shrank under her touch.

"What do you think that is?" she asked me, again pointing with her stick. "That, where those cobwebs are?"

"I can't guess what it is, ma'am."

"It's a great cake. A bride cake. Mine!"

She looked all round the room in a glaring manner, and then said, leaning on me while her hand twitched my shoulder, "Come, come, come! Walk me, walk me!"

I concluded from this that the work I had to do was to walk Miss Havisham round and round the room. I started at once, while she leaned upon my shoulder. After a while she said, "Call Estella!" so I went out on the landing and did as I was asked.

Estella arrived with the three women and the gentleman I had encountered not long before.

"Dear Miss Havisham," said Miss Sarah Pocket. "How well you look!"

"I do not," returned Miss Havisham. "I am yellow skin and bone."

Camilla brightened when Miss Pocket met with this rebuff. She murmured to Miss Havisham, "Poor dear soul! Certainly she is not to be expected to look well, poor thing. The idea!"

"And how are you?" said Miss Havisham to Camilla. As we were close to Camilla then, I would have stopped as a matter of course. But Miss

Havisham urged me on right past her. We swept on, and I felt that I was highly obnoxious to Camilla.

"Thank you, Miss Havisham," she returned, "I am as well as can be expected."

"Why, what's the matter with you?" asked Miss Havisham, with exceeding sharpness.

"Nothing worth mentioning," replied Camilla. "I don't wish to make a display of my feelings. But I have thought of you more in the night than I am quite equal to."

"Then don't think of me," retorted Miss Havisham.

"Very easily said!" remarked Camilla, as she broke into tears. "Raymond here knows what medications I am obliged to take in the night, when I think with anxiety of those I love. But as to not thinking of you in the night—impossible!" Here, a burst of tears.

The Raymond referred to turned out to be the gentleman present. He came to his wife's rescue by stating, "Camilla, my dear, it is well known that your family feelings are affecting you so much that one of your legs is growing shorter than the other."

"I am not aware," observed the lady who had not yet spoken, "that to think of any person is to make a great claim upon that person, my dear."

Miss Sarah Pocket, whom I now saw to be a little dry brown old woman, with a small face that might have been made of walnut shells, and a large mouth like a cat's without the whiskers, supported this position.

"There's Matthew!" said Camilla. "Never coming here to see how Miss Havisham is!"

When this same Matthew was mentioned, Miss Havisham stopped me and herself.

"Matthew will come and see me at last," said Miss Havisham, sternly, "when I am laid on that table. That will be his place—there," striking the table with her stick, "at my head! And yours will be there! And your husband's there! And Sarah Pocket's there! And Georgiana's—the third lady present—there! Now you all know where to take your stations when you come to feast upon me. And now go!"

At the mention of each name, she had struck the table with her stick in a new place. She now said, "Walk me, walk me!" and we went on again. Estella led the guests out the front door. Miss Havisham still walked with her hand on my shoulder, but more and more slowly. At last she stopped before the fire, and said, after muttering and looking at it for a few seconds, "This is my birthday, Pip."

I was going to wish her many happy returns, when she lifted her stick.

"I don't suffer it to be spoken of. I don't suffer those who were here just now, or any one, to speak of it. They come here on the day, but they dare not refer to it."

Of course I made no further effort to refer to it.

"On this day of the year, long before you were born, this heap of decay," stabbing with her crutched stick at the pile of cobwebs engulfing the centerpiece on the table but not touching it, "was brought here. It and I have worn away together. The mice have gnawed at it, and sharper teeth than the teeth of mice have gnawed at me."

She held the head of her stick against her heart as she stood looking at the table. She in her once white dress, all yellow and withered. The once white cloth all yellow and withered. Everything around, in a state to crumble under a touch.

"When the ruin is complete," said she, with a ghastly look, "and when they lay me dead, in my bride's dress on the bride's table—which shall be done, and which will be the finished curse upon him—so much the better if it is done on this day!"

At length, coming out of her distraught state, Miss Havisham said, "Let me see you two play cards." With that, we returned to her room, and sat down as before. I was beggared, as before. And again, as before, Miss Havisham watched us all the time. Often she directed my attention to Estella's beauty, and made me notice it the more by trying her jewels on Estella's dress and hair.

Estella continued to treat me as before. But now she did not condescend to speak. When we had played some half-dozen games, a day was appointed for my return. I was taken down into the yard to be fed in the former dog-like manner. For a while, I was left to wander about as I liked.

I decided to stroll about the garden. To my surprise, I encountered a pale young gentleman with red eyelids and light hair.

"Hello!" said he.

"Hello," I replied.

"Come and fight," said the pale young gentleman.

What could I do but follow him? We proceeded to a retired corner of the garden, formed by the junction of two walls and screened by some rubbish. I judged him to be about my own age, but he was much taller, and he had a way of spinning himself about that was quite impressive.

My heart failed me when I saw him squaring at me, as though he were selecting the bone he would break. You can imagine my surprise when I let out the first blow and saw him lying on his back, looking up at me with a bloody nose.

But he was on his feet directly and began squaring again. Once again I was amazed to see him on his back again, looking up at me out of a black eye.

His spirit inspired me with great respect. He seemed to have no strength, and he never once hit me hard. He was always getting knocked down, but he would be up again in a moment. At last he fell with the back of his head against the wall. Even after that, he got up and turned round and round confusedly a few times. Then he fell down and called out, "That means you have won."

When I got into the courtyard, I found Estella waiting with the keys. There was a bright flush upon her face, as though she had just watched something to delight her. She beckoned me to come closer.

"Come here! You may kiss me, if you like."

I kissed her cheek as she turned it to me. But I felt that the kiss was given to the coarse common boy as a piece of money might have been, and that it was worth nothing.

What with the birthday visitors, and the cards, and the fight, my stay had lasted very long. When I neared home, the light from Joe's furnace was flinging a path of fire across the road.

On the appointed day, I returned to Miss Havisham's. On the landing between Miss Havisham's own room and that other room in which the long table was laid out, I saw a wheelchair. It had been placed there since my last visit, and it had become a part of our regular routine. When she was tired of walking with her hand upon my shoulder, I would push her about in the wheelchair. It was soon arranged that I should return every other day at noon for these purposes.

As we became more used to one another, Miss Havisham talked more to me. She asked me what I was going to be. I told her I was going to be apprenticed to Joe. She never gave me any money, or anything but my daily dinner. And she never offered to pay me for my services.

Estella always let me in and out, but never told me I might kiss her again. Sometimes she would coldly tolerate me. Sometimes she would condescend to me. Sometimes she would be friendly to me. And sometimes she would tell me that she hated me. Miss Havisham would often ask me in a whisper, or when we were alone, "Does she grow prettier and prettier, Pip?" And when I said yes (for indeed she did), she would seem to enjoy it greedily. We continued to play at cards, to amuse Miss Havisham. Occasionally, Miss Havisham would hug her and murmur something in her ear that sounded like, "Break their hearts, my pride and hope, break their hearts and have no mercy!"

We went on in this way for a long time. Then, one day, Miss Havisham stopped short as she and I were walking. She leaned on my shoulder and said with some displeasure, "You are growing tall, Pip!"

I thought it best to hint, by staring at the ceiling, that this might be the result of circumstances over which I had no control.

On the next day of my attendance, when our usual exercise was over, she stayed me with a movement of her impatient fingers:

"Tell me the name again of that blacksmith of yours."

"Joe Gargery, ma'am."

"Meaning the master you were to be apprenticed to?"

"Yes, Miss Havisham."

"You had better be apprenticed at once. Would Gargery come here with you, and bring your apprentice papers, do you think?"

I said that he would be honored to be asked.

"Then let him come."

"At any particular time, Miss Havisham?"

"There, there! I know nothing about times. Let him come soon, and come alone with you."

When I got home at night, and delivered this message to Joe, my sister "went on the Rampage," more than ever before. She asked me and Joe whether we supposed she was a doormat under our feet, and how we dared to use her so. In her rage at being excluded, she threw a candlestick at Joe and burst into loud sobbing. Then she got out the dust-pan—which was always a very bad sign—put on her coarse apron, and began cleaning up to a terrible extent. Not satisfied with a dry cleaning, she took to a pail and scrubbing brush, and cleaned us out of house and home, so that we stood shivering in the backyard. It was ten o'clock at night before we ventured to creep in again. She asked Joe why he hadn't married a slave. Joe offered no answer, poor fellow, but stood feeling his whiskers and looking sadly at me, as if he thought it really might have been a better idea.

Two days later, Joe put on his Sunday clothes to accompany me to Miss Havisham's. I felt bad, because I knew he made himself so dreadfully uncomfortable, entirely on my account. It was for my sake that he pulled up his shirt collar so very high that it made the hair on his head stand up like a tuft of feathers.

At breakfast time my sister declared her intention of going to town with us, and being left at Uncle Pumblechook's. She was to be called for "when we had done with our fine ladies," as she put it.

When we came to Pumblechook's, my sister bounced in and left us. As it was almost noon, Joe and I went straight to Miss Havisham's house. Estella opened the gate as usual. Estella took no notice of either of us, but led us the way that I knew so well. Estella told me we were both to go in, so I took Joe by the coat-cuff and conducted him into Miss Havisham's presence. She was seated at her dressing table and looked round at us immediately.

"Oh!" said she to Joe. "You are the husband of the sister of this boy?"

It was eventually established that Joe was indeed that husband. It was also confirmed that I was to be apprenticed to Joe, and that I had no objection to my future in that trade.

"Have you brought his apprentice papers with you?" asked Miss Havisham. I took the papers out of his hand and gave them to Miss Havisham.

Miss Havisham then picked up from the table beside her a little bag. "Pip deserves to be paid for his time here," she said. "There are five-and-twenty guineas in this bag. Give it to your master, Pip."

I did so. "Goodbye, Pip!" said Miss Havisham. "Let them out, Estella."

"Am I to come again, Miss Havisham?" I asked.

"No. Gargery is your master now. Gargery! One word!"

Thus calling him back as I went out of the door, I heard her say to Joe, "The boy has been a good boy here, and that is his reward."

In another minute we were outside the gate, and it was locked, and Estella was gone.

When we stood in the daylight alone again, Joe backed up against a wall and said to me, "Astonishing!" And there he remained so long, saying "Astonishing" so often, that I began to think his senses were never coming back. At length, though, he regained his senses, and we proceeded to Pumblechook's. There, we found my sister sitting with that detested corn merchant.

"Well?" cried my sister, addressing us both at once. "And what's happened to you? I wonder you condescend to come back to such poor society as this, I am sure I do! And what did she give to this worthless boy, what I've brought up by my own hand?"

"She giv' him," said Joe, "nothing."

Mrs. Joe was going to break out, but Joe went on.

"What she giv'," said Joe, "she giv' to his friends. And by his friends, were her explanation, I mean into the hands of his sister Mrs. J. Gargery. Them were her words."

My sister looked at Pumblechook. He nodded at her and at the fire, as if he had known all about it beforehand.

"And how much have you got?" asked my sister.

"What would present company say to ten pound?" demanded Joe.

"They'd say," returned my sister, curtly, "pretty well. Not too much, but pretty well."

"It's more than that, then," said Joe.

That dreadful interloper, Pumblechook, immediately nodded, and said, as though he had helped arrange the payment, "It's more than that, Mum."

"To make an end of it," said Joe, delightedly handing the bag to my sister, "it's five-and-twenty pound."

"It's five-and-twenty pound, Mum," echoed

that basest of swindlers, Pumblechook, rising to shake hands with her. "And it's no more than you deserve (as I said when my opinion was asked), and I wish you joy of the money!"

"Goodness knows, Uncle Pumblechook," said my sister, grasping the money, "we're deeply beholden to you."

"Never mind me, Mum," returned that diabolical corn dealer. "It was all my pleasure. But this boy must be officially apprenticed right away. I'll be happy to see to it."

With that, we marched directly to the Town Hall. Here, in a corner, my apprentice papers were duly signed and finalized, and I was officially apprenticed to Joe.

By the time I got into my little bedroom, I was truly wretched. I was nearly certain that I should never like Joe's trade. I had liked it once, but not any more.

It is a miserable thing to feel ashamed of home. Home had never been a very pleasant place to me, because of my sister's temper. But Joe had made the place at least tolerable for me. Furthermore, I had believed in Joe's forge as the glowing road to manhood and independence. Within a single year, all this was changed. Now, it was all coarse and common. I had started my apprenticeship as a blacksmith. What I dreaded most was that I, being at my grimiest and commonest, should lift up my eyes and see Estella looking in at one of the wooden windows of the forge. I was haunted by the fear that she would, sooner or later, find me out. She would see me with black face and hands, doing the coarsest part of my work, and would exult over me and despise me.

One Sunday I inquired of Joe, "Don't you think I ought to pay Miss Havisham a visit?"

"Well, Pip," returned Joe, slowly considering, "what for?"

"What for, Joe? What is any visit made for?"

"She might think you wanted something."

"Don't you think I might say that I did not, Joe?"

"You might, old chap," said Joe. "And she might believe it. Similarly she mightn't. You see, Pip, Miss Havisham done the handsome thing by you. When Miss Havisham done the handsome thing by you, she called me back to say to me as that were all you were going to get."

"But, Joe. Here I am, in the first year of my apprenticeship. I have never thanked Miss Havisham, or asked after her, or shown that I remember her. As we are rather slack just now, maybe you could give me the afternoon off tomorrow. I think I would go uptown and make a call on Miss Est—Havisham."

"Which her name," said Joe, gravely, "ain't Estavisham, Pip, unless she have been rechris'ened."

"I know, Joe, I know. It was a slip of mine. What do you think of it, Joe?"

Joe thought that if I thought well of it, he thought well of it. And so it was arranged.

Now Joe kept a journeyman, at weekly wages, whose name was Orlick. He was a broad-shouldered dark fellow of great strength, never in a hurry, and always slouching. On Sundays he mostly lazed about or stood against ricks and barns.

Orlick had no liking for me. When I was very small, he told me that the Devil lived in a back corner of the forge. He said also that it was necessary to make up the fire, once in seven years, with a live boy, and that I might consider myself fuel. When I became Joe's apprentice, Orlick liked me still less.

Orlick was at work, next day, when I reminded Joe of my half-holiday. Orlick then said, leaning on his hammer, "Now, master! Sure you're not a going to favor only one of us. If Young Pip has a half-holiday, do as much for Old Orlick." I suppose he was about twenty-five years of age, but he usually spoke of himself as an ancient person.

"Why, what'll you do with a half-holiday, if you get it?" said Joe.

"What'll I do with it! What'll he do with it? I'll do as much with it as him," said Orlick. "Come. No favoring in this shop. Be a man!"

After both men had hammered some on the anvil, and sent showers of sparks flying into the air, Joe turned to Orlick and said, "As in general you stick to your work as well as most men, let it be a half-holiday for all."

My sister had been standing silent in the yard, within hearing. She instantly looked in at one of the windows.

"Like you, you fool!" said she to Joe, "giving holidays to great idle fools like that. I wish I was his master!"

"You'd be everybody's master, if you could," retorted Orlick, with an ill-favored grin.

"Let her alone," said Joe.

"I'd be more than a match for all rogues, especially you, who are the blackest-looking and the worst villain of all!"

"You're a foul shrew, Mother Gargery," growled the journeyman.

"Let her alone, will you?" said Joe.

"What did you say?" cried my sister, beginning to scream. "What did you say? What did that fellow Orlick say to me, Pip? What did he call me, with my husband standing by? O! O! O!" Each of these exclamations was a shriek. "What was the name he gave me before the base man who swore to defend me? O! Hold me! O!"

"Ah-h-h!" growled Orlick, between his teeth, "I'd hold you, if you was my wife. I'd hold you under the pump, and choke it out of you."

"I tell you, let her alone," said Joe.

"Oh! To hear him!" cried my sister, with a clap of her hands and a scream at the same time—which was her next stage. "To hear the names he's giving me! That Orlick! In my own house! Me, a married woman! With my husband standing by! O! O!" Here my sister, after a fit of clappings and screamings, beat her hands upon her chest and upon her knees, and threw her cap off, and pulled her hair down—the last stages on her road to frenzy. Being by this time a perfect Fury and a complete success, she made a dash at the door, which I had fortunately locked.

What could the wretched Joe do now, but stand up to his journeyman and challenge him. In a

moment they were at one another, like two giants. But, if any man in that neighborhood could stand up long against Joe, I never saw the man. Orlick was very soon among the coal dust and in no hurry to come out of it. Then, Joe unlocked the door and picked up my sister. She had fainted at the window (but not before first seeing the fight). Joe carried her into the house and helped her revive.

Not long after, I found Joe and Orlick sweeping up, without any other traces of anger than a slit in one of Orlick's nostrils. A pot of beer had appeared from the Jolly Bargemen, and they were sharing it by turns in a peaceable manner.

I got dressed and made my way to Miss Havisham's. I don't recall how many times I passed and repassed the gate before I summoned the courage to ring.

Miss Sarah Pocket came to the gate. No Estella. Miss Pocket let me in, showing no enthusiasm whatsoever. She conducted me to Miss Havisham.

Everything was unchanged, and Miss Havisham was alone. "Well?" said she, fixing her eyes upon me. "I hope you want nothing? You'll get nothing."

"No, indeed, Miss Havisham. I only wanted you to know that I am doing very well in my apprenticeship, and am always much obliged to you."

"There, there!" with the old restless fingers. "Visit me now and then. Come on your birthday.—Ay!" she cried suddenly turning herself and her chair toward me, "You are looking round for Estella? Hey?"

I had been looking round—in fact, for Estella—and I stammered that I hoped she was well.

"Abroad," said Miss Havisham, "getting a proper education for a lady; far out of reach; prettier than ever; admired by all who see her. Do you feel that you have lost her?"

There was such a malignant enjoyment in her utterance of the last words, and she broke into such a disagreeable laugh, that I was at a loss what to say. She spared me the trouble by dismissing me. When the gate was closed upon me, I felt more than ever ashamed and dissatisfied with my home and with my trade and with everything.

I lingered about well into twilight, growing

more dejected as the sky darkened. My spirits were not lifted at all when I ran into Mr. Wopsle. But, since the night was growing dark, I was not displeased to have Mr. Wopsle accompany me home. There was a heavy mist out, and it fell wet and thick. The street lamp was a blur, and its rays looked solid against the fog. We were noticing this, when we came upon a man slouching against the wall of a building.

"Hello!" we said, stopping. "Orlick, there?"

"Yeah!" he answered, slouching out. "By the way, the guns is going again."

"At the Hulks?" said I.

"Ay! There's some of the prisoners flown from the cages. The guns have been going since dark. You'll hear one presently."

Indeed, we had not walked many yards further, when the well-remembered boom came toward us. Deadened by the mist, the sound rolled away along the low grounds by the river, as if it were pursuing and threatening the fugitives.

It was very dark, very wet, very muddy, and so we splashed along. Now and then, the sound of the signal cannon broke upon us again.

Thus, we came to our village. The way by which we approached it took us past the Three Jolly Bargemen. The inn appeared to be in an unaccustomed state of commotion, with the door wide open. Mr. Wopsle dropped in to ask what was the matter (thinking that a convict had been taken), but came running out in a great hurry.

"There's something wrong," said he, without stopping, "up at your place, Pip. We must run there at once!"

"What is it?" I asked, keeping up with him. So did Orlick, at my side.

"I can't quite understand. The house seems to have been broken into when Joe Gargery was out. Supposed by convicts. Somebody has been attacked and hurt."

We were running too fast to allow conversation, and we made no stop until we got into our kitchen. A big crowd was there. There was a doctor, and there was Joe, and there was a group of women. The people drew back when they saw me. On the kitchen floor I saw my sister—lying unconscious. She had been knocked down by a vicious blow on the back of the head, dealt by some unknown hand.

Over the next several days, there was considerable discussion about who might have attacked my sister.

Joe had been at the Three Jolly Bargemen, smoking his pipe, from a quarter after eight o'clock to a quarter before ten. While he was there, my sister had been seen standing at the kitchen door, and had wished good night to a farm laborer going home. The man could not be certain when he saw her, except that it must have been before nine. When Joe went home at five minutes before ten, he found her struck down on the floor, and promptly called in assistance. The fire had not then burnt unusually low, nor was the snuff of the candle very long. The candle, however, had been blown out.

Nothing had been taken away from any part of the house. Neither, beyond the blowing out of the candle, was there any disarrangement of the kitchen. But, there was one remarkable piece of evidence on the spot. She had been struck with something blunt and heavy, on the head and spine. After the blows were dealt, something heavy had been thrown down at her with considerable violence, as she lay on her face. And on the ground beside her, when Joe picked her up, was a convict's leg-iron, which had been filed apart.

Now Joe, examining this iron with a blacksmith's eye, declared it to have been filed some time ago. Policemen summoned from the Hulks confirmed Joe's opinion. They could not say when it had left the prison-ships to which it undoubtedly had once belonged. But they were certain that that particular iron had not been worn by either of two convicts who had escaped last night. Further, one of those two was already retaken, and had not freed himself of his iron.

I believed the iron to be my convict's iron—the iron I had seen and heard him filing at, on the marshes. However, my mind did not accuse him of having put it to its latest use. I believed one of two other persons became possessed of it and used it in this cruel manner. Either Orlick, or the strange man at the Three Jolly Bargemen who had shown me the file.

Now, as to Orlick. He had been seen about town all the evening, mostly drinking in several public houses, and he had come back with me and Mr. Wopsle. There was nothing against him, except the quarrel. But my sister had quarreled with him, and with everybody else about her, ten thousand times. As to the strange man with the file, I simply did not know what to believe.

It was horrible to think that I had provided the weapon, however innocently, but I could hardly think otherwise. I suffered unspeakable trouble and guilt while I considered whether I should tell Joe the full story of the convict in the marshes. For months I debated what to do, but I managed to hold my tongue.

For a very long interval, my sister lay very ill in bed. Her sight was disturbed, so that she saw objects multiplied, and grasped at imaginary teacups and wine glasses. Her hearing was greatly impaired; her memory also; and her speech could not be understood. When, at last, she came round so far as to be helped downstairs, it was still necessary to keep my slate always by her. That way, she could indicate in writing what she could not express in speech. As she was a poor speller, and as Joe was a poor reader, extraordinary complications arose between them. I was always called in to solve these puzzles. Thus, I was able to substitute mutton for medicine, tea for Joe, and the baker for bacon, to mention only a fraction of the difficulties between Joe and his wife.

However, her temper was greatly improved, and she was patient. Her limbs began to tremble regularly. Sometimes, at intervals of two or three months, she would put her hands to her head and fall into a deep and silent depression. We were at a loss to find a suitable attendant for her, until Mr. Wopsle's great aunt's granddaughter announced that she would be pleased to move in with us and take care of my sister. This young woman, whom everyone called Biddy, became a blessing to our household.

Biddy's first triumph in her new office was to solve a difficulty that had completely baffled me. Again and again, my sister had traced upon the slate a character that looked like a T. She then indicated that she was most eager to have it. I had in vain tried everything that began with a T, from tar to toast and tub. At length it had come into my head that the sign looked like a hammer. But, when I paraded before her all the hammers in the forge, she shook her head no. I explained all this to Biddy.

"Why, of course!" cried Biddy, with an exultant face. "Don't you see? It's him!"

Orlick, without a doubt! She had lost his name, and could only signify him by his hammer. We told him why we wanted him to come into the kitchen, and he slowly laid down his hammer, wiped his brow with his arm, and came slouching out.

I confess that I expected to see my sister denounce him, and that I was disappointed by the different result. She showed every possible desire to be on good terms with him. After that day, a day rarely passed without her drawing the hammer on her slate, and without Orlick's slouching in and standing doggedly before her, as if he knew no more than I did what to make of it.

I now fell into a regular routine of apprenticeship life. When my birthday arrived, I paid another visit to Miss Havisham. Miss Sarah Pocket was still on duty at the gate. I found Miss Havisham just as I had left her, and she spoke of Estella in the very same way.

"So!" she said, without being startled or surprised, "the days have worn away, have they?"

"Yes, ma'am. Today is—"

"There, there, there!" with the impatient movement of her fingers. "I don't want to know." The interview lasted but a few minutes. She gave me a guinea when I was going, and told me to come again on my next birthday. This became an annual custom.

Everything remained unchanged about the dull old house, the yellow light in the darkened room, and the faded figure in the chair by the dressing table glass. I felt as if Time had stopped in that mysterious place, while I and everything else outside it grew older. Daylight never entered the house. As for me, I continued to hate my trade and to be ashamed of home.

Slowly, however, I became conscious of a change in Biddy. Her shoes were polished, her hair grew bright and neat, her hands were always clean. She was not beautiful—she was common, and could not be like Estella—but she was pleasant and sweet-tempered. She had not been with us more than a year, when I observed to myself one evening that she had curiously thoughtful and attentive eyes. Indeed, her eyes were very pretty and very good.

As I leaned back in my wooden chair and looked at Biddy sewing, I began to think her rather an extraordinary girl.

"You are one of those, Biddy," said I, "who make the most of every chance. You never had a chance before you came here, and see how improved you are!"

Biddy looked at me for an instant and went on with her sewing. I thought I saw a tear well up in her eye.

"Biddy!" I exclaimed, in amazement. "Why, you are crying!"

"No, I am not," said Biddy, looking up and laughing. "What put that in your head?"

What could have put it in my head, but the glistening of a tear as it dropped on her work?

"We must talk together a little more," I said. "Let us have a quiet walk on the marshes next

Sunday, Biddy, and a long chat."

Joe undertook the care of my sister on that Sunday afternoon, and Biddy and I went out together. It was summertime, and lovely weather. We passed the village and the church and the churchyard, and were out on the marshes. We could see the sails of the ships as they sailed on. When we came to the riverside and sat down on the bank, with the water rippling at our feet, I resolved that it was a good time and place for the admission of Biddy into my inner confidence.

"Biddy," said I, after binding her to secrecy, "I want to be a gentleman."

"Oh, I wouldn't, if I was you!" she returned. "I don't think it would be such a good thing."

"Biddy," said I, with some severity, "I have particular reasons for wanting to be a gentleman."

"You know best, Pip. But don't you think you are happier as you are?"

"Biddy," I exclaimed, impatiently, "I am not at all happy as I am. I am disgusted with my trade and with my life. I never shall be anything but miserable, unless I can lead a very different sort of life from the life I lead now. If I could have settled down and been but half as fond of the forge as I was when I was little, I know it would have been much better for me. But now I know I am only coarse and common."

Biddy turned her face suddenly toward mine, and looked far more attentively at me than she had looked at the sailing ships.

"It was neither a very true nor a very polite thing to say," she remarked, directing her eyes to the ships again. "Who said it?"

I was unsure of how to reply, but I answered, "The beautiful young lady at Miss Havisham's, and she's more beautiful than anybody ever was, and I admire her dreadfully, and I want to be a gentleman on her account." Having made this lunatic confession, I began to throw my torn-up grass into the river, as if I had some thoughts of following it.

"Do you want to be a gentleman to spite her, or to gain her over?" Biddy quietly asked me, after a pause.

"I don't know," I moodily answered.

"Because, if it is to spite her," Biddy pursued, "I should think—but you know best—that might be better done by caring nothing for her words. And if it is to gain her over, I should think—but you know best—she was not worth gaining over."

Exactly what I myself had thought, many times. "It may be all quite true," said I to Biddy, "but I admire her dreadfully."

Biddy was the wisest of girls, and she tried to reason no more with me. She put her hand, which was a comfortable hand though roughened by work, upon my hands, one after another. Then she softly patted my shoulder in a soothing way, while with my face upon my sleeve, I cried a little—exactly as I had done in the brewery yard.

"I am glad of one thing," said Biddy, "and that is, that you have felt you could give me your confidence, Pip. Of course you know you may depend upon my keeping it and always so far deserving it." So, with a quiet sigh for me, Biddy rose from the bank, and said, with a fresh and pleasant change of voice, "Shall we walk a little further, or go home?"

"Biddy," I cried, getting up, putting my arm round her neck, and giving her a light kiss on the cheek, "I shall always tell you everything."

"Till you're a gentleman," said Biddy.

"You know I never shall be, so that's always."

"Ah!" said Biddy, quite in a whisper, as she looked away at the ships. And then repeated, with her former pleasant change, "Shall we walk a little further, or go home?"

I said to Biddy we would walk a little further, and we did so. The summer afternoon gave way to the summer evening, and it was very beautiful. I began to consider whether I was not more naturally and wholesomely situated, after all, in these circumstances, than playing beggar my neighbor by candlelight in the room with the stopped clocks, and being despised by Estella. I thought it would be very good for me if I could get her out of my head, with all the rest of those remembrances and fancies, and could go to work determined to relish what I had to do, and stick to it, and make the best of it. I asked myself whether, if Estella were beside me at that moment instead of Biddy, she would make me miserable. I was obliged to admit that she certainly would, and I said to myself, "Pip, what a fool you are!"

We talked a good deal as we walked, and all that Biddy said seemed right. Biddy was never insulting. She would have derived only pain, and no pleasure, from giving me pain. She would far rather have wounded her own heart than mine. How could it be, then, that I did not like her much the better of the two?

When we came near the churchyard, we had to cross an embankment. There started up, from the gate, or from the rushes, or from the ooze, Old Orlick.

"Halloa!" he growled, "where are you two going?"

"Where should we be going, but home?"

"Well then," said he, "I'll see you home!"

Biddy was much against his going with us, and said to me in a whisper, "Don't let him come; I don't like him." As I did not like him either, I took the liberty of saying that we thanked him, but we didn't need seeing home. He received that piece of information with a yell of laughter, and dropped back, but came slouching after us at a little distance.

I was curious to know whether Biddy suspected him of having had a hand in that murderous attack on my sister. So, I asked her why she did not like him.

"Oh!" she replied, glancing over her shoulder as he slouched after us, "because I—I am afraid he likes me."

"Did he ever tell you he liked you?" I asked, indignantly.

"No," said Biddy, glancing over her shoulder again, "he never told me so. But he dances at me, whenever he can catch my eye."

I was very angry about Old Orlick's daring to admire her.

"But it makes no difference to you," said Biddy, with a hint of regret in her tone of voice.

"No, Biddy, it makes no difference to me. Only I don't like it. I don't approve of it."

"Nor I neither," said Biddy. "Though that makes no difference to you."

"Exactly," said I.

I kept an eye on Orlick after that night. Whenever I saw that he had a chance to dance before Biddy, I got between them, to obscure that demonstration. He had become established in the forge, by reason of my sister's sudden fancy for him. Otherwise, I should have tried to get him dismissed. He quite understood and returned my feelings, as I had reason to know thereafter.

It was in the fourth year of my apprenticeship to Joe, and it was a Saturday night. I was part of a group assembled round the fire at the Three Jolly Bargemen. We listened to Mr. Wopsle as he read a newspaper account concerning a local murder.

I became aware of a strange gentleman looking on. He bit the side of a great forefinger as he watched the group of faces. This individual had about him an air of authority not to be disputed.

"From information I have received," said he, looking round at us, "I have reason to believe there is a blacksmith among you, by name Joseph—or Joe—Gargery. Which is the man?"

"Here is the man," said Joe.

The strange gentleman beckoned him out of his place, and Joe went.

"You have an apprentice," pursued the stranger, "commonly known as Pip? Is he here?"

"I am here!" I cried.

The stranger did not recognize me. However, I recognized him as the gentleman I had met on the stairs during my second visit to Miss Havisham. Now that I stood before him with his hand upon my shoulder, I observed again his large head, his dark complexion, his deep-set eyes, his bushy black eyebrows, his large watchchain, his strong black dots of beard and whisker, and even the smell of scented soap on his great hand.

"I wish to have a private conference with you two," said he, when he had surveyed me at his leisure. "It will take a little time. Perhaps we had better go to your place of residence."

Amidst a wondering silence, we three walked out of the Jolly Bargemen, and in a wondering silence walked home. While going along, the strange gentleman occasionally looked at me, and occasionally bit the side of his finger. We reached our house and settled down in the parlor, which was feebly lighted by one candle.

It began with the strange gentleman's sitting down at the table, drawing the candle to him, and looking over some entries in his pocket notebook. He then put away the notebook and set the candle a little aside.

"My name," he said, "is Jaggers, and I am a lawyer in London. I am rather well known. I have unusual business to transact with you. I begin by explaining that it is not my idea. If my advice had been asked, I should have advised against it. It was not asked, and you see me here. I am acting as the confidential agent of another.

"Now, Joseph Gargery, I bear an offer to relieve you of this young fellow. You would not object to cancel his legal obligation to serve as an apprentice under you, at his request and for his good? You would want nothing for so doing?"

"Lord forbid that I should want anything for not standing in Pip's way," said Joe, staring.

"Lord forbidding is pious, but not to the purpose," returned Mr. Jaggers. "The question is, Would you want anything? Do you want anything?"

"The answer is," returned Joe, sternly, "no."

I thought Mr. Jaggers glanced at Joe, as if he considered him a fool for not asking for any reward. But I was too much bewildered, between breathless curiosity and surprise, to be sure of it.

"Very well," said Mr. Jaggers. "Remember the admission you have made, and don't try to change your mind."

"Who's a-going to try?" retorted Joe.

"I don't say anybody is. Now, I return to this young fellow. And the communication I have got to make is, that he has great expectations."

Joe and I gasped, and looked at one another.

"I am instructed to communicate to him," said Mr. Jaggers, throwing his finger at me sideways, "that he will come into a handsome quantity of wealth. Further, it is the desire of the present possessor of that money, that he be immediately removed from this place, and be brought up as a gentleman—in a word, as a young fellow of great expectations."

My dream was coming true! Miss Havisham was going to make my fortune on a grand scale.

"Now, Mr. Pip," pursued the lawyer, "I address the rest of what I have to say, to you. You are to understand, first, that it is the request of the person from whom I take my instructions, that you always bear the name of Pip. You will have no objection, I dare say, to this request. But if you have any objection, this is the time to mention it."

My heart was beating so fast, and there was such a singing in my ears, that I could scarcely stammer that I had no objection.

"I should think not! Now you are to understand, secondly, Mr. Pip, that the name of the person who is your liberal benefactor remains a profound secret, until the person chooses to reveal it. I am authorized to mention that it is the intention of that person to reveal it first hand by word of mouth to yourself. When or where that intention may be carried out, I cannot say. It may be years in the future. Now, you are to understand that you are prohibited from inquiring about the identity of this individual in all the communications you may have with me. If you have a suspicion, keep that suspicion to yourself. This condition is laid down. Your acceptance of it is the only remaining condition that I am charged with, by the person from whom I take my instructions. That person is the person from whom you derive your expectations, and the secret is solely held by that person and by me. If you have any objection to it, this is the time to mention it. Speak out."

Once more, I stammered with difficulty that I had no objection.

"I should think not! Now, Mr. Pip, I have done with conditions. We come next to mere details of arrangement. Although I have used the term 'expectations' more than once, you are not endowed with expectations only. There is already lodged, in my hands, a sum of money amply sufficient for your suitable education and maintenance. You will please consider me your guardian. Oh!" for I was going to thank him, "I tell you at once, I am paid for my services, or I shouldn't render them. Now, you must be better educated, in accordance with your altered position. Are you ready to start right away?"

I stammered yes.

"Good. There is a certain tutor, of whom I have some knowledge, who I think might suit the purpose," said Mr. Jaggers. "The gentleman I speak of is one Mr. Matthew Pocket."

Ah! I recognized the name directly. Miss Havisham's relation. The Matthew whose place was to be at Miss Havisham's head, when she lay dead in her bride's dress on the bride's table.

"You know the name?" said Mr. Jaggers, looking shrewdly at me, and then shutting his eyes while he waited for my answer.

My answer was that I had heard of the name.

"Oh!" said he. "You have heard of the name. But the question is, what do you say of it?"

I said I would gladly try that gentleman.

"Good. You had better try him in his own house. The way shall be prepared for you, and you can see his son first, who is in London. When will you come to London?"

I said (glancing at Joe, who stood looking on, motionless), that I supposed I could come directly.

"First," said Mr. Jaggers, "you should have some new clothes to come in, and they should not be working clothes. Say a week from today. You'll want some money. Shall I leave you twenty guineas?"

He produced a long purse, with the greatest coolness, and counted them out on the table and pushed them over to me.

"Well, Joseph Gargery? You look dumbfounded?"

"I am!" said Joe, in a very decided manner.

"It was understood that you wanted nothing for yourself, remember?"

"It were understood." said Joe. "And it are understood."

"But what," said Mr. Jaggers, swinging his purse, "what if it was in my instructions to make you a present, as compensation?"

"As compensation what for?" Joe demanded.

"For the loss of his services."

Joe gently laid his hand upon my shoulder. He was like the steam-hammer, that can crush a man or pat an eggshell, in his combination of strength with gentleness. "Pip is welcome," said Joe, "to go free with his services, to honor and fortun'. But if you think as money can make compensation to me for the loss of the little child—what come to the forge—and ever the best of friends!—"

O dear good Joe, whom I was so ready to leave and so unthankful to, I see you again, with your muscular blacksmith's arm before your eyes, and your broad chest heaving, and your voice dying away. O dear good faithful tender Joe, I feel the loving tremble of your hand upon my arm, as solemnly this day as if it had been the rustle of an angel's wing!

I begged Joe to be comforted, for (as he said) we had ever been the best of friends, and (as I said) we ever would be so. Joe wiped his eyes with his disengaged wrist, as if he were bent on gouging himself, but said not another word.

Mr. Jaggers had looked on at this, as one who recognized in Joe the village idiot. When it was over, he said, weighing in his hand the purse he had ceased to swing, "Now, Joseph Gargery, I warn you this is your last chance. No half measures with me. If you mean to take a present that I have been instructed to make you, speak out, and you shall have it. If on the contrary you mean to say—" Here, to his great amazement, he was stopped by Joe's suddenly making menacing gestures.

"Which I meantersay," cried Joe, "that if you come into my place bull-baiting and badgering me, come out! Which I meantersay, if you're a man, come on and let's fight it out!"

I drew Joe away, and he immediately became quiet. He only repeated softly that he was not going to be bull-baited and badgered in his own place. Mr. Jaggers had risen when Joe demonstrated, and had backed near the door. Without showing any inclination to come in again, he there delivered his parting remarks. They were these:

"Well, Mr. Pip, I think the sooner you leave here—as you are to be a gentleman—the better. Let's agree to a week from today. You shall receive my printed address in the meantime. When you reach London, come straight to me." With that, he began to retrace his steps to the Jolly Bargemen, where he had left a hired carriage. I ran after him and called out, "I beg your pardon, Mr. Jaggers."

"Halloa!" said he, facing round, "what's the matter?"

"I wish to keep to your directions, so I thought I had better ask. Would there be any objection to my saying goodbye to any one I know, before I go away?"

"No," said he.

"I don't mean in the village only, but uptown?"

"No," said he. "No objection."

I thanked him and ran home again, and there I found Joe seated by the kitchen fire with a hand on each knee, gazing intently at the burning coals. I too sat down before the fire and gazed at the coals, and nothing was said for a long time.

My sister was in her cushioned chair in her corner, and Biddy sat at her needlework before the fire. The more I looked into the glowing coals, the more incapable I became of looking at Joe. The longer the silence lasted, the more unable I felt to speak.

At length I got out, "Joe, have you told Biddy?"

"No, Pip," returned Joe, still looking at the fire, and holding his knees tight, "which I left it to yourself, Pip."

"I would rather you told, Joe."

"Pip's a gentleman of fortun' then," said Joe, "and God bless him in it!"

Biddy dropped her work and looked at me. Joe held his knees and looked at me. I looked at both of them. After a pause, they both heartily congratulated me. But there was a certain touch of sadness in their congratulations that I rather resented.

Biddy then tried to convey to my sister some idea of what had happened. To the best of my belief, her efforts entirely failed. She laughed and nodded her head a great many times, and even repeated, after Biddy, the words "Pip" and "Property."

I sat with my elbow on my knee and my face upon my hand, looking into the fire, as those two talked about my going away, and about what they should do without me.

I soon exchanged an affectionate good night with Biddy and Joe and went up to bed. When I got into my little room, I sat down and took a long look at it. It was a mean little room that I should soon be parted from and raised above, forever. It was furnished with things from my youth. I fell into the same confused division of mind between it and the better rooms to which I was going, as I had been in so often between the forge and Miss Havisham's, and Biddy and Estella.

I put my light out and crept into bed. It was an uneasy bed now, and I never slept the old sound sleep in it any more.

When I awoke the next morning, my spirits were much improved. Joe and Biddy were very sympathetic and pleasant when I spoke of our approaching separation. After breakfast, Joe brought out my official apprentice papers, and we put them in the fire. I felt that I was free.

That afternoon I paid a visit to the churchyard and the marshes one last time. I could not help thinking about the fugitive whom I had once seen limping among those graves, ragged and shivering, with his felon iron and badge! My comfort was that it happened a long time ago, and that he had doubtless been taken to a distant prison. In any event, he was dead to me, and might be actually dead as well. I thought, too, of Miss Havisham, and whether she intended me for Estella.

The next day, I put on my best clothes and went into town. I presented myself before Mr. Trabb, the tailor. Mr. Trabb was having his breakfast in the parlor behind his shop. Not thinking it worth his while to come out to me, he called me in to him.

"Well!" said Mr. Trabb, "how are you, and what can I do for you?"

"Mr. Trabb," said I, "it's an unpleasant thing to have to mention, because it looks like boasting. But I have come into some money."

A change passed over Mr. Trabb. He forgot about his breakfast and came out to meet me, exclaiming, "Lord bless my soul!"

"I am going up to my guardian in London," said I, casually drawing some guineas out of my pocket and looking at them. "I would like you to make me a fashionable suit of clothes to go in."

"My dear sir," said Mr. Trabb, as he respectfully bowed." May I venture to congratulate you? Would you do me the favor of stepping into the shop?"

Mr. Trabb's helper was the most ill-mannered boy in all that countryside. When I had entered he was sweeping the shop, knocking the broom against all possible corners and obstacles.

"Hold that noise," said Mr. Trabb, with the greatest sternness, "or I'll knock your head off! Do me the favor to be seated, sir." As I took my seat, the tailor presented me with several bolts of cloth of various colors and patterns. I selected the materials for a suit, with the assistance of Mr. Trabb's judgment. Mr. Trabb then measured me up and down and across, precisely writing down the numbers. It was agreed that he would deliver the finished garment to Mr. Pumblechook's on Thursday evening.

The last word was flung at the boy, who had not the least notion what it meant. But I saw him collapse as his master escorted me out. My first experience of the stupendous power of money was that it had laid Trabb's boy upon his back.

After this memorable event, I went to the hatter's, and the bootmaker's, and the stocking-maker's. I also went to the coach office and booked passage for seven o'clock on Saturday morning. It was not necessary to explain everywhere that I had come into a handsome property. However, whenever I said anything to that effect, I observed that the tradesman ceased his lazy peering out the window and paid attention to me. When I had ordered everything I wanted, I directed my steps toward Pumblechook's. As I approached that gentleman's place of business, I saw him standing at his door.

He was waiting for me with great impatience. He had been out early with his carriage, and had called at the forge and heard the news.

"My dear friend," said Mr. Pumblechook, taking me by both hands, "I give you joy of your good fortune. Well deserved, well deserved! To think that I should have been the humble instrument of leading up to this, is a proud reward. My dear young friend," said Mr. Pumblechook, "if you will allow me to call you so—"

I murmured "Certainly," and Mr. Pumblechook took me by both hands again. "My dear young friend," said Mr. Pumblechook, "you must be hungry, you must be exhausted. Be seated. Here is some chicken and some tongue plus a few other delicacies for you. And may I—may I—?"

This "May I" meant "might I shake hands?" I consented, and he did so enthusiastically, and then sat down again.

"Here is wine," said Mr. Pumblechook. "Let us drink. And may I—may I?"

I said he might, and he shook hands with me again. He then emptied his glass and turned it upside down. I did the same. If I had turned myself upside down before drinking, the wine could not have gone more directly to my head.

After several more "May I's" and handshakes, I mentioned to Mr. Pumblechook that I wished to have my new clothes sent to his house. He was ecstatic on my so distinguishing him. He also made known to me, for the first time in my life, and certainly after having kept his secret wonderfully well, that he had always said of me, "That boy is no common boy, and mark me, his fortun' will be no common fortun'."

We shook hands for the hundredth time at least, and I pursued my way home.

Friday morning I went to Mr. Pumblechook's, to put on my new clothes and pay my visit to Miss Havisham. Mr. Pumblechook was not at home, it being market day. So I made my way to Miss Havisham's. Sarah Pocket came to the gate and positively reeled back when she saw me so changed.

"You?" said she. "You, good gracious! What do you want?"

"I am going to London, Miss Pocket," said I, "and I want to say goodbye to Miss Havisham."

She left me locked outside the gate, while she went to ask if I were to be admitted. After a very short delay, she returned and took me up, staring at me all the way.

Miss Havisham was taking exercise in the room with the long spread table, leaning on her crutch stick. The room was lighted as before. At the sound of our entrance, she stopped and turned. She was then just beside the rotted bride cake.

"Don't go, Sarah," she said. "Well, Pip?"

"I start for London, Miss Havisham, tomorrow, and I thought you would not mind my taking leave of you."

"This is a grand figure, Pip," said she, making her crutch stick play round me, as if she, the fairy godmother who had changed me, were bestowing the finishing gift.

"I have come into such good fortune since I saw you last, Miss Havisham," I murmured. "And I am so grateful for it, Miss Havisham!"

"Ay, ay!" said she, looking at the envious Sarah with delight. "I have seen Mr. Jaggers. I have heard about it, Pip. So you go tomorrow?"

"Yes, Miss Havisham."

"And you are adopted by a rich person?"

"Yes, Miss Havisham."

"Not named?"

"No, Miss Havisham."

"And Mr. Jaggers is made your guardian?"

"Yes, Miss Havisham."

She quite gloated on these questions and answers, so keen was her enjoyment of Sarah Pocket's jealous dismay. "Well!" she went on, "you have a promising career before you. Be good—deserve it—and obey Mr. Jaggers's instructions." She looked at me, and looked at Sarah. Sarah's hurtful expression put a cruel smile on Miss Havisham's face. "Goodbye, Pip!—you will always keep the name of Pip, you know."

"Yes, Miss Havisham."

"Goodbye, Pip!"

She stretched out her hand. I went down on my knee and put it to my lips. She looked at Sarah Pocket with triumph in her weird eyes. And so I left my fairy godmother, with both her hands on her crutch stick, standing in the midst of the dimly lighted room beside the rotten bride cake that was hidden in cobwebs.

Sarah Pocket conducted me down. She could not get over my appearance. I said "Goodbye, Miss Pocket," but she merely stared, and did not seem collected enough to know that I had spoken.

And now, those six days, which were to have run out so slowly, had run out fast and were gone. Tomorrow looked me in the face more steadily than I could look at it. As the six evenings had dwindled away, to five, to four, to three, to two, I had become more and more appreciative of the society of Joe and Biddy. On my last evening, I dressed myself in my new clothes for their delight. We had a hot supper on the occasion, graced by the inevitable roast fowl. We were all in very low spirits.

Early the next morning, Biddy prepared my breakfast. It was a hurried meal with no taste in it. After it was over, I got up and declared, "Well! I suppose I must be off!" Then I kissed my sister, who was laughing and nodding and shaking in her usual chair, and kissed Biddy, and threw my arms around Joe's neck. Then I took up my little suitcase and walked out. The last I saw of them was dear old Joe waving his strong right arm above his head, crying huskily "Hooroar!" and Biddy putting her apron to her face.

I walked away at a good pace. The village was very peaceful and quiet, and the light mists were solemnly rising. Perhaps under the influence of such tranquility, I broke into tears. It was by a post at the end of the village. I laid my hand upon it, and said, "Goodbye O my dear, dear friend!"

I felt better after I had cried. Yet, when I was on the coach, and it was clear of the town, I deliberated with an aching heart whether I would not get down when we changed horses and walk back. We changed, and we changed many times again. Still I found myself riding in the coach. The mists had all solemnly risen now, and the world lay spread before me.

THIS IS THE END OF THE FIRST STAGE
OF PIP'S EXPECTATIONS.

VOLUME 2

The journey from our town to London was a of about five hours. It was a little past midday when we reached the city.

At the time, we Britons were convinced that we had the best of everything. Otherwise, I might have concluded that London was rather ugly, crooked, narrow, and dirty.

Mr. Jaggers had duly sent me his address. It was close by the coach office. I hired a local carriage to take me to my destination.

I scarcely had time to enjoy the coach when I observed the coachman beginning to get down, as if we were going to stop presently. And stop we presently did, in a gloomy street, at certain offices with an open door, whereon was painted MR. JAGGERS.

"How much?" I asked the coachman.

The coachman answered, "A shilling—unless you wish to make it more."

I naturally said I had no wish to make it more.

"Then it must be a shilling," observed the coachman. "I don't want to get into trouble. I know him!" He darkly closed an eye at Mr. Jaggers's name, and shook his head.

I went into the front office with my little suitcase in my hand and asked, Was Mr. Jaggers at home?

"He is not," returned the clerk. "He is in court at present. Am I addressing Mr. Pip?"

I nodded my head.

"Mr. Jaggers left word for you to wait in his room. He couldn't say how long he might be, having a case on. But since his time is valuable, he won't be longer than he can help."

With those words, the clerk opened a door and ushered me into an inner chamber at the back. Mr. Jaggers's room was lighted by a skylight only, and was a most dismal place. There were some odd objects about, such as an old rusty pistol, a sword in a scabbard, several strange-looking boxes and packages, and two dreadful casts on a shelf, their faces peculiarly swollen. Mr. Jaggers's own high-backed chair was of deadly black horsehair, with rows of brass nails round it, like a coffin. I fancied I could see how he leaned back in it, and bit his forefinger at the clients.

I sat down in the client's chair and became fascinated by the dismal atmosphere of the place. I wondered whether the two swollen faces were of Mr. Jaggers's family. Of course I had no experience of a London summer day, and my spirits may have been oppressed by the hot exhausted air, and by the dust

and grit that lay thick on everything. But I sat wondering and waiting in Mr. Jaggers's close room, until I really could not bear the two casts on the shelf above Mr. Jaggers's chair, and got up and went out.

When I told the clerk that I would take a walk outside while I waited, he advised me to go round the corner and I should find myself in the neighborhood known as Smithfield. I did so. The shameful place, smeared with filth and fat and blood and foam, seemed to stick to me. So I rubbed it off with all possible speed by turning into a street where I saw the great black dome of Saint Paul's bulging at me from behind a grim stone building. A bystander said it was Newgate Prison. From the quantity of people standing about, smelling strongly of spirits and beer, I inferred that the trials were on.

While I looked about me here, an exceedingly dirty and partially drunk servant of justice showed me where the gallows was kept, and also where people were publicly whipped. Then he showed me the

Debtors' Door, out of which convicted persons came to be hanged. This was horrible and gave me a sickening idea of London.

I dropped into the office to ask if Mr. Jaggers had come in yet. I found he had not, and I strolled out again along a street known as Bartholomew Close. I became aware that other people were waiting for Mr. Jaggers, as well as I. There were two men of suspicious appearance whispering together. One of them said to the other, when they passed me, "Jaggers would do it if it was to be done." There was a knot of three men and two women standing at a corner. One of the women was crying on her dirty shawl, and the other comforted her by saying, "Jaggers is defending him, Melia. What more could you want?" These testimonies to the popularity of my guardian made a deep impression on me, and I admired and wondered more than ever.

At length, I saw Mr. Jaggers coming across the road toward me. The others saw him at the same time, and there was quite a rush at him. Mr. Jaggers put a hand on my shoulder and addressed himself to his followers.

First, he spoke to the two suspicious men. "I have nothing to say to you at present," said Mr. Jaggers. "As to the result, it's a toss-up. I told you from the first it was a toss-up. Have you paid Wemmick?"

"We made the money up this morning, sir," said one of the men, submissively.

"I don't ask you when you made it up, or where, or whether you made it up at all. Has Wemmick got it?"

"Yes, sir," said both the men together.

"Very well; then you may go."

"We thought, Mr. Jaggers—" one of the men began, pulling off his hat.

"That's what I told you not to do," said Mr. Jaggers. "You thought! I think for you. If I want you, I know where to find you. I don't want you to find me. I won't hear a word."

The two men looked at one another and humbly fell back and were heard no more. My guardian discharged the remaining supplicants in the same bullying manner. Without further interruption, we reached the front office.

My guardian took me into his own room. While he ate lunch from a sandwich-box, he informed me what arrangements he had made for me. I was to go to "Barnard's Inn," a residence where young Mr. Pocket lived. I was to remain with young Mr. Pocket until Monday. On Monday I was to go with him to his father's house to see how I liked it. Also, I was told what my allowance was to be. It was a very generous one. I was also given the business cards of certain tradesmen I was to buy clothes and other necessities from.

Being more than satisfied with these arrangements, I asked Mr. Jaggers if I could send for a coach. He said it was not worthwhile, for Barnard's Inn was very close. Wemmick would walk round with me, if I pleased. I then found that Wemmick was the clerk in the next room. We made our way to Barnard's Inn.

As we went along, I had a chance to observe what Mr. Wemmick looked like in the light of day. I found him to be rather short in stature, with a square wooden face. From the frayed condition of his clothes, I judged him to be a bachelor. He had glittering eyes—small, keen, and black—and thin wide lips. His age appeared to be from forty to fifty years.

"So you were never in London before?" said Mr. Wemmick to me.

"No," said I. "Is it a very wicked place?"

"You may get cheated, robbed, and murdered, in London. But there are plenty of people anywhere who'll do that for you. They'll do it, if there's anything to be got by it."

I was still looking sideways at his block of a face, when he said here we were at Barnard's Inn. I had supposed that establishment to be a hotel kept by Mr. Barnard. I now found Barnard to be a fiction, and his inn the dingiest collection of shabby buildings ever squeezed together.

We passed through a nondescript gate that opened on a melancholy little square that looked to me like a flat burying ground. I thought it had the most dismal trees in it, and the most dismal sparrows, and the most dismal cats, and the most dismal houses (in number half a dozen or so), that I had ever seen. The windows of the rooms into which those houses were divided, were in every stage of dilapidated blind and curtain, crippled flowerpot, cracked glass, and dusty decay. My nose was assaulted by dry rot and wet rot and all the silent rots that rot in neglected roof and cellar—rot of rat and mouse and bug and coaching stables near at hand.

Mr. Wemmick conducted me up a flight of stairs, which appeared to me to be slowly collapsing into sawdust, to a set of chambers on the top floor. MR. POCKET, JUN., was painted on the door, and there was a label on the letterbox, "Return shortly."

"He hardly thought you'd come so soon," Mr. Wemmick explained. "You don't want me any more?"

"No, thank you," said I.

"As I keep the cash," Mr. Wemmick observed, "we shall most likely meet pretty often. Good day."

"Good day."

I concluded that London was decidedly overrated.

I whiled away the time by writing my name with my finger several times in the dirt of every pane in the window, before I heard footsteps on the stairs. Gradually there arose before me the hat, head, neckcloth, waistcoat, trousers, and boots, of a member of society of about my own standing. He had a paper bag under each arm and a container of strawberries in one hand, and was out of breath.

"Mr. Pip?" said he.

"Mr. Pocket?" said I.

"Dear me!" he exclaimed. "I am extremely sorry. I thought you would arrive later. The fact is, I have been out on your account—not that that is any excuse—for I thought, coming from the country, you might like a little fruit after dinner, and I went to Covent Garden Market to buy the best."

As I gazed at Mr. Pocket, I felt as if my eyes would start out of my head. In truth, I began to think this was a dream.

"Pray come in," said Mr. Pocket, Junior. "Allow me to lead the way. Things are pretty basic here, but I hope you'll be able to make out tolerably well till Monday. My father thought you would get on more agreeably with me than with him, and might like to take a walk about London. I am sure I shall be very happy to show London to you. This is our sitting room—just such chairs and tables and carpet and so forth, you see, as they could spare from home. This is my little bedroom; rather musty, but Barnard's is musty. This is your bedroom. The furniture's hired for the occasion, but I trust it will suit your needs.

As I stood opposite to Mr. Pocket, Junior, I saw

the amazed look come into his own eyes that I knew to be in mine, and he said, falling back:

"Lord bless me, you're the prowling boy!"

"And you," said I, "are the pale young gentleman! And the first time we met, in Miss Havisham's yard, we had a fight?"

The pale young gentleman and I stood looking at each other until we both burst out laughing. "The idea of its being you!" said he. "The idea of its being you!" said I. And then we looked at one another afresh and laughed again.

"You hadn't come into your good fortune when we first met?" said Herbert Pocket, for that was his name.

"No," said I.

"I heard it happened very lately. I was rather on the lookout for good fortune then."

"Indeed?"

"Yes. Miss Havisham had sent for me, to see if she could take a fancy to me. But she didn't. If I had come out of it successfully, I suppose I should have been provided for. Perhaps I should have been—what's the word?—to Estella."

"What word?" I asked, with sudden seriousness.

He was arranging his fruit on plates while we talked, and this task distracted him. "Betrothed, engaged," he explained, still busy with the fruit.

"How did you bear your disappointment?" I asked.

"Oh fine!" said he. "She's a tyrant."

"Miss Havisham?"

"I don't say no to that, but I meant Estella. That girl's hard and mean-spirited. She's been brought up by Miss Havisham to wreak revenge on all the male sex."

"What relation is she to Miss Havisham?"

"None," said he. "Only adopted."

"Why should she wreak revenge on all the male sex?"

"Lord, Mr. Pip!" said he. "Don't you know?"

"No," said I.

"Dear me! It's quite a story, and shall be saved till dinnertime. Mr. Jaggers is your guardian, I understand?" he went on.

"Yes."

"You know he is Miss Havisham's man of business and lawyer. She trusts him in all matters. He suggested my father for your tutor. My father is Miss Havisham's cousin, but they are not on good terms."

Herbert Pocket had a frank and easy way with him. I have never met anyone who seemed so incapable of doing anything secret and mean. There was something wonderfully hopeful about him. At the same time, I sensed that he would never be very successful or rich. He did not have a handsome face. However, his face was better than handsome, being extremely friendly and cheerful.

As he was so communicative, I felt confident in telling him my small story. I laid stress on my being forbidden to inquire who my benefactor was. I further mentioned that as I had been brought up a country blacksmith, I knew very little about proper manners. I said I would be grateful if he would give me a hint whenever he saw me behaving wrongly.

"With pleasure," said he, "though I predict that you'll need very few hints. We shall be often together, and I should like to remove any formality between us. Will you do me the favor to begin at once to call me by my Christian name, Herbert?"

I thanked him, and said I would. I informed him in exchange that my Christian name was Philip.

"I don't take to Philip," said he, smiling, "for it sounds like a boy who was so lazy that he fell into a pond, or so fat that he couldn't see out of his eyes. I tell you what I should like. We are so harmonious, and you have been a blacksmith—would you mind it?"

"I shouldn't mind anything that you propose," I answered, "but I don't understand you."

"Would you mind Handel for a familiar name? There's a charming piece of music by Handel, called 'The Harmonious Blacksmith.'"

"I should like it very much."

"Then, my dear Handel," said he, "here is the dinner."

We had made some progress in the dinner, when I reminded Herbert of his promise to tell me about Miss Havisham.

"True," he replied. "I'll honor it at once. But first, allow me to mention that in London it is not the custom to put the knife in the mouth—for fear of accidents—and that while the fork is reserved for that use, it is not put further in than necessary."

He offered these friendly suggestions in such a lively way, that we both laughed and I scarcely blushed.

"Now," he pursued, "concerning Miss Havisham. Miss Havisham, you must know, was a spoiled child. Her mother died when she was a baby, and her father denied her nothing. Her father was a country gentleman down in your part of the world, and was a brewer. Mr. Havisham was very rich and very proud. So was his daughter."

"Miss Havisham was an only child?" I hazarded.

"I am coming to that. No, she was not an only child. She had a half-brother. Her father secretly married again—his cook, I rather think. They had a boy. The daughter knew nothing about this. In due course, the second wife died. When she was dead, he first told his daughter what he had done. The son became a part of the family, living in the house you are acquainted with. As the son became a young man, he turned out riotous, extravagant, undutiful—altogether bad. His father disinherited him. But he softened when he was dying, and left him well off, though not nearly so well off as Miss

Havisham. Take another glass of wine. Please excuse my mentioning that society does not expect one to be so enthusiastic in emptying one's glass, as to turn it bottom upward with the rim on one's nose."

I thanked him and apologized. He said, "Not at all," and resumed.

"Miss Havisham was now a rich heiress. You may suppose she was sought after by many suitors as a great match. Her half-brother had now ample means again. However, reckless behavior plunged him into debt. He and his half-sister had a bitter falling-out. It is suspected that he cherished a deep grudge against her, as having turned his father's anger against him. Now, I come to the cruel part of the story—merely breaking off, my dear Handel, to remark that a dinner napkin does not get packed into a glass at the end of the meal."

Again I thanked him and apologized, and again he said cheerfully, "Not at all, I am sure!" and resumed.

"There appeared upon the scene a certain man, who ardently professed his love to Miss Havisham. I never saw him, for this happened twenty-five years ago. My father insists that this person was no gentleman, although he pretended to be one. My father says no varnish can hide the grain of the wood. Well! This man pursued Miss Havisham and proclaimed that he was devoted to her. She fell passionately in love with him. She perfectly idolized him. He preyed upon her innocent affections so as to extract great sums of money from her. He persuaded her to buy her brother out of a share in the brewery at an immense price. Your guardian was not at that time in Miss Havisham's councils. She was too much in love to be advised by any one. Her relations were poor and scheming, with the exception of my father. He was poor enough, but not one to take advantage. He was the only independent one among them. He warned her that she was doing too much for this man, and was placing herself too much in his power. She took the first opportunity of angrily ordering my father out of the house, in his presence, and my father has never seen her since.

"The marriage day was fixed. The wedding dresses were bought. The honeymoon was planned. The wedding guests were invited. The day came, but not the bridegroom. He wrote her a letter—"

"Which she received," I struck in, "when she was dressing for her marriage? At twenty minutes to nine?"

"At the hour and minute," said Herbert, nodding, "at which she afterward stopped all the clocks. What was in the letter, further than that it most heartlessly broke the marriage off, I don't know. When she recovered from a bad illness that she had, she laid the whole place waste, as you have seen it. She has never since looked upon the light of day."

"Is that all the story?" I asked.

"All I know of it. But I have forgotten one thing. It has been said that the man to whom she gave her misplaced confidence, acted throughout in concert with her half-brother. It was a conspiracy between them, and they shared the profits."

"What became of the two men?" I asked.

"They fell into deeper shame and degradation—if there can be deeper—and ruin."

"Are they alive now?"

"I don't know."

"You said just now, that Estella was not related to Miss Havisham, but adopted. When adopted?"

Herbert shrugged his shoulders. "There has always been an Estella, since I have heard of a Miss Havisham. I know no more. And now, Handel, there is a perfectly open understanding between us. All that I know about Miss Havisham, you know."

"And all that I know," I retorted, "you know."

That settled the matter, and we became very relaxed and sociable. At length I asked him what he did for a living. He replied, "An insurer of ships." I suppose he saw me glancing about the room in search of some tokens of shipping, for he added, "in downtown London."

I had grand ideas of the wealth and importance of insurers of ships. But then I recalled my impression that Herbert Pocket would never be very successful or rich. The insurer of ships went on to elaborate. "I shall not rest satisfied with merely employing my capital in insuring ships. I shall become a partner in a life insurance company. I shall also do a little in the mining way. I think I shall also become an international trader," said he, leaning back in his chair, "to the East Indies, for silks, scarves, spices, dyes, and precious woods."

"And the profits are large?" said I.

"Tremendous!" said he. "I think I shall trade, also, to the West Indies for sugar, tobacco, and rum. Also to Ceylon, especially for elephants' tusks."

"You will want a good many ships," said I.

"A perfect fleet," said he.

Quite overpowered by the scope of his ambitions, especially compared to my own, I asked him where the ships he presently insured sailed to.

"I haven't begun insuring yet," he replied. "I am looking about me."

Somehow, that pursuit seemed more in keeping with his apartment at Barnard's Inn.

"Yes," he said. "I am in a counting house, and looking about me."

"Is a counting house profitable?" I asked.

"Do you mean to me?" he asked, in reply.

"Yes; to you."

"Why, n-no; not to me. It doesn't pay me anything. But the thing is that you look about you. That's the grand thing. You are in a counting-house, you know, and you look about you. Then the time comes when you see your opening. And you go in, and you swoop upon it, and you make your fortune!"

Having practically made his fortune in his own mind, he was so pleasant that we got on famously. In the evening we went out for a walk in the streets and then bought half-price seats to the theatre. Next day we went to church at Westminster Abbey. In the afternoon we walked in the parks. I wondered who shod all the horses there, and wished Joe did.

The next afternoon, Herbert accompanied me on the coach to his family home in Hammersmith. From the coaching station it was a short walk to Mr. Pocket's house. Lifting the latch of a gate, we passed into a little garden overlooking the river, where Mr. Pocket's children were playing. There I perceived that Mr. and Mrs. Pocket's children were not growing up or being brought up, but were tumbling up.

Mrs. Pocket was sitting on a garden chair under a tree, reading, with her legs upon another garden chair. Two nursemaids in charge of the children were looking about them while the children played. "Mamma," said Herbert, "this is young Mr. Pip." Mrs. Pocket greeted me with a friendly smile.

"Master Alick and Miss Jane," cried one of the nurses to two of the children. "If you go a bouncing up against them bushes you'll fall over into the river and be drownded, and what'll your pa say then?"

At the same time, this nurse picked up Mrs. Pocket's handkerchief and said, "If that don't make six times you've dropped it, Mum!" Upon which Mrs. Pocket laughed and said, "Thank you, Flopson." She then resumed her book. But before she could have read half a dozen lines, she fixed her eyes upon me, and said, "I hope your mamma is quite well?" This unexpected inquiry put me in a state of total confusion. Luckily, the nurse came to my rescue.

"Well!" she cried, picking up the pocket handkerchief, "if that don't make seven times! What ARE you a-doing of this afternoon, Mum!" Mrs. Pocket received her property, at first with a look of unutterable surprise as if she had never seen it before, and then with a laugh of recognition, and said, "Thank you, Flopson." Forgetting me, she went on reading.

I found that there were no fewer than six little Pockets present, in various stages of tumbling up. I had scarcely arrived at the total when a seventh was heard, wailing mightily.

"If there ain't Baby!" said Flopson. "See what's the trouble, Millers."

Millers, who was the other nurse, retired into the house, and by degrees the child's wailing was hushed and stopped.

All this commotion had lasted but a very short time, when Mrs. Pocket issued summary orders that they were all to be taken into the house for a nap. I thus discovered that the nurture of the little Pockets consisted of alternately tumbling up and lying down.

At this juncture, Mr. Pocket came out of the house and joined us. He said he was glad to see me, and he hoped I was not sorry to see him. Mr. Pocket was a young-looking man, in spite of very gray hair and large black eyebrows. "Belinda," he said to his wife, "I hope you have welcomed Mr. Pip?" She looked up from her book and said, "Yes." She then smiled upon me in an absent state of mind and asked me if I liked the taste of orange-flower water.

Mr. Pocket took me into the house and showed me my room. It was pleasant and comfortable. He then knocked at the doors of two other similar rooms and introduced me to their occupants, by name Drummle and Startop. Drummle, a heavy-set, old-looking young man, was whistling. Startop, younger in years and appearance, was reading and holding his head, as if he were afraid it might explode from too much knowledge.

By degrees I learned about Mr. Pocket's profession. After receiving his education at Harrow and Cambridge, he encountered a streak of bad luck and missed opportunities. Now he hired himself out as an editor and proofreader. By what he earned in this capacity, as well as what he collected from lodgers in his house, he managed to maintain the house in which I presently found myself.

After two or three days, when I had purchased all that I needed and had established myself in my room, Mr. Pocket and I had a long talk together. He knew more of my intended career than I knew myself. Mr. Jaggers had directed that I was not to be educated for any specific profession. Instead, Jaggers had directed that I should be so educated that I could "hold my own" with other young men in prosperous circumstances.

Mr. Pocket advised my visiting certain places in London, for the purpose of acquiring the knowledge I needed. He would serve as explainer and director of all my studies.

These points were readily settled, and we two began to work in earnest. It occurred to me that if I could retain my bedroom in Barnard's Inn, my life would be pleasant. Mr. Pocket did not object to this arrangement but said I must first obtain Mr. Jaggers's approval. So I went off to that gentleman's office in London.

Mr. Jaggers consented and directed me to obtain some spending money from his assistant Mr. Wemmick. We fell into a discussion of many things. "Have you dined with Mr. Jaggers yet?" Wemmick inquired.

"Not yet."

"Well," said Wemmick, "when you go to dine with Mr. Jaggers, look at his housekeeper."

"Shall I see something very uncommon?"

"Well," said Wemmick, "you'll see a wild beast tamed."

I told him I would do so. As I was leaving, he asked me if I would like to devote five minutes to seeing Mr. Jaggers "at it?"

I replied in the affirmative, curious to know what Mr. Jaggers would be "at." We made our way to a crowded criminal court. My guardian had a woman under cross-examination. If anybody wouldn't make an admission, he proclaimed, "I'll have it out of you!" If anybody made an admission, he called out, "Now I have got you!" The magistrates shivered in his presence. Which side he was on, I couldn't make out, for he seemed to me to be grinding the whole place in a mill.

Bentley Drummle was a sulky fellow and not very bright. Idle, proud, and suspicious, he came of rich people down in Somersetshire.

Startop had been spoiled by a weak mother and kept at home when he ought to have been at school. He had a woman's delicacy of feature. It was but natural that I should take to him much more kindly than to Drummle.

Herbert was my close companion and friend. He often visited me while I lived in the family home. And I spent many an evening in London in the apartment I shared with him.

When I had been in Mr. Pocket's family a month or two, Mr. and Mrs. Camilla turned up. Camilla was Mr. Pocket's sister. Georgiana, whom I had seen at Miss Havisham's on the same occasion, also turned up. She was a cousin and a very unpleasant woman. These people hated me for my good fortune, which they contrasted with their own empty lives.

These were the surroundings among which I

settled down and applied myself to my education. I soon developed expensive habits and began to spend a good bit of money. But through good and evil I stuck to my books. Between Mr. Pocket and Herbert, I learned fast.

I had not seen Mr. Wemmick for some weeks. I thought I would write him a note and propose to go home with him on a certain evening. He replied that it would give him much pleasure, and that he would expect me at the office at six o'clock. I arrived at the appointed time, and we walked to his tiny house. On the way he inquired, "You haven't dined with Mr. Jaggers yet?"

"Not yet."

"I expect you'll have an invitation tomorrow. He's going to ask your pals, too. Three of 'em, ain't there?"

Although I did not consider Drummle as one of my friends, I answered, "Yes."

"Well, he's going to ask the whole gang."

Once at Wemmick's house, he showed me his collection of professional souvenirs. There was the pen with which a celebrated forgery had been committed. He revealed a razor or two, that had been used in murderous crimes. Some locks of hair were on display. He also showed me several handwritten confessions written under pressure. He valued these particularly, as being, to use his own words, "every one of 'em lies, sir."

Supper was splendid, as was breakfast the next morning. At half-past eight precisely we started for Wemmick's office, and arrived not long after.

As Wemmick had predicted, my guardian invited me and my friends for dinner the very next evening. We were all to meet him at his office, from which he promised to lead us to his home. He offered this invitation as he was washing his hands with his scented soap. Mr. Jaggers was in the habit of washing his hands and wiping them clean, whenever he came in from a criminal court or dismissed a client from his room.

The following evening we gathered at his office. He conducted us to Gerrard Street, Soho. His house was somewhat stately, but sadly in need of painting, and with dirty windows. He took out his key and opened the door, and we all went into a stone hall, bare, gloomy, and little used. We climbed up a dark brown staircase to a series of three dark brown rooms. There were carved garlands on the paneled walls, and as he stood among them giving us welcome, I know what kind of loops I thought they looked like.

Dinner was served in the best of these rooms. There was a bookcase in the room. The volumes were all about evidence, criminal law, criminal biography, trials, acts of Parliament, and such things. The furniture was all very solid and good, like his watch-chain. It had an official look, however, and there was nothing merely ornamental to be seen. In a corner was a little table of papers with a shaded lamp, so he could do office work at home in the evening.

Of my three companions, Mr. Jaggers seemed principally interested in Drummle.

"Pip," said he, putting his large hand on my shoulder and moving me to the window, "Who's the Spider?"

"The spider?" said I.

"The blotchy, sprawly, sulky fellow."

"That's Bentley Drummle," I replied. "The one with the delicate face is Startop."

Not showing the least interest in "the one with the delicate face," he returned, "Bentley Drummle is his name, is it? I like the look of that fellow."

He immediately began to talk to Drummle. I was looking at the two, when there came between me and them, the housekeeper, with the first dish for the table.

She was a woman of about forty, I supposed. Rather tall, of a graceful figure, extremely pale, with large faded eyes, and a quantity of streaming hair. Her lips were parted as if she were panting, and her face bore a curious expression of suddenness and flutter.

She set the dish down, touched my guardian quietly on the arm with a finger to notify that dinner was ready, and vanished. We took our seats at the round table, and my guardian kept Drummle on one side of him, while Startop sat on the other. It was a noble dish of fish that the housekeeper had put on table. It was followed by roast lamb and then chicken. For each course, Mr. Jaggers presented us with clean plates and silverware. There were also sauces, wines, and all the accessories we wanted. I observed that whenever the housekeeper was in the room, she kept her eyes attentively on my guardian. She would remove her hands from any dish she put before him, hesitatingly, as if she dreaded his calling her back.

Dinner went off gaily. When we got to the cheese, our conversation turned to our relative physical strength. Drummle insisted he was the strongest of us three. He got so wound up that he bared his arm and flexed it to show how muscular it was. Then Startop and I did the same, all in a rather ridiculous manner.

At that very moment, the housekeeper was clearing the table. With a suddenness that surprised us all, my guardian clapped his large hand on the housekeeper's, like a trap, as she stretched it across the table.

"If you talk of strength," said Mr. Jaggers, "I'll show you a wrist. Molly, let them see your wrist."

Her entrapped hand was on the table, but she had already put her other hand behind her waist.

"Master," she said, in a low voice, with her eyes attentively and pleadingly fixed upon him. "Don't."

"I'll show you a wrist," repeated Mr. Jaggers, with an immovable determination to show it. "Molly, let them see your wrist."

"Master," she again murmured. "Please!"

"Molly," said Mr. Jaggers, not looking at her, but obstinately looking at the opposite side of the room, "let them see both your wrists. Show them. Come!"

He took his hand from hers and turned that wrist up on the table. She brought her other hand from behind her, and held the two out side by side. The second wrist was much disfigured—deeply scarred. When she held her hands out, she took her eyes from Mr. Jaggers, and turned them watchfully on every one of the rest of us in succession.

"There's power here," said Mr. Jaggers, coolly tracing out the sinews with his forefinger. "Very few men have the power of wrist that this woman has. It's remarkable what mere force of grip there is in these hands. I have had occasion to notice many hands. I never saw stronger hands than these."

The moment he ceased, she looked at him again. "That'll do, Molly," said Mr. Jaggers, giving her a slight nod. She withdrew her hands and went out of the room. Mr. Jaggers then refilled our glasses with wine.

"At half-past nine, gentlemen," said he, "we must break up. Pray make the best use of your time. I am glad to see you all. Mr. Drummle, I drink to you."

This only made Drummle more boorish and talkative, until he became downright intolerable. Through it all, Mr. Jaggers followed him with the same strange interest.

In our boyish want of discretion I dare say we took too much to drink, and I know we talked too much.

"Gentlemen," said Mr. Jaggers, deliberately putting down his glass, and hauling out his gold watch by its massive chain, "I am exceedingly sorry to announce that it's half-past nine."

On this hint we all rose, expressed our thanks for the evening, and departed.

MY DEAR MR. PIP,

I write this by request of Mr. Gargery, to let you know that he is going to London in company with Mr. Wopsle and would be glad to be allowed to see you. He would call at Barnard's Hotel Tuesday morning at nine o'clock. If not agreeable please leave word. Your poor sister is much the same as when you left. We talk of you in the kitchen every night and wonder what you are doing. If you consider this to be an unwarranted liberty, excuse it for the love of poor old days.

Your ever obliged, and affectionate servant,

BIDDY

P.S. He wishes me most particular to write what larks. He says you will understand. I hope and do not doubt it will be agreeable to see him even though you are a gentleman, for you had ever a good heart, and he is a worthy man. I have read him all excepting only the last

little sentence, and he wishes me most particular to write again what larks.

I received this letter on Monday morning. Therefore its appointment was for the next day. Let me confess the feelings I had about Joe's coming.

I did not look forward to the visit with any pleasure, though I was bound to Joe by so many ties. No; I was actually quite agitated by the prospect of his arrival. If I could have kept him away by paying money, I would have paid money. I was greatly relieved that he was coming to Barnard's Inn, not to Hammersmith (where Mr. Pocket kept house), and consequently would not meet Bentley Drummle. I had little objection to his being seen by Herbert or his father, for both of whom I felt respect. However, I had the sharpest objection to his being seen by Drummle, whom I held in contempt. So, throughout life, our worst weaknesses and meannesses are usually committed for the sake of the people whom we most despise.

By this time, I had arranged for the services of a young boy to act as my occasional attendant. I had clothed him in a blue coat, yellow vest, white cravat and trousers, and top boots. This youth was ordered to be on duty at eight on Tuesday morning in the hall, which was all of two feet square. Herbert suggested certain things for breakfast that he thought Joe would like.

I came into town Monday night to be ready for Joe. I got up early in the morning and fixed up the sitting room and breakfast table to assume their most splendid appearance. Unfortunately the morning was drizzly, and an angel could not have concealed the fact that Barnard was shedding sooty tears outside the window.

As the time approached, I would have liked to run away. However, my young attendant was in the hall, and presently I heard Joe on the staircase. I knew it was Joe, by his clumsy manner of coming upstairs and by the time it took him to read the names on the other floors as he made his ascent. When at last he stopped outside our door, I could hear his finger tracing over the painted letters of my name. Finally he gave a faint single rap, and Pepper (my attendant's name) announced, "Mr. Gargery!" I thought he never would have done wiping his feet, and that I must have gone out to lift him off the mat, but at last he came in.

"Joe, how are you, Joe?"

"Pip, how AIR you, Pip?"

With his good honest face all glowing and shining, and his hat put down on the floor between us, he caught both my hands and worked them up and down, as if I had been a new patented pump.

"I am glad to see you, Joe. Give me your hat."

But Joe, taking it up carefully with both hands, like a bird's nest with eggs in it, wouldn't hear of parting with that piece of property, and persisted in standing talking over it in a most uncomfortable way.

"Which you have growed," said Joe, "and swelled, and gentle-folked. As to be sure you are a honor to your king and country."

"And you, Joe, look wonderfully well."

"Thank God," said Joe. "And your sister, she's no worse than she were. And Biddy, she's ever right and ready. And all friends is no worser, ceptin' Wopsle. He's had a drop."

All this time, Joe was rolling his eyes round and round the room, and round and round the flowered pattern of my dressing-gown.

"Had a drop, Joe?"

"Why yes," said Joe, lowering his voice, "he's left the Church, and went into the playacting. Which the playacting have likeways brought him to London along with me. I come to see him in a play here in London."

At his moment, Herbert entered the room. I presented Joe to Herbert, who held out his hand. But Joe nervously backed away from it.

"Your servant, Sir," said Joe, "which I hope as you and Pip keep your healths in this close spot. I wouldn't keep a pig in it myself—not in the case that I wished him to fatten wholesome and to eat with a meller flavor on him."

Having borne this flattering testimony to the merits of our dwelling place, we sat down to table.

"Do you take tea, or coffee, Mr. Gargery?" asked Herbert.

"Thankee, Sir," said Joe, stiff from head to foot, "I'll take whichever is most agreeable to yourself."

"What do you say to coffee?"

"Thankee, Sir," returned Joe.

The meal did not go well. Joe, obviously uneasy, fell into lengthy intervals of meditation, with his fork midway between his plate and his mouth. He sat so far from the table, and dropped so much more than he ate, that I was heartily glad when Herbert left us for the city.

I had neither the good sense nor the good feeling to know that this was all my fault. If I had been more welcoming toward Joe, Joe would have been easier with me. I felt impatient with him and out of temper with him. I sensed Joe realized how I felt about him.

"Us two being now alone, Sir," began Joe, "and me having the intentions and abilities to stay not many minutes more, I will now mention what have led to my having the present honor of being in your presence. This is how it were. I were at the Bargemen t'other night, Pip, when there come up in his shay-cart, Pumblechook. His word were, 'Joseph, Miss Havisham she wish to speak to you.'"

"Next day, Sir," said Joe, "having cleaned myself, I go and I see Miss Havisham."

"Her words were then as follering: 'Mr. Gargery. You air in correspondence with Mr. Pip?' When I said I were, she said, 'Tell him that Estella has come home and would be glad to see him.'"

I felt my face fire up as I looked at Joe. He declared, "I have now concluded, Sir. And, Pip, I wish you ever well and ever prospering to a greater and a greater heighth."

"But you are not going now, Joe?"

"Yes I am," said Joe.

"But you are coming back to dinner, Joe?"

"No I am not," said Joe.

Our eyes met, and all the "Sir" melted out of that manly heart as he gave me his hand.

"Pip, dear old chap, life is made of ever so many partings. One man's a blacksmith, and one's a goldsmith. Diwisions among such must come, and must be met as they come. If there's been any fault at all today, it's mine. You and me is not two figures to be together in London, nor anywheres else but what is private. I'm wrong out of the forge. You won't find half so much fault in me if you think of me in my forge dress, with my hammer in my hand, or even my pipe. You won't find half so much fault in me if, supposing as you should ever wish to see me, you come and put your head in at the forge window and see Joe the blacksmith, there, at the old anvil, in the old burnt apron, sticking to the old work. And so GOD bless you, dear old Pip, old chap, GOD bless you!"

I had not been mistaken in my feeling that there was a simple dignity in him. He touched me gently on the forehead and went out. As soon as I could recover myself sufficiently, I hurried out after him and looked for him in the neighboring streets. But he was gone.

I decided that I must go to our town next day. And, feeling bad about my behavior toward Joe, I decided that I must stay at Joe's house. When the next day dawned, however, I was not by any means convinced on the last point. I began to invent reasons and make excuses for putting up at the Blue Boar. I should be an inconvenience at Joe's. I was not expected. My bed would not be ready. I concluded that I would stay at the Blue Boar.

I had arranged passage on the afternoon coach, which would leave London at two o'clock. As winter had now come round, I should not arrive at my destination until two or three hours after dark.

At that time it was customary to carry convicts down to the dockyards by stagecoach. I had no cause to be surprised when Herbert, meeting me in the yard, came up and told me there were two convicts going down with me.

"See! There they are," said Herbert, "coming out of the Tap. What a degraded and vile sight it is!"

They had a guard with them, and all three came out wiping their mouths on their hands. The two convicts were handcuffed together, and had irons on their legs—irons of a pattern that I knew well. They wore the uniform that I likewise knew well. Their keeper had a brace of pistols and carried a thick-knobbed bludgeon under his arm. One was a taller and stouter man than the other, but I knew his half-closed eye at one glance. There stood the man whom I had seen on the bench at the Three Jolly Bargemen on a Saturday night.

I could tell he didn't recognize me. The convicts hauled themselves up on the coach as well as they could. The convict I had recognized sat behind me with his breath on the hair of my head.

"Goodbye, Handel!" Herbert called out as we started. I thought what a blessed fortune it was, that he had found another name for me than Pip.

It is impossible to express with what acuteness I felt the convict's breathing, not only on the back of my head, but all along my spine. It set my very teeth on edge.

The weather was miserably raw, and the two convicts cursed the cold. We habitually dozed and shivered and were silent. I dozed off, myself, in considering the question whether I ought to restore a couple of pounds sterling to this creature before losing sight of him, and how it could best be done.

Once again I dozed off. When I awoke, the first words I heard one of the convicts say were, "Two one-pound notes."

"How did he get 'em?" said the convict I had never seen.

"How should I know?" returned the other. "At any rate, I asked him, You're a going to be discharged? The answer was yes. Then he asked me to find out that boy that had fed him and kep' his secret, and give him them two one-pound notes. I said I would. And I did. But then he was tried again for prison breaking, and got made a Lifer."

The coincidence of our being together on the coach filled me with dread. I resolved to alight as soon as we reached my town, and I did. As to the convicts, they went their way with the coach, and I knew at what point they would be spirited off to the river.

I could not have said what I was afraid of, for my fear was altogether undefined and vague, but there was great fear upon me. I made my way directly to the Blue Boar. There I took my dinner and spent the night.

I woke up the next morning thinking about my patroness and painting brilliant pictures of her plans for me. She had adopted Estella; she had as good as adopted me, and it must be her intent to bring us together.

I arrived at the gate at my accustomed time. After ringing the bell, I tried to keep the beating of my heart moderately quiet. I heard the side door open. I heard steps come across the court. I turned away from the gate and pretended not to hear, even when the gate swung on its rusty hinges.

Being at last touched on the shoulder, I started and turned. I was stunned to see before me a man in a sober gray outfit. He was the last man I should have expected to see at Miss Havisham's door.

"Orlick!"

"Ah, young master, there's more changes than yours. But come in, come in."

I entered. Orlick closed the gate, locked it, and took the key out. "Yes!" said he, facing round, after preceding me a few steps toward the house. "Here I am!"

"How did you come here?"

"I come here," he retorted, "on my legs. I had my box brought alongside me in a cart."

"Are you here for good?"

"I ain't here for harm, young master, I suppose?"

I was not so sure of that. By this time we had come to the house. His room was just within the side door, with a little window looking on the courtyard. Certain keys were hanging on the wall, to which he now added the gate key.

"There used to be no porter here," I said.

"No," said he, "not till it got about that there was no protection on the premises, and it come to be considered dangerous, with convicts here about. And then I was recommended to the place as a man who could give another man as good as he brought, and I took it. It's easier than bellowing and hammering, I'm sure."

My eye had been caught by a gun with a brass bound stock over the chimneypiece, and his eye had followed mine.

"Well," said I, not wishing further conversation, "shall I go up to Miss Havisham?"

"Don't ask me," he retorted. "My orders ends here, young master. I give this here bell a rap with this here hammer, and you go on along the passage till you meet somebody."

"I am expected, I believe?"

"Burn me twice over, if I can say!" said he.

Upon that, I turned down the long passage which I had first trodden in my thick boots, and he made his bell sound. At the end of the passage, I found Sarah Pocket.

"Oh!" said she. "You, is it, Mr. Pip?"

"It is, Miss Pocket. I am glad to tell you that Mr. Pocket and family are all well."

"Are they any wiser?" said Sarah, with a dismal shake of the head. "They had better be wiser, than well. Ah, Matthew, Matthew! You know your way, sir?"

I had gone up the staircase in the dark many a time, and I ascended it now. I tapped in my old way at the door of Miss Havisham's room. "Pip's rap," I heard her say. "Come in, Pip."

She was in her chair near the old table, in the old dress, with her two hands crossed on her stick, her chin resting on them, and her eyes on the fire. Sitting near her, holding the white shoe that had never been worn, was an elegant lady whom I had never seen.

"Come in, Pip," Miss Havisham continued to mutter, without looking round or up. "Come in, Pip, how do you do, Pip? So, you kiss my hand as if I were a queen, eh?—Well?"

She looked up at me suddenly, only moving her eyes, and repeated in a grimly playful manner, "Well?"

"I heard, Miss Havisham," said I, rather at a loss, "that you were so kind as to wish me to come and see you, and I came directly."

"Well?"

The lady whom I had never seen before lifted up her eyes and looked archly at me. Then I saw that the eyes were Estella's eyes. But she was so much changed, was so much more beautiful, so much more womanly. I imagined, as I looked at her, that I had slipped hopelessly back into the coarse and common boy again. How distant and unequal I felt! How inaccessible she was!

She gave me her hand. I stammered something about the pleasure I felt in seeing her again, and about my having looked forward to it for a long, long time.

"Is he changed?" Miss Havisham asked her.

"Very much," said Estella, looking at me.

"Less coarse and common?" said Miss Havisham, playing with Estella's hair.

Estella laughed, and looked at the shoe in her hand, and laughed again, and looked at me, and put the shoe down. She treated me as a boy still, but she lured me on.

We sat in the dreamy room among the old strange influences which had so made an impression upon me. I learned that she had but just come home from France, and that she was going to London.

It was settled that I should stay there all the rest of the day, and return to the hotel at night, and to London tomorrow. When we had conversed for a while, Miss Havisham sent us two out to walk in the neglected garden. On our coming in by-and-by, she said, I should wheel her about a little as in past times.

So, Estella and I went out into the garden by the gate through which I had strayed to my encounter with the pale young gentleman, now Herbert. I trembled and worshipped the very hem of her dress. She was quite composed and most decidedly not worshipping the hem of mine. As we drew near to the place of encounter, she asked about Herbert Pocket.

"He and I are great friends now."

"Are you?"

"Yes."

"Since your change of fortune and prospects, you have changed your companions," said Estella.

"Naturally," said I.

"And necessarily," she added, in a haughty tone. "What was fit company for you once, would be quite unfit company for you now."

In my conscience, I doubt very much whether I had any lingering intention left, of going to see Joe. But if I had, this observation put it to flight.

"You had no idea of your impending good fortune, in those times?" said Estella.

"Not the least."

She walked at my side with an air of maturity and superiority. It painfully contrasted with the air of youthfulness and submission with which I walked at hers.

During our walk around the overgrown garden, I reminded her where she had come out of the house and given me meat and drink. She said, "I don't remember."

"Not remember that you made me cry?" said I.

"No," said she. I truly believe that her not remembering made me cry again, inwardly—and that is the sharpest crying of all.

"You must know," said Estella, condescending to me as a brilliant and beautiful woman might, "that I have no heart—if that has anything to do with my memory."

I took the liberty of stating that I doubted that.

"Oh! I have a heart to be stabbed in or shot in, I have no doubt," said Estella. "And, of course, if it ceased to beat, I should cease to be. But you know what I mean. I have no softness there, no—sympathy—sentiment. If we are to be thrown much together, you had better believe it at once. No!" imperiously stopping me as I opened my lips. "I have not bestowed my tenderness anywhere. I have never had any such thing. Let us make one more round of the garden, and then go in. Come!"

Her handsome dress trailed upon the ground. She held it in one hand now, and with the other lightly touched my shoulder as we walked. We walked round the ruined garden twice or three times more. For me it was all in glorious bloom. If the green and yellow growth of weed in the chinks of the old wall had been the most precious flowers that ever grew, it could not have been more cherished in my memory.

There was no difference of years between us

that might divide us. We were of nearly the same age. But the air of inaccessibility which her beauty and her manner gave her tormented me in the midst of my delight. And my torment was deepened by my conviction that our patroness had chosen us for one another. Wretched boy!

At last we went back into the house. There I heard, with surprise, that my guardian had come down to see Miss Havisham on business, and would come back to dinner. Miss Havisham was in her chair and waiting for me.

It was like pushing the chair itself back into the past, when we began the old slow circuit round about the ashes of the bridal feast. But, in the funereal room, Estella looked more bright and beautiful than before, and I was under stronger enchantment.

Estella left to prepare herself for dinner, and Miss Havisham and I were left alone. She turned to me and said in a whisper: "Is she beautiful, graceful, well-grown? Do you admire her?"

"Everybody must who sees her, Miss Havisham."

She drew an arm round my neck, and drew my head close down to hers as she sat in the chair. "Love her, love her, love her! If she favors you, love her. If she wounds you, love her. If she tears your heart to pieces—and as it gets older and stronger, it will tear deeper—love her, love her, love her!"

Never had I seen such passionate eagerness as was joined to her utterance of these words. I could feel the muscles of the thin arm round my neck swell with the vehemence that possessed her.

"Hear me, Pip! I adopted her to be loved. I bred her and educated her, to be loved. I developed her into what she is, that she might be loved. Love her!"

"I'll tell you," said she, in the same hurried passionate whisper, "what real love is. It is blind devotion, unquestioning self-humiliation, utter submission, trust and belief against yourself and against the whole world, giving up your whole heart and soul to the smiter—as I did!"

When she said that, and a wild cry that followed, I caught her round the waist. For she rose up in the chair, in her shroud of a dress, and struck at the air as if she would as soon have struck herself against the wall and fallen dead.

All this passed in a few seconds. As I drew her down into her chair, I was conscious of a scent that I knew. Turning, I saw my guardian in the room.

He always carried (I have not yet mentioned it, I think) a pocket-handkerchief of rich silk and of imposing proportions, which was of great value to him in his profession. I have seen him so terrify a client or a witness by ceremoniously unfolding this pocket-handkerchief as if he were immediately going to blow his nose, and then pausing, as if he knew he should not have time to do it before such client or witness committed himself, that the self-committal has followed directly, quite as a matter of course. When I saw him in the room, he had this expressive pocket-handkerchief in both hands, and was looking at us.

Miss Havisham had seen him as soon as I, and was (like everybody else) afraid of him. She made a strong attempt to compose herself.

"And so you are here, Pip?"

I told him when I had arrived, and how Miss Havisham had wished me to come and see Estella. To which he replied, "Ah! Very fine young lady!" Then he pushed Miss Havisham in her chair around the room.

"Well, Pip! How often have you seen Miss Estella before?" said he, when he came to a stop.

"How often?"

"Ah! How many times? Ten thousand times?"

"Oh! Certainly not so many."

"Twice?"

"Jaggers," interposed Miss Havisham, much to my relief, "leave my Pip alone, and go with him to your dinner."

He complied, and we groped our way down the dark stairs together. While we were on our way, he asked me how often I had seen Miss Havisham eat and drink.

I considered, and said, "Never."

"And never will, Pip," he retorted, with a frowning smile. "She has never allowed herself to be seen doing either, since she began this present life of hers. She wanders about in the night, and then lays hands on such food as she takes."

"Pray, sir," said I, "may I ask you a question?"

"You may," said he, "and I may decline to answer it. Put your question."

"Estella's last name. Is it Havisham or—?" I had nothing to add.

"Or what?" said he.

"Is it Havisham?"

"It is Havisham."

This brought us to the dinner table, where Estella and Sarah Pocket awaited us. Mr. Jaggers presided; Estella sat opposite him; I faced Sarah Pocket. We dined very well. We were waited on by a maidservant whom I had never seen in all my comings and goings, but who, for anything I know, had been in that mysterious house the whole time. After dinner, a bottle of choice old port was placed before my guardian, and the two ladies left us.

Anything to equal the determined silence of Mr. Jaggers under that roof, I never saw elsewhere. He kept his very looks to himself, and scarcely directed his eyes to Estella's face once during dinner. When she spoke to him, he listened, and in due course answered, but never looked at her. On the other hand, she often looked at him, with interest and curiosity, if not distrust. Throughout dinner he took a dry delight in making Sarah Pocket turn various shades of green and yellow. This he did by often referring in conversation with me to my expectations.

After dinner Miss Pocket left us, while we three went up to Miss Havisham's room and played at whist. Miss Havisham placed some of the most beautiful jewels from her dressing table into Estella's hair, and about her dress. She appeared even more dazzling than ever.

We played until nine o'clock. It was arranged that when Estella came to London, I should be notified in advance and should meet her at the coach. I then said good night and walked back to the Boar.

Far into the night, Miss Havisham's words, "Love her, love her, love her!" sounded in my ears. At least a hundred times, I declared to my pillow, "I love her, I love her, I love her!" Then, a burst of gratitude came upon me, that she should be destined for me, once the blacksmith's boy. I thought if she were, as I feared, by no means rapturously grateful for that destiny yet, when would she begin to be interested in me? When should I awaken the heart within her, that was mute and sleeping now?

Ah me! I thought those were high and great emotions. But I never thought there was anything low and small in my keeping away from Joe, because I knew she would be contemptuous of him. The thought brought tears into my eyes. But they soon dried— God forgive me!—soon dried.

After considering the matter while I was dressing at the Blue Boar in the morning, I resolved to tell my guardian that I doubted Orlick was the right sort of man to fill a post of trust at Miss Havisham's. "Why, of course he is not the right sort of man, Pip," said my guardian. "That's because the man who fills the post of trust never is the right sort of man." He listened in a satisfied manner while I told him what knowledge I had of Orlick. "Very good, Pip," he observed, when I had concluded, "I'll go round presently, and pay our friend off." Rather alarmed by this summary action, I was for a little delay. Mr. Jaggers, however, would hear nothing of it.

As we were going back together to London by the midday coach, I told my guardian that I would like to walk through town and get picked up by the coach on its way to London. My guardian said he would alert the coachman to stop, and I went on my way.

It was interesting to be in the quiet old town once more, and it was not disagreeable to be recognized and stared after. My position was a distinguished one, and I was not at all dissatisfied with it. But then Fate threw me in the way of that mischievous rascal, Trabb's boy.

Casting my eyes ahead, I beheld Trabb's boy approaching, lashing himself with an empty blue bag. I decided that I would greet him with a polite though not overly familiar look on my face. When he came upon me, suddenly the knees of Trabb's boy knocked together, his hair uprose, his cap fell off, he trembled violently in every limb, staggered out into the road, and crying to the populace, "Hold me! I'm so frightened!" feigned to be in a paroxysm of terror, occasioned by the dignity of my appearance. As I passed him, his teeth loudly chattered in his head. Pretending extreme humiliation, he prostrated himself in the dust.

This was a hard thing to bear, but this was nothing. I had not advanced another two hundred yards, when, to my surprise and indignation, I again beheld Trabb's boy approaching. He was coming round a narrow corner. His blue bag was slung over his shoulder. When he spied me, he acted in the same way as before. But this time he staggered round and round me with knees more afflicted, and with uplifted hands as if begging for mercy. His pretended sufferings were hailed with the greatest joy by a knot of spectators, and I felt utterly confounded.

I continued down the street to the post office, when I again beheld Trabb's boy shooting round by a back way. He was strutting along the pavement toward me on the opposite side of the street, attended by a company of delighted young friends to whom he from time to time exclaimed, with a wave of his hand, "Don't know yah!" As he passed me, he pulled up his shirt collar, held an arm akimbo, and smirked extravagantly by, wriggling his elbows and body, and drawling to his attendants, "Don't know yah, don't know yah, 'pon my soul don't know yah!"

Feeling humiliated and disgraced, I really do not see what I could have done except endure. However, I did write to Mr. Trabb to say that I must decline to deal further with him so long as he continued to employ that young man.

The coach, with Mr. Jaggers inside, came up in due time, and I took my box seat again. I arrived in London safe—but not sound, for my heart was gone. As soon as I arrived, I sent a codfish and barrel of oysters to Joe (as apology for not having gone myself), and then went on to Barnard's Inn.

I found Herbert dining on cold meat. He welcomed me back, and I joined him at dinner. When we finished, I said to Herbert, "My dear Herbert, I have something very particular to tell you."

"My dear Handel," he returned, "I shall esteem and respect your confidence."

"It concerns myself, Herbert," said I, "and one other person."

Herbert crossed his feet, looked at the fire, and waited for me to go on.

"Herbert," said I, laying my hand upon his knee, "I love—I adore—Estella."

Instead of being transfixed, Herbert replied in an easy matter-of-course way, "Exactly. Well?"

"Well, Herbert? Is that all you say? Well?"

"What next, I mean?" said Herbert. "Of course I know that."

"How do you know it?" said I.

"How do I know it, Handel? Why, from you."

"I never told you."

"Told me! You have never told me when you have got your hair cut, but I have had senses to perceive it. You have always adored her, ever since I have known you. You brought your adoration and your suitcase here, together. Told me! Why, you have always told me all day long. When you told me your own story, you told me plainly that you began adoring her the first time you saw her, when you were very young indeed."

"Very well, then," said I, "I have never left off adoring her. And she has come back, a most beautiful and most elegant creature. And I saw her yesterday. And if I adored her before, I now doubly adore her."

"Lucky for you then, Handel," said Herbert, "that you have been chosen for her. Have you any idea yet, of Estella's views on the adoration question?"

I shook my head gloomily. "Oh! She is thousands of miles away from me," said I.

"Patience, my dear Handel; time enough, time enough. But you have something more to say?"

"I am ashamed to say it," I returned, "and yet it's no worse to say it than to think it. You call me a lucky fellow. Of course, I am. I was a blacksmith's boy just yesterday. I am—what shall I say I am—today?"

"Say, a good fellow, if you want a phrase," returned Herbert, smiling.

"When I ask what I am to call myself today, Herbert," I went on, "I tell you what I have in my thoughts. You say I am lucky. I know I have done nothing to raise myself in life, and that Fortune alone has raised me. That is being very lucky. And yet, when I think of Estella—"

"And when don't you, you know?" Herbert threw in.

"—Then, my dear Herbert, I cannot tell you how dependent and uncertain I feel, and how exposed to hundreds of chances. On the constancy of one person (naming no person) all my expectations depend. And I have not the vaguest idea what these expectations might be!"

"Now, Handel," Herbert replied, in his gay hopeful way, "Could you believe that of all men in London, Mr. Jaggers would continue to be in contact with you unless he were sure of his ground?"

I said I could not deny that this was a strong point.

"I should think it was a strong point," said Herbert. "As to the rest, you must bide your guardian's time, and he must bide his client's time. You'll be twenty-one before you know it, and then perhaps you'll find out more."

"What a hopeful disposition you have!" said I, gratefully admiring his cheery ways.

"Now, Handel, I want to make myself seriously disagreeable to you for a moment—positively repulsive."

"You won't succeed," said I.

"Oh yes I shall!" said he. "I have been thinking since we have been talking with our feet by the fire, that Estella surely cannot be a condition of your inheritance, if she was never referred to by your guardian. Am I right that he never referred to her in any way? Never even hinted, for instance, that your patron might have views as to your marriage ultimately?"

"Never."

"Now, Handel, not being bound to her, can you not detach yourself from her? I told you I should be disagreeable. Think of her bringing-up, and think of Miss Havisham. Think of what she is herself (now I am repulsive, and you hate me). This may lead to miserable things."

"I know it, Herbert," said I, with my head still turned away, "but I can't help it."

"You can't detach yourself?"

"No. Impossible!"

"You can't try, Handel?"

"No. Impossible!"

"Well!" said Herbert, getting up with a lively

shake as if he had been asleep, and stirring the fire; "now I'll endeavor to make myself agreeable again!"

So he went round the room and shook the curtains out, put the chairs in their places, tidied the books and so forth that were lying about, looked into the hall, peeped into the letter box, shut the door, and came back to his chair by the fire. Finally, after a number of false starts, Herbert announced that he was engaged to be married. "But it's a secret," he admonished me.

I told him his secret was safe with me. "May I ask her name?" I said.

"Name of Clara," said Herbert.

"Live in London?"

"Yes. Perhaps I ought to mention," said Herbert, "that she is rather below my mother's nonsensical family notions. Her father had to do with the provisioning of passenger ships."

"What is he now?" said I.

"He's an invalid now," replied Herbert.

"Living on—?"

"On the second floor," said Herbert. Which was not at all what I meant, for I had intended my question to apply to his means of livelihood. "I have never seen him, for he has always kept his room overhead, since I have known Clara. But I have heard him constantly. He sometimes roars, and knocks at the floor with some frightful instrument."

"Don't you expect to see him?" said I.

"Oh yes, I constantly expect to see him," returned Herbert, "because I never hear him, without expecting him to come tumbling through the ceiling. But I don't know how long the rafters may hold."

When he had once more laughed heartily, he told me that the moment he began to earn money, it was his intention to marry this young lady. He added as a self-evident proposition, "But you can't marry, you know, while you're looking about you."

Miserably I went to bed, and miserably thought of Estella. I miserably dreamed that my expectations were all canceled, and that I had to give my hand in marriage to Herbert's Clara.

One day when I was busy with my books and Mr. Pocket, I received a note by the post. The writing on the envelope threw me into a great flutter. Though I had never seen the handwriting in which it was addressed, I knew whose hand it was. It had no set beginning, as "Dear Mr. Pip," or "Dear Pip," or "Dear Sir, " or "Dear Anything," but said as follows:

> **I am to come to London the day after tomorrow by the midday coach. I believe it was settled you should meet me? At all events Miss Havisham has that impression, and I write in obedience to it. She sends you her regard.**
>
> **Yours, ESTELLA**

If there had been time, I would have ordered several suits of clothes for this occasion. As there was not, I had to be content with those I had. My appetite vanished instantly, and I knew no peace or rest until the day arrived. Not that its arrival brought me either. I was more agitated than ever, and began haunting the coach office before the coach had even left the Blue Boar in our town. While I waited, whom should I meet but Mr. Wemmick?

"Halloa, Mr. Pip," said he; "how do you do? I should hardly have thought this was your beat."

I explained that I was waiting to meet somebody who was coming up by coach, and I inquired after his house and father.

"Both flourishing, thankye," said Wemmick. He then inquired, "Where do you think I am going?"

"To the office?" said I, for he was tending in that direction.

"Next thing to it," returned Wemmick, "I am going to Newgate Prison. We are handling a robbery case at present, and I have been down the road to examine the scene of the crime. Now I must have a word or two with our client."

"Did your client commit the robbery?" I asked.

"Bless your soul and body, no," answered Wemmick. "But he is accused of it. Would you like to have a look at Newgate? Have you time to spare?"

I had so much time to spare that the proposal came as a relief. We were at Newgate in a few minutes. We passed through the corridor where some chains were hanging up on the bare walls into the interior of the jail. It was visiting time when Wemmick took me in. A potman was going his rounds with beer. The prisoners, behind bars, were buying beer and talking to friends, and an ugly, disorderly, depressing scene it was.

Wemmick walked among the prisoners, much as a gardener might walk among his plants. He was highly popular, though something of the state of Mr. Jaggers hung about him too, forbidding approach beyond certain limits. His personal recognition of each successive client was expressed by a nod, and in his settling his hat a little easier on his head with both hands, and then putting his hands in his pockets. In one or two instances, there was a difficulty respecting the raising of fees. Then Mr. Wemmick, backing as far as possible from the insufficient money produced, said, "It's no use, my boy. I'm only a subordinate. I can't take it. If you are unable to pay the fee, my boy, you had better address yourself to a principal. There are plenty of principals in the profession, you know, and what is not worth the while of one, may be worth the while of another. That's my recommendation to you, speaking as a subordinate. Now, who's next?"

Thus, we walked through Wemmick's greenhouse.

As we came out of the prison, I found that the great importance of my guardian was appreciated by the jailers, no less than by those whom they held in charge. "Well, Mr. Wemmick," said the turnkey, who kept us between the two studded and spiked lodge gates, and who carefully locked one before he unlocked the other, "what's Mr. Jaggers going to do with that waterside murder? Is he going to make it manslaughter, or what's he going to make of it?"

"Why don't you ask him?" returned Wemmick.

"Oh yes, I dare say!" said the turnkey.

"Now, that's the way with them here, Mr. Pip," remarked Wemmick. "They don't mind what they ask of me, the subordinate, but you'll never catch 'em asking any questions of my principal."

We descended the steps into the street and made our way to Little Britain. Suppliants for Mr. Jaggers's attention were lingering about as usual. I returned to my watch in the street of the coach office. With some three hours before the coach would arrive, I thought of the beautiful young Estella, proud and refined, coming toward me, and I thought with absolute abhorrence of the contrast between the jail and her. I wished that Wemmick had not met me, or that I had not yielded to him and gone with him, so that, of all days in the year on this day, I might not have had Newgate in my breath and on my clothes. I beat the prison dust off my feet as I walked to and fro, and I shook it out of my clothes. So contaminated did I feel, remembering who was coming, that the coach came quickly after all, and I saw her face at the coach window and her hand waving to me.

In her furred traveling dress, Estella seemed more delicately beautiful than ever. We stood in the Inn Yard while she pointed out her luggage to me. When it was all collected I remembered—having forgotten everything but herself in the meanwhile—that I knew nothing of her destination.

"I am going to the town of Richmond, located in Surrey," she told me. The distance is ten miles. I am to have a carriage, and you are to take me. This is my purse, and you are to pay my charges out of it. Oh, you must take the purse! We have no choice, you and I, but to obey our instructions. We are not free to follow our own devices, you and I."

As she looked at me in giving me the purse, I hoped there was an inner meaning in her words.

"A carriage will have to be sent for, Estella. Will you rest here a little?"

"Yes, I am to rest here a little, and I am to drink some tea, and you are to take care of me the while."

She drew her arm through mine, as if it must be done, and we went to a simple tearoom.

"Where are you going to, at Richmond?" I asked Estella.

"I am going to live," said she, "at a great expense, with a lady there, who has the power of taking me about, and introducing me, and showing people to me and showing me to people."

"I suppose you will be glad of variety and admiration?"

"Yes, I suppose so. How do you thrive with Mr. Pocket?"

"I live quite pleasantly there; at least—" It appeared to me that I was losing a chance.

"At least?" repeated Estella.

"As pleasantly as I could anywhere, away from you."

"You silly boy," said Estella, quite calmly, "how can you talk such nonsense? Your friend Mr. Matthew, I believe, is superior to the rest of his family?"

"Very superior indeed. He is nobody's enemy—"

"Don't add but his own," interposed Estella, "for I hate that class of man. But he really is disinterested, and above small jealousy and spite, I have heard?"

"I am sure I have every reason to say so."

"You have not every reason to say so of the rest of his people," said Estella, nodding at me with an expression that was at once grave and encouraging.

"You should know that they beset Miss Havisham with reports and insinuations to your disadvantage. They watch you, misrepresent you, and write letters about you (anonymous sometimes). You are the torment and the occupation of their lives. You can scarcely realize the hatred those people feel for you."

"They do me no harm, I hope?"

Instead of answering, Estella burst out laughing.

"I hope I may suppose that you would not be amused if they did me any harm," I said.

"No, no, you may be sure of that," said Estella. "You may be certain that I laugh because they fail. Oh, those people with Miss Havisham, and the tortures they undergo!" She laughed again, and while her laughter was genuine, it seemed too much for the occasion. I thought there must really be something more here than I knew. She saw the thought in my mind and answered it.

"It is not easy for even you," said Estella, "to know what satisfaction it gives me to see those people thwarted. You were not brought up in that strange house from a mere baby. I was. You had not your little wits sharpened by their intriguing against you, under the mask of sympathy and pity. I had."

It was no laughing matter with Estella now.

"You may set your mind at rest," said Estella, "that these people never will jeopardize your standing with Miss Havisham. There is my hand upon it."

As she gave it to me playfully, I held it and put it to my lips. "You ridiculous boy," said Estella, "will you never take warning? Or do you kiss my hand in the same spirit in which I once let you kiss my cheek?"

"What spirit was that?" said I.

"I must think a moment. A spirit of contempt for the fawners and plotters."

"If I say yes, may I kiss the cheek again?"

"You should have asked before you touched the hand. But, yes, if you like."

I leaned down, and her calm face was like a statue's. "Now," said Estella, gliding away the instant I touched her cheek, "you are to take care that I have some tea, and you are to take me to Richmond."

Her reverting to this tone, as if our association were forced upon us, gave me pain. In truth, everything in our association gave me pain. Whatever her tone with me happened to be, I could put no trust in it, and build no hope on it. Yet I went on, against trust and against hope. Why repeat it a thousand times? So it always was.

Estella took her tea, and then we got into our post-coach and drove away. Turning into Cheapside and rattling up Newgate Street, we were soon under the prison walls of which I was so ashamed.

"What place is that?" Estella asked me.

I made a foolish pretence of not at first recognizing it, and then told her. As she looked at it, and drew in her head again, murmuring "Wretches!" I would not have confessed to my visit for any sum.

"Mr. Jaggers," said I, by way of putting it neatly on somebody else, "has the reputation of being more in the secrets of that dismal place than any man in London."

"He is more in the secrets of every place, I think," said Estella, in a low voice.

"You have been accustomed to see him often, I suppose?"

"I have been accustomed to see him at uncertain intervals, ever since I can remember. But I know him no better now, than I did before I could speak plainly. What is your own experience of him? Do you advance with him?"

"Once accustomed to his distrustful manner," said I, "I have done very well."

"Are you close friends?"

"I have dined with him at his private house."

"I fancy," said Estella, shrinking, "that must be a curious place."

"It is a curious place."

We fell into conversation about London. The great city was almost new to her, she told me, for she had never left Miss Havisham's neighborhood until she had gone to France. And then she had merely passed through London in going and returning. I asked her if my guardian had any charge of her while she remained here. To that she emphatically said "God forbid!" and no more.

When we passed through Hammersmith, I showed her where Mr. Matthew Pocket lived, and said it was no great distance from Richmond, and that I hoped I should see her sometimes.

"Oh yes, you are to see me. You are to come when you think proper."

I inquired if it was a large household she was going to join.

"No; there are only two; mother and daughter. The mother is a lady of some station, though not averse to increasing her income."

"I wonder Miss Havisham could part with you again so soon."

"It is a part of Miss Havisham's plans for me, Pip," said Estella, with a sigh, as if she were tired. "I am to write to her constantly and see her regularly, and report how I go on—I and the jewels—for they are nearly all mine now."

It was the first time she had ever called me by

my name. Of course she did so, purposely, and knew that I should treasure it.

We came to Richmond all too soon and ended our journey at a dignified old house. We rang the bell, and two cherry-colored maids came fluttering out to receive Estella. The doorway soon absorbed her boxes, and she gave me her hand and a smile, and said good night, and was absorbed likewise. I stood looking at the house, thinking how happy I should be if I lived there with her, and knowing that I never was happy with her, but always miserable.

With an aching heart, I got into the carriage to be taken back to Hammersmith. I got out with a worse heartache, and in that condition I went up to bed.

As I had grown accustomed to my expectations, I had begun to notice their effect upon myself and those around me. Their influence on my own character, I realized, was not all good. I lived in a state of chronic uneasiness respecting my behavior to Joe. My conscience was not by any means comfortable about Biddy. I sometimes thought that I should have been happier and better if I had never seen Miss Havisham's face, and had risen to manhood content to be partners with Joe in the honest old forge. Many an evening, when I sat alone looking at the fire, I thought there was no fire like the forge fire and the kitchen fire at home.

Concerning the influence of my position on others, I perceived that it was not beneficial to anybody. Above all, it was not beneficial to Herbert. My lavish habits led his easy nature into expenses that he could not afford, corrupted the simplicity of his life, and disturbed his peace with anxieties and regrets.

I began to contract a quantity of debt. Herbert soon followed down this path. At Startop's suggestion, we put ourselves down for election into a club called The Finches of the Grove. I never could divine the object of that organization, except that the members should dine expensively once a fortnight, should quarrel among themselves as much as possible after dinner, and cause six waiters to get drunk on the stairs.

The Finches spent their money lavishly. The hotel where we dined was in Covent Garden, an expensive section of London. The first Finch I saw, when I had the honor of joining the Grove, was Bentley Drummle. He was floundering about town in a horse and carriage of his own, and doing a great deal of damage to the posts at the street corners. Occasionally, he shot himself out of his wagon headforemost. On one occasion I observed him deliver himself at the door of the Grove in this unintentional way—like coals. But here I anticipate a little. I was not a Finch, and could not be, according to the sacred laws of the society, until I came of age.

In my confidence in my own resources, I would willingly have taken Herbert's expenses on myself. However, Herbert was proud, and I could make no such proposal to him. So he got into difficulties in every direction, and continued to look about him for a way to earn money. When we gradually fell into keeping late hours and late company, I noticed that he looked about him with a desponding eye at breakfast time; that he began to look about him more hopefully about midday; that he drooped when he came into dinner; that he seemed to see a sum of money floating his way after dinner; that he all but grasped that money toward midnight; and that at about two o'clock in the morning, he became so deeply despondent again as to talk of buying a rifle and going to America, with a general purpose of compelling buffaloes to make his fortune.

We spent as much money as we could, and got as little for it as people could make up their minds to give us. We were always more or less miserable, and most of our acquaintances were in the same condition. There was a fiction among us that we were constantly enjoying ourselves, and a skeleton truth that we never did. To the best of my belief, our case was in the last aspect a rather common one.

Every morning, with an air ever new, Herbert went into central London to look about him. I do not remember that I ever saw him do anything else but look about him. If we all did what we undertake to do, as faithfully as Herbert did, we might live in a Republic of the Virtues. He had nothing else to do, poor fellow.

At certain times—meaning at uncertain times, for they depended on our mood—I would say to Herbert, as if it were a remarkable discovery, "My dear Herbert, we are getting on badly."

"My dear Handel," Herbert would say to me,

in all sincerity, "if you will believe me, those very words were on my lips, by a strange coincidence."

"Then, Herbert," I would respond, "let us look into our affairs."

We always derived profound satisfaction from making an appointment for this purpose. We ordered something rather special for dinner, with a bottle of something similarly out of the common way, in order that our minds might be fortified for the occasion. Dinner over, we produced a bundle of pens, a generous supply of ink, and a goodly show of writing and blotting paper.

I would then take a sheet of paper, and write across the top of it, in a neat hand, the heading, "Memorandum of Pip's debts." Herbert would also take a sheet of paper, and write across it, "Memorandum of Herbert's debts."

Each of us would then refer to a confused heap of papers at his side, which had been thrown into drawers, worn into holes in pockets, half-burnt in lighting candles, stuck for weeks into the looking glass, and otherwise damaged. The sound of our pens going refreshed us exceedingly, so much so that I sometimes found it difficult to distinguish between copying the amounts and actually paying the money. As commendable behavior, the two seemed about equal.

When we had written a little while, I would ask Herbert how he got on. Herbert would be scratching his head in a most rueful manner at the sight of his accumulating figures.

"They are mounting up, Handel," Herbert would say. "Upon my life, they are mounting up."

"Be firm, Herbert," I would retort, plying my own pen with great energy. "Look the thing in the face. Look into your affairs. Stare them out of countenance."

"So I would, Handel, only they are staring me out of countenance."

However, my determined manner would have its effect, and Herbert would fall to work again.

I established with myself, on these occasions, the reputation of a first-rate man of business—prompt, decisive, energetic, clear, cool-headed. When I had got all my responsibilities down upon my list, I compared each with the bill, and ticked it off.

There was a calm, a rest, a virtuous hush, following these examinations of our debts that gave me, for the time, an admirable opinion of myself. Soothed by my exertions, my method, and Herbert's compliments, I would feel like a bank of some sort, rather than a private individual.

We shut our outer door on these solemn occasions, in order that we might not be interrupted. I had fallen into my serene state one evening, when we heard a letter dropped through the slit in the said door. "It's for you, Handel," said Herbert, going out and coming back with it, "and I hope there is nothing the matter." This was in allusion to its heavy black seal and border.

The letter was signed TRABB & CO. Its contents were simply that they begged to inform me that Mrs. J. Gargery had departed this life on Monday last, at twenty minutes past six in the evening, and that my attendance was requested at the burial on Monday next at three o'clock in the afternoon.

It was the first time that a grave had opened in my road of life. The figure of my sister in her chair by the kitchen fire haunted me night and day. I could not imagine that the place could possibly exist without her. Even though she had seldom or never been in my thoughts of late, I had now the strangest ideas that she was coming toward me in the street, or that she would presently knock at the door. In my rooms too, there was a recurrent suggestion of the sound of her voice or the turn of her face or figure, as if she were still alive and had been often there.

Whatever my fortunes might have been, I could scarcely have recalled my sister with much tenderness. But I suppose there is a shock of regret which may exist without much tenderness. Under its influence, I was seized with a violent indignation against the assailant from whom she had suffered so much. I felt that with sufficient proof, I could have revengefully pursued Orlick, or anyone else, to the last extremity.

I wrote to Joe to offer consolation and to assure him that I should come to the funeral. On the assigned day, I went home early in the morning and alighted at the Blue Boar in good time to walk over to the forge.

It was fine summer weather again. As I walked along, the times when I was a little helpless creature, and my sister did not spare me, vividly returned. But they returned with a gentle tone upon them.

At last I came within sight of the house. Poor dear Joe, entangled in a little black cloak tied in a large bow under his chin, was seated apart at the upper end of the room. I bent down and said to him, "Dear Joe, how are you?"

He replied, "Pip, old chap, you knowed her when she were a fine figure of a—" and clasped my hand and said no more.

Biddy, looking very neat and modest in her black dress, went quietly here and there and was very helpful. The air of the parlor was faint with the smell of sweet cake. Beside it on the refreshment table was a cut-up plum cake. There were also cut-up oranges, and sandwiches, and biscuits, and two decanters, one full of port, and one of sherry. Standing at this table, I became conscious of the servile Pumblechook in a black cloak. He was alternately stuffing himself, and making excessively humble movements to catch my attention. The moment he succeeded, he came over to me (breathing sherry and crumbs), and said in a subdued voice, "May I, dear sir?" and did. I then spotted Mr. and Mrs. Hubble. At the appropriate signal from Trabb, we were all going to form a procession and proceed mournfully through the village.

"Which I meantersay, Pip," Joe whispered me, as we were being "formed" in the parlor, two and two, "which I meantersay, sir, as I would in preference have carried her to the church myself, along with three or four friendly ones wot come to it with willing harts and arms, but it were considered wot the neighbours would look down on such and would be of opinions as it were wanting in respect."

"Pocket-handkerchiefs out, all!" cried Mr. Trabb at this point, in a business-like voice. "Pocket-handkerchiefs out! We are ready!"

So, we all put our pocket-handkerchiefs to our faces, as if our noses were bleeding, and filed out two and two; Joe and I; Biddy and Pumblechook; Mr. and Mrs. Hubble. The remains of my poor sister had been brought round by the kitchen door, and we all marched dolefully toward the village.

The neighbors highly approved of these arrangements, and we were much admired as we went through the village. By and by, we came to the church near the marshes. We went into the churchyard, close to the graves of my unknown parents, Philip and Georgiana. And there, my sister was laid quietly in the earth while the larks sang high above it. A light wind strewed the ground with beautiful shadows of clouds and trees.

When they were all gone, the house felt more

wholesome. Soon afterwards, Biddy, Joe, and I had a cold dinner together. We dined in the best parlor, not in the old kitchen, and Joe was so exceedingly particular what he did with his knife and fork and the saltshaker and what not, that there was great restraint upon us. But after dinner, when I made him take his pipe, and when I had loitered with him about the forge, and when we sat down together on the great block of stone outside it, we got on better. I noticed that after the funeral Joe changed his clothes so as to make a compromise between his Sunday dress and working dress. It was only in the latter the dear fellow looked natural.

He was very much pleased by my asking if I might sleep in my own little room, and I was pleased too. When the shadows of evening were closing in, I took an opportunity of getting into the garden with Biddy for a little talk.

"Biddy," said I, "I think you might have written to me about these sad matters."

"Do you, Mr. Pip?" said Biddy. "I should have written if I had thought that."

"Don't suppose that I mean to be unkind, Biddy, when I say I consider that you ought to have thought that."

"Do you, Mr. Pip?"

She was so quiet, and had such an orderly, good, and pretty way with her, that I did not like the thought of making her cry again. After looking a little at her downcast eyes as she walked beside me, I gave up that point.

"I suppose it will be difficult for you to remain here now, Biddy dear?"

"Oh! I can't do so, Mr. Pip," said Biddy, in a tone of regret, but still of quiet conviction. "I have been speaking to Mrs. Hubble, and I am going to her tomorrow. I hope we shall be able to take some care of Mr. Gargery, together, until he settles down."

"How are you going to live, Biddy? If you want any mo—"

"How am I going to live?" repeated Biddy, striking in, with a momentary flush upon her face. "I'll tell you, Mr. Pip. I am going to try to get the place of teacher in the new school nearly finished here. I can be well recommended by all the neighbors, and I hope I can be industrious and patient, and teach myself while I teach others."

"I think you would always improve, Biddy, under any circumstances."

I walked a little further with Biddy, looking silently at her downcast eyes.

"I have not heard the particulars of my sister's death, Biddy."

"They are very slight, poor thing. She had been in one of her bad states—though they had got better of late, rather than worse—for four days, when she came out of it in the evening, just at teatime, and said quite plainly, 'Joe.' As she had never said any word for a long while, I ran and fetched in Mr. Gargery from the forge. She made signs to me that she wanted him to sit down close to her, and wanted me to put her arms round his neck. So I put them round his neck, and she laid her head down on his shoulder quite content and satisfied. And so she presently said 'Joe' again, and once 'Pardon,' and once 'Pip.' And so she never lifted her head up any more, and it was just an hour later when we laid her down on her own bed, because we found she was gone."

Biddy cried, and the darkening garden, and the lane, and the stars that were coming out, were blurred in my own sight.

"Nothing was ever discovered, Biddy?"

"Nothing."

"Do you know what is become of Orlick?"

"I should think from the color of his clothes that he is working in the quarries."

"You have seen him, then?—Why are you looking at that dark tree in the lane?"

"I saw him there, on the night she died."

"That was not the last time either, Biddy?"

"No; I have seen him there, since we have been walking here.—It is of no use," said Biddy, laying her hand upon my arm, as I prepared to run out, "you know I would not deceive you. He was not there a minute, and he is gone."

I was indignant to learn that she was still pursued by this fellow, and I felt furious toward him. I told her so, and told her that I would spend any money or take any pains to drive him out of that country. By degrees she led me into more restrained talk, and she told me how Joe loved me, and how Joe never complained of anything—she didn't say, of me; she had no need; I knew what she meant—but ever did his duty in his way of life, with a strong hand, a quiet tongue, and a gentle heart.

"Indeed, it would be hard to say too much for him," said I. "And Biddy, we must often speak of these things, for of course I shall be often down here now. I am not going to leave poor Joe alone."

Biddy said not a single word.

"Biddy, don't you hear me?"

"Yes, Mr. Pip."

"Not to mention your calling me Mr. Pip—which appears to me to be in bad taste, Biddy—what do you mean?"

"What do I mean?" asked Biddy, timidly.

"Biddy," said I, in a self-asserting manner, "I must request to know what you mean by this?"

"By this?" said Biddy.

"Now, don't echo," I retorted. "You used not to echo, Biddy."

"Used not!" said Biddy. "O Mr. Pip! Used!"

Well! I rather thought I would give up that point too. After another silent turn in the garden, I addressed her again.

"Biddy," said I, "I made a remark respecting my coming down here often, to see Joe, which you received with a marked silence. Have the goodness, Biddy, to tell me why."

"Are you quite sure, then, that you will come to see him often?" asked Biddy, stopping in the narrow garden walk, and looking at me under the stars with a clear and honest eye.

"Oh dear me!" said I, as if I found myself compelled to give up Biddy in despair. "Don't say any more, if you please, Biddy. This shocks me very much."

For which reason I kept Biddy at a distance during supper, and, when I went up to my own old little room, took a rather formal leave of her. I spent a restless night, thinking what an unkindness, what an injury, what an injustice, Biddy had done me.

I was scheduled to leave next day. Early in the morning, I looked in, unseen, at one of the wooden windows of the forge. Joe was already at work. The glow of health and strength upon his face made it show as if the bright sun of the life in store for him were shining on it.

"Goodbye, dear Joe!—No, don't wipe it off—for God's sake, give me your blackened hand!—I shall be down soon, and often."

"Never too soon, sir," said Joe, "and never too often, Pip!"

Biddy was waiting for me at the kitchen door, with a mug of new milk and a crust of bread. "Biddy," said I, when I gave her my hand at parting, "I am not angry, but I am hurt."

"No, don't be hurt," she pleaded quite pathetically. "Let only me be hurt, if I have been ungenerous."

Once more, the mists were rising as I walked away. If they disclosed to me, as I suspect they did, that I should not come back, and that Biddy was quite right, all I can say is—they were quite right too.

Herbert and I went on from bad to worse, increasing our debts. And Time went on, as he has a way of doing; and I came of age—in fulfillment of Herbert's prediction, that I should do so before I knew where I was.

Herbert himself had come of age, eight months before me. As he had nothing else than his majority to come into, the event did not make a profound sensation in Barnard's Inn. But we had looked forward to my twenty-first birthday, with a crowd of speculations and anticipations, for we had both considered that my guardian could hardly help saying something definite on that occasion.

I had taken care to let Wemmick know when my birthday was. On the day before it, I received an official note from Wemmick, informing me that Mr. Jaggers would be glad if I would call upon him at five in the afternoon of the special day. This convinced us that something great was to happen, and threw me into an unusual flutter when I repaired to my guardian's office, a model of punctuality.

In the outer office Wemmick offered me his congratulations, and incidentally rubbed the side of his nose with a folded piece of tissue paper that I liked the look of. But he said nothing respecting it, and motioned me with a nod into my guardian's room. It was November, and my guardian was standing before his fire, leaning his back against the chimneypiece, with his hands under his coattails.

"Well, Pip," said he, "I must call you Mr. Pip today. Congratulations, Mr. Pip."

We shook hands, and I thanked him.

"Take a chair, Mr. Pip," said my guardian.

As I sat down, and he preserved his attitude and bent his brows at his boots, I felt at a disadvantage, which reminded me of that old time when I had been put upon a tombstone. The two ghastly casts on the shelf were not far from him, and their expression was as if they were making an attempt to attend to the conversation.

"Now my young friend," my guardian began, as if I were a witness in the box, "I am going to have a word or two with you."

"If you please, sir."

"What do you suppose," said Mr. Jaggers, bending forward to look at the ground, and then throwing his head back to look at the ceiling, "what do you suppose you are living at the rate of?"

"At the rate of, sir?"

"At," repeated Mr. Jaggers, still looking at the

ceiling, "the—rate—of?" And then looked all round the room, and paused with his pocket-handkerchief in his hand, halfway to his nose.

I had looked into my affairs so often, that I had thoroughly destroyed any slight notion I might ever have had of their bearings. Reluctantly, I confessed myself quite unable to answer the question. This reply seemed agreeable to Mr. Jaggers, who said, "I thought so!" and blew his nose with an air of satisfaction.

"Now, I have asked you a question, my friend," said Mr. Jaggers. "Have you anything to ask me?"

"Of course it would be a great relief to me to ask you several questions, sir. But I remember your prohibition."

"Ask one," said Mr. Jaggers.

"Is my benefactor to be made known to me today?"

"No. Ask another."

"Is that confidence to be imparted to me soon?"

"Waive that, a moment," said Mr. Jaggers, "and ask another."

I looked about me, but there appeared to be now no possible escape from the inquiry, "Have—I—anything to receive, sir?" On that, Mr. Jaggers said, triumphantly, "I thought we should come to it!" and called to Wemmick to give him that piece of paper. Wemmick appeared, handed it in, and disappeared.

"Now, Mr. Pip," said Mr. Jaggers, "attend, if you please. You have been drawing pretty freely here. Your name occurs pretty often in Wemmick's cashbook. But you are in debt, of course?"

"I am afraid I must say yes, sir."

"You know you must say yes, don't you?" said Mr. Jaggers.

"Yes, sir."

"I don't ask you what you owe, because you don't know; and if you did know, you wouldn't tell me; you would say less. Yes, yes, my friend," cried Mr. Jaggers, waving his forefinger to stop me, as I made a show of protesting. "It's likely enough that you think you wouldn't, but you would. You'll excuse me, but I know better than you. Now, take this piece of paper in your hand. You have got it? Very good. Now, unfold it and tell me what it is."

"This is a banknote," said I, "for five hundred pounds."

"That is a banknote," repeated Mr. Jaggers, "for five hundred pounds. And a very handsome sum of money too, I think. You consider it so?

"How could I do otherwise!"

"Ah! But answer the question," said Mr. Jaggers.

"Undoubtedly."

"You consider it, undoubtedly, a handsome sum of money. Now, that handsome sum of money, Pip, is your own. It is a present to you on this day, in earnest of your expectations. And at the rate of that handsome sum of money per year, and at no higher rate, you are to live until the donor of the whole amount appears. That is to say, you will now take your money affairs entirely into your own hands, and you will draw from Wemmick one hundred and twenty-five pounds per quarter, until you are in communication with the donor, and no longer with the mere agent. As I have told you before, I am the mere agent. I carry out my instructions, and I am paid for doing so. I think them unwise, but I am not paid for giving any opinion on their merits.

I was beginning to express my gratitude to my benefactor for his generosity, when Mr. Jaggers stopped me. "I am not paid, Pip," said he, coolly, "to carry your words to any one." Then he gathered up his coattails, as he had gathered up the subject, and stood frowning at his boots as if he suspected them of designs against him.

After a pause, I remarked, "There was a question just now, Mr. Jaggers, which you desired me to waive for a moment. I hope I am doing nothing wrong in asking it again?"

"What is it?" said he.

"Is it likely," I said, after hesitating, "that my patron, the donor you have spoken of, Mr. Jaggers, will soon—" there I delicately stopped.

"Will soon what?" asked Mr. Jaggers. "That's no question as it stands, you know."

"Will soon come to London," said I, after casting about for a precise form of words, "or summon me anywhere else?"

"Now here," replied Mr. Jaggers, fixing me for the first time with his dark deep-set eyes, "we must revert to the evening when we first encountered one another in your village. What did I tell you then, Pip?"

"You told me, Mr. Jaggers, that it might be years away when that person appeared."

"Just so," said Mr. Jaggers. "That's my answer."

As we looked full at one another, I felt my breath come quicker in my strong desire to get something out of him.

"Do you suppose it will still be years hence, Mr. Jaggers?" I inquired.

Mr. Jaggers shook his head—not in saying no to the question, but in dismissing the notion that he could be got to answer it.

"Come!" said Mr. Jaggers, warming the backs of his legs with the backs of his warmed hands, "I'll be plain with you, my friend Pip. That's a question I must not be asked. You'll understand that, better, when I tell you it's a question that might compromise me. Come! I'll go a little further with you. I'll say something more."

He bent down so low to frown at his boots, that he was able to rub the calves of his legs in the pause he made.

"When that person comes forward," said Mr. Jaggers, straightening himself, "you and that person will settle your own affairs. When that person comes forward, my part in this business will cease. When that person comes forward, it will not be necessary for me to know anything about it. And that's all I have got to say."

We looked at one another until I withdrew my eyes, and looked thoughtfully at the floor. From this last speech I assumed that Miss Havisham, for some reason or no reason, had not taken him into her confidence as to her designing me for Estella, and that he resented this. When I raised my eyes again, I found that he had been shrewdly looking at me all the time, and was doing so still.

"If that is all you have to say, sir," I remarked, "there can be nothing left for me to say."

He nodded assent, and pulled out his watch, and asked me where I was going to dine. I replied at my own chambers, with Herbert. As a necessary politeness, I asked him if he would favor us with his company, and he promptly accepted the invitation. He insisted on walking home with me, in order that I might make no extra preparation for him. But first he had a letter or two to write, and (of course) had his hands to wash. So, I said I would go into the outer office and talk to Wemmick.

The fact was, that when the five hundred pounds had come into my pocket, a thought had come into my head which had been often there before. It appeared to me that Wemmick was a good person to advise with, concerning such thought.

He had already locked up his safe and made preparations for going home. He had left his desk and had raked his fire low, put his hat and great-coat ready, and was beating himself all over the chest with his safe-key, as an athletic exercise after business.

"Mr. Wemmick," said I, "I want to ask your opinion. I am very desirous to serve a friend."

Wemmick tightened his lips and shook his head, as if he were dead against any fatal weakness of that sort.

"This friend," I pursued, "is trying to get on in commercial life. However, he has no money and finds it difficult and disheartening to make a beginning. Now, I want somehow to help him to a beginning."

"With money down?" said Wemmick, in a tone drier than any sawdust.

"With some money down," I replied.

"Mr. Pip," said Wemmick, "I should like just to run over with you on my fingers, if you please, the names of the various bridges across the Thames River in London." He then proceeded to name each one.

"I don't understand you," said I.

"Choose your bridge, Mr. Pip," returned Wemmick, "and take a walk upon your bridge, and pitch your money into the Thames over the center arch of your bridge, and you know the end of it. Serve a friend with it, and you may know the end of it too—but it's a less pleasant and profitable end."

"This is very discouraging," said I.

"Meant to be so," said Wemmick.

"Then is it your opinion," I inquired, with some little indignation, "that a man should never—"

"—Offer money to a friend?" said Wemmick. "Certainly he should not. Unless he wants to get rid of the friend."

"And that," said I, "is your deliberate opinion, Mr. Wemmick?"

"That," he returned, "is my deliberate opinion in this office."

"Ah!" said I, pressing him, for I thought I saw him near a loophole here. "Would that be your opinion if presented at your home in Walworth?"

"Mr. Pip," he replied, with gravity, "Walworth is one place, and this office is another. They must not be confounded together. My Walworth sentiments must be taken at Walworth. None but my official sentiments can be taken in this office."

"Very well," said I, much relieved, "then I shall look you up at Walworth, you may depend upon it."

"Mr. Pip," he returned, "you will be welcome there, in a private and personal capacity."

We had held this conversation in a low voice, well knowing my guardian's ears to be the sharpest of the sharp. As he now appeared in his doorway, toweling his hands, Wemmick put on his greatcoat and stood by to snuff out the candles. We all three went into the street together, and from the doorstep Wemmick turned his way, and Mr. Jaggers and I turned ours.

The following Sunday I went to Wemmick's home in Walworth to hear his out-of-office views on my proposal to share my good fortune. When I arrived, I was admitted by Wemmick's aged father.

"My son, sir," said the old man, "rather thought that you might happen to drop in, and he left word that he would soon be home from his afternoon's walk. He is very regular in his walks, is my son. Very regular in everything, is my son."

I nodded at the old gentleman, and we went in and sat down by the fireside. After a short while, Wemmick arrived, accompanied by a lady known as Miss Skiffins. Miss Skiffins was of a wooden appearance and might have been some two or three years younger than Wemmick.

While Miss Skiffins was taking off her bonnet, Wemmick invited me to take a walk with him, and I seized the opportunity.

I informed Wemmick that I was anxious on behalf of Herbert Pocket. I then explained our relationship and the affection I felt toward my friend. Finally, I told Wemmick that I wished my own good fortune to reflect upon Herbert. At the same time, I added, I did not want Herbert to know that I was acting as his benefactor.

Wemmick was silent for a little while, and then said with a kind of start, "Well you know, Mr. Pip, I must tell you one thing. This is devilish good of you." He went on to say that Miss Skiffins's brother was an accountant and agent. "I'll look him up and go to work for you," Wemmick said.

"I thank you ten thousand times."

We made our way back to Wemmick's residence. We all had something warm to drink. Miss Skiffins mixed the drink, and I observed that she and Wemmick drank out of one glass. Of course I knew better than to offer to see Miss Skiffins home, and under the circumstances I thought I had best go first, which I did.

Before a week was out, I received a note from Wemmick, postmarked Walworth. The note said that he would be glad if I could come and see him again concerning the matter of Herbert Pocket. So, I went out to Walworth again, and yet again, and yet again. The upshot was, that we found a worthy young merchant or shipping-broker, not long established in business, who needed an assistant and some working capital. If the business prospered, he would no doubt need a partner some day. This gentleman and I signed secret agreements of which Herbert was the subject. I paid him half of my five hundred pounds immediately. I also agreed to make additional payments in the future out of my income. Miss Skiffins's brother conducted the negotiation. Wemmick also assisted.

The whole business was so cleverly managed, that Herbert had not the least suspicion of my hand being in it. I never shall forget the radiant look on his face, when he told me he had been hired by one Clarriker (the young merchant's name). That night I had a good cry to think that my expectations had done some good to somebody.

A great event in my life, the turning point of my life, now opens on my view. But, before I proceed to narrate it, and before I pass on to all the changes it involved, I must give one chapter to Estella. It is not much to give to the theme that so long filled my heart.

If that dignified old house in Richmond where Estella now lived should ever come to be haunted when I am dead, it will be haunted, surely, by my ghost. O the many, many nights and days through which the restless spirit within me haunted that house when Estella lived there! Let my body be where it would, my spirit was always wandering, wandering, wandering, about that house.

The lady with whom Estella was placed, Mrs. Brandley by name, was a widow, with one daughter several years older than Estella. The mother looked young, and the daughter looked old. They were in what is called a good position, and visited, and were visited by, numbers of people. Little, if any, community of feeling subsisted between them and Estella, but the understanding was established that they were necessary to her, and that she was necessary to them. Mrs. Brandley had been a friend of Miss Havisham's before the time of her seclusion.

In Mrs. Brandley's house and out of Mrs. Brandley's house, I suffered every kind and degree of torture that Estella could cause me. The nature of my relations with her, which placed me on terms of familiarity without placing me on terms of favor, was responsible for my agony. She made use of me to tease other admirers. The privilege of calling her by her name and hearing her call me by mine served only to aggravate of my trials.

She had admirers without end. No doubt my jealousy made an admirer of every one who went near her; but there were more than enough of them without that.

I saw her often at Richmond. I heard of her often in town. And I used often to take her and the Brandleys for a row on the water. There were picnics, holidays, plays, operas, concerts, parties, all sorts of pleasures, through which I pursued her—and they were all miseries to me. I never had one hour's happiness in her society, and yet my mind ceaselessly harped on the happiness of having her with me unto death.

Throughout this part of our relationship—and it lasted, as will presently be seen, for what I then thought a long time—she habitually behaved as though our association was forced upon us. There were other times when she would suddenly stop this behavior and would seem to pity me.

"Pip, Pip," she said one evening, when we sat apart at a darkening window of the house in Richmond. "Will you never take warning?"

"Of what?"

"Of me."

"Warning not to be attracted by you, do you mean, Estella?"

"Do I mean! If you don't know what I mean, you are blind."

I should have replied that Love was commonly said to be blind, but instead I held my tongue.

After looking at the twilight outside, for a little while, she went on to say, "The time has come round when Miss Havisham wishes to have me for a day at Satis. You are to take me there, and bring me back, if you will. Can you take me?"

"Can I take you, Estella!"

"You can then? The day after tomorrow, if you please. You are to pay all charges out of my purse. You hear the condition of your going?"

"And must obey," said I.

This was all the preparation I received for that visit, or for others like it. Miss Havisham never wrote to me, nor had I ever so much as seen her handwriting. We went there two days later, and we found her in the room where I had first beheld her. There was no change in Satis House.

She was even more dreadfully fond of Estella than she had been when I last saw them together. There was something positively dreadful in the energy of her looks and embraces. She hung upon Estella's beauty, hung upon her words, hung upon her gestures, and sat chewing on her own trembling fingers while she looked at her, as though she were devouring the beautiful creature she had reared.

From Estella she looked at me, with a searching glance that seemed to pry into my heart and probe its wounds. "How does she use you, Pip; how does she use you?" she asked me again, with her witch-like eagerness, even in Estella's hearing. But, when we sat by her flickering fire at night, she was most dreadful. For then, keeping Estella's hand drawn through her arm and clutched in her own hand, she extorted from her the names and conditions of the men whom she had attracted. As Miss Havisham dwelt upon this roll, with the intensity of a mind mortally hurt and diseased, she sat with her other hand on her crutch stick, and her chin on that, and her wan bright eyes glaring at me, looking like a ghost.

I realized that Estella was instructed to wreak Miss Havisham's revenge on men. Furthermore, she was not to be given to me until she had done so for a while. I saw in this, the reason for my being put off so long. And I saw, in this, the shadow of the darkened and unhealthy house in which her life was hidden from the sun.

The candles that lighted that room of hers were placed in sconces on the wall. They were high from the ground, and they burnt with the steady dullness of artificial light in air that is seldom renewed. I looked round at them, and at the pale gloom they made, and at the stopped clock, and at the withered articles of bridal dress upon the table and the ground, and at her own awful figure with its ghostly reflection thrown large by the fire upon the ceiling and the wall. My thoughts passed into the great room across the landing where the table was spread, and I saw the falls of the cobwebs from the center-piece, in the crawlings of the spiders on the cloth, in the tracks of the mice as they betook their little quickened hearts behind the panels, and in the gropings and pausings of the beetles on the floor.

It happened on this visit that some sharp words arose between Estella and Miss Havisham. It was the first time I had ever seen them angry with each other.

We were seated by the fire, as just now described, and Miss Havisham still had Estella's arm drawn through her own, and still clutched Estella's hand in hers, when Estella gradually began to detach herself.

"What!" said Miss Havisham, flashing her eyes upon her, "are you tired of me?"

"Only a little tired of myself," replied Estella, disengaging her arm, and moving to the great chimneypiece, where she stood looking down at the fire.

"Speak the truth, you ingrate!" cried Miss Havisham, passionately striking her stick upon the floor. "You are tired of me."

Estella looked at her with perfect composure, and again looked down at the fire. Her graceful figure and her beautiful face expressed a self-possessed indifference to the wild heat of the other, that was almost cruel.

"You stock and stone!" exclaimed Miss Havisham. "You cold, cold heart!"

"What?" said Estella, preserving her attitude of indifference as she leaned against the great mantel. "Do you reproach me for being cold? You?"

"Are you not?" was the fierce retort.

"You should know," said Estella. "I am what you have made me. Take all the praise, take all the blame. Take all the success, take all the failure; in short, take me."

"O, look at her, look at her!" cried Miss Havisham, bitterly. "Look at her, so hard and thankless, on the hearth where she was reared! Where I took her to my heart when it was first bleeding from its stabs, and where I have lavished years of tenderness upon her!"

"At least I was no party to the agreement," said Estella. "But what do you want of me? You have been very good to me, and I owe everything to you. What would you have?"

"Love," replied the other.

"You have it."

"I have not," said Miss Havisham.

"Mother by adoption," retorted Estella, never departing from the easy grace of her attitude, never raising her voice as the other did, never yielding either to anger or tenderness. "Mother by adoption, I have said that I owe everything to you. All I possess is freely yours. All that you have given me, is at your command to have again. Beyond that, I have nothing. And if you ask me to give you what you never gave me, my gratitude and duty cannot do the impossible."

"Did I never give her love!" cried Miss Havisham, turning wildly to me. "Did I never give her a burning love, inseparable from jealousy at all times, and from sharp pain, while she speaks thus to me! Let her call me mad, let her call me mad!"

"Why should I call you mad," returned Estella, "I, of all people? Does anyone live, who knows what set purposes you have, half as well as I do? Does anyone live, who knows what a steady memory you have, half as well as I do? I who have sat on this same hearth on the little stool that is even now beside you there, learning your lessons and looking up into your face, when your face was strange and frightened me!"

"Soon forgotten!" moaned Miss Havisham. "Times soon forgotten!"

"No, not forgotten," retorted Estella. "Not forgotten, but treasured up in my memory. When have you found me false to your teaching? When have you found me unmindful of your lessons? Be just to me."

"So proud, so proud!" moaned Miss Havisham, pushing away her gray hair with both her hands.

"Who taught me to be proud?" returned Estella. "Who praised me when I learned my lesson?"

"So hard, so hard!" moaned Miss Havisham, with her former action.

"Who taught me to be hard?" returned Estella. "Who praised me when I learned my lesson?"

"But to be proud and hard to me!" Miss Havisham quite shrieked, as she stretched out her arms. "Estella, Estella, Estella, to be proud and hard to me!"

Estella looked at her for a moment with a kind of calm wonder, but was not otherwise disturbed. When the moment passed, she looked down at the fire again.

"I cannot think," said Estella, raising her eyes after a silence, "why you should be so unreasonable when I come to see you after a separation. I have never forgotten your wrongs and their causes. I have never been unfaithful to you or your schooling. I have never shown any weakness that I can charge myself with."

"Would it be weakness to return my love?" exclaimed Miss Havisham. "But yes, yes, you would call it so!"

Miss Havisham had settled down, I hardly knew how, upon the floor, among the faded bridal relics with which it was strewn. I took advantage of the moment to leave the room. When I left, Estella was still standing by the great mantel, just as she had stood throughout. Miss Havisham's gray hair was all adrift upon the ground, among the other bridal wrecks, and was a miserable sight to see.

It was with a sad heart that I walked in the starlight for an hour and more, about the courtyard, and about the ruined garden. When I at last took courage to return to the room, I found Estella sitting at Miss Havisham's knee, taking up some stitches in one of those old articles of dress that were dropping to pieces. Afterward, Estella and I played at cards, as we used to do. And so the evening wore away, and I went to bed.

I lay in that separate building across the courtyard. It was the first time I had ever lain down to rest in Satis House, and sleep refused to come near me. A thousand Miss Havishams haunted me. She was on this side of my pillow, on that, at the head of the bed, at the foot, behind the half-opened door of the dressing room, in the dressing room, in the room overhead, in the room beneath—everywhere. Toward two o'clock, I realized I could not sleep. I therefore got up and put on my clothes. I went out across the yard into the long stone passage, intending to enter the outer courtyard and walk there to clear my mind. But I was no sooner in the passage than I extinguished my candle. There was Miss Havisham going along it in a ghostly manner, making a low cry. I followed her at a distance and saw her go up the staircase. She carried a bare candle in her hand and was a most unearthly object by its light. Standing at the bottom of the staircase, I felt the mildewed air of the feast chamber, without seeing her open the door. I heard her walking there, and so across into her own room, never ceasing the low cry. After a time, I tried to find my way back, but I could not in the dark. Until some streaks of day strayed in and showed me the way, I heard her footstep, saw her light pass above, and heard her ceaseless low cry.

Before we left next day, there was no revival of the difference between her and Estella, nor did I ever witness a repetition. Nor did Miss Havisham's manner toward Estella change in any way, except that I believed it to have something like fear added to its former characteristics.

It is impossible to turn this leaf of my life, without putting Bentley Drummle's name upon it.

There was a certain occasion when the Finches were assembled in force, and when good feeling was being promoted in the usual manner by nobody's agreeing with anybody else. The presiding Finch called the Grove to order and called upon Mr. Drummle to toast a lady. What was my indignant surprise when he called upon the company to pledge him to "Estella!"

"Estella who?" said I.

"Never you mind," retorted Drummle.

"Estella of where?" said I. "You are bound to say of where." Which he was, as a Finch.

"Of Richmond, gentlemen," said Drummle, "and a peerless beauty."

"I know that lady," said Herbert, across the table, when the toast had been honored.

"Do you?" said Drummle.

"And so do I," I added, with a scarlet face.

"Do you?" said Drummle. "Oh, Lord!"

This remark infuriated me, as I suspected Drummle had no familiarity at all with the lady in question. When I insisted that was the case, Drummle himself grew incensed and offered to bring a note from Estella asserting that the two were acquainted. I held him to his promise. The very next day, before the assembled Finches, Drummle produced a polite avowal in Estella's hand, saying that she had had the honor of dancing with him several times.

I cannot adequately express what pain it gave me to think that Estella should show any favor to a contemptible, clumsy, sulky imbecile, so very far below the average. I would have been miserable no matter who it was she had favored. But a worthier object would have caused me less distress.

I soon discovered that Drummle had begun to follow her closely, and that she allowed him to do it. As I also pursued her, we crossed one another every day. Estella held him on, now with encouragement, now with discouragement, now almost flattering him, now openly despising him, now knowing him very well, now scarcely remembering who he was.

At a certain Assembly Ball at Richmond, where Estella had outshone all other beauties, this blundering Drummle so hung about her, and with so much toleration on her part, that I resolved to speak to her concerning him.

"Estella," said I, "do look at that fellow in the corner yonder, who is looking over here at us."

"Why should I look at him?" returned Estella, with her eyes on me instead. "What is there in that fellow that I need look at?"

"Indeed, that is the very question I want to ask

you," said I. "For he has been hovering about you all night."

"Moths, and all sorts of ugly creatures," replied Estella, with a glance toward him, "hover about a lighted candle. Can the candle help it?"

"No" I returned; "but cannot Estella help it?"

"Well!" said she, laughing, after a moment, "perhaps. Yes. Anything you like."

"But, Estella, do hear me speak. It makes me wretched that you should encourage a man so generally despised as Drummle."

Now, if I could have believed that she favored Drummle with any idea of making me—me—wretched, I should have been in better heart about it. However, she put me so entirely out of the question, that I could believe nothing of the kind.

"Do you deceive and entrap him, Estella?"

"Yes, and many others—all of them but you."

And now that I have given the one chapter to the theme that so filled my heart, and so often made it ache and ache again, I pass on to the event that had such a remarkable influence upon my life.

I was twenty-three years old. Not another word had I heard to enlighten me on the subject of my expectations, and my twenty-third birthday was a week gone. Herbert and I had left Barnard's Inn more than a year ago, and we now lived in the Temple district of London. Our chambers were in Garden Court, down by the river.

Mr. Pocket and I had for some time parted company as to our original relations, though we continued on the best terms. I developed a strong taste for reading and read regularly many hours a day. The occupation I had uncovered for Herbert was progressing well. Indeed, on the night I am to relate, his business had taken him to France.

I was alone, dispirited and anxious. It was wretched weather, stormy and wet. Day after day, a vast heavy veil had been driving over London from the East, and it drove still, as if in the East there were an Eternity of cloud and wind. So furious had been the gusts, that high buildings in town had had the lead stripped off their roofs. In the country, trees had been torn up. Gloomy accounts of shipwreck and death had come in from the coast. Violent blasts of rain had accompanied these rages of wind. The day just ending had been the worst of all. When the rain came and dashed against the windows, I thought that I might have been transported to a storm-beaten lighthouse.

I read with my watch upon the table, planning to close my book at eleven o'clock. When I shut it, I was astonished to hear a footstep on the stair.

Remembering that the staircase lights were blown out by the storm, I took up my reading lamp and went out to the stairhead. Whoever was below had stopped on seeing my lamp, for all was quiet.

"There is some one down there, is there not?" I called out, looking down.

"Yes," said a voice from the darkness beneath.

"What floor do you want?"

"The top. Mr. Pip."

"That is my name. There is nothing the matter?"

"Nothing the matter," returned the voice. And the man came on.

I stood with my lamp held out over the stair rail, and he came slowly within its light. I beheld a face that was strange to me, looking up with an incomprehensible air of being touched and pleased by the sight of me.

Moving the lamp as the man moved, I made out that he was substantially dressed, but roughly, like a voyager by sea. He had long iron-gray hair. His age was about sixty. He appeared to be a muscular man, strong on his legs, browned and hardened by exposure to weather. As he ascended the last stair or two, and the light of my lamp included us both, I saw, with a stupid kind of amazement, that he was holding out both his hands to me.

"Pray what is your business?" I asked him.

"My business?" he repeated, pausing. "Ah! Yes. I will explain my business, by your leave."

"Do you wish to come in?"

"Yes," he replied. "I wish to come in, Master."

I took him into the room I had just left. Setting the lamp on the table, I asked him, as civilly as I could, to explain himself.

He looked about him with the strangest air—an air of wondering pleasure as if he had some part in the things he admired—and he pulled off a rough outer coat, and his hat. Then, I saw that his head was bald, and that the long iron-gray hair grew only on its sides. But, I saw nothing that in the least explained him. On the contrary, I saw him once more holding out both his hands to me.

"What do you mean?" said I, half suspecting him to be mad.

He stopped looking at me, and slowly rubbed his right hand over his head. "It's disapinting to a man," he said, in a coarse, broken voice, "arter having looked for'ard so distant, and come so fur; but you're not to blame for that—neither on us is to blame for that. I'll speak in half a minute. Give me half a minute, please."

He sat down on a chair that stood before the fire and covered his forehead with his large brown hands. I looked at him attentively then, and recoiled a little from him. But I did not know him.

"There's no one else here," said he, looking over his shoulder, "is there?"

"Why do you, a stranger coming into my rooms at this time of the night, ask that question?" said I.

"You're a game one," he returned, shaking his head at me with a deliberate affection. "I'm glad you've grow'd up a game one!"

I knew him! I could not recall a single feature, but I knew him! If the wind and the rain had driven away the intervening years, had scattered all the intervening objects, had swept us to the churchyard where we first stood face to face on such different levels, I could not have known my convict more distinctly than I knew him now, as he sat in the chair before the fire. No need to take a file from his pocket and show it to me. No need to take the handkerchief from his neck and twist it round his head. No need to hug himself with both his arms and take a shivering turn across the room, looking back at me for recognition. I knew him before he gave me any of those signs, though a moment before, I had not the least idea of his identity.

He came back to where I stood, and again held out both his hands. Not knowing what to do—for, in my astonishment I had lost my self-possession—

I reluctantly gave him my hands. He grasped them heartily, raised them to his lips, kissed them, and still held them.

"You acted noble, my boy," said he. "Noble, Pip! And I have never forgot it!"

At a change in his manner as if he were even going to embrace me, I laid a hand upon his chest and held him away.

"Stay!" said I. "Keep off! If you are grateful to me for what I did when I was a little child, I hope you have shown your gratitude by mending your way of life. If you have come here to thank me, it was not necessary. Still, however you have found me out, there must be something good in the feeling that has brought you here. I will not repulse you, but surely you must understand that—I—"

My attention was so attracted by the singularity of his fixed look at me, that the words died away on my tongue.

"You was a-saying," he observed, when we had confronted one another in silence, "that surely I must understand. What, surely, must I understand?"

"That I cannot wish to renew that chance interaction with you of long ago, under these different circumstances. I am glad to believe you have repented and recovered yourself. I am glad to tell you so. I am glad that, thinking I deserve to be thanked, you have come to thank me. But our ways are different ways, nonetheless. You are wet, and you look weary. Will you drink something before you go?"

He had replaced his neckerchief loosely, and had stood, keenly observant of me, biting a long end of it. "I think," he answered, still with the end at his mouth and still observant of me, "that I will drink—I thank you—afore I go."

There was a tray ready on a side table. I brought it to the table near the fire, and asked him what he would have. He touched one of the bottles without looking at it or speaking, and I made him some hot rum-and-water. I tried to keep my hand steady while I did so, but his look at me as he leaned back in his chair with the long draggled end of his neckerchief between his teeth—evidently forgotten—made my hand very difficult to master. When at last I put the glass to him, I saw with amazement that his eyes were full of tears.

Up to this time I had remained standing, so as to indicate that I wished him to go. But I was softened by the softened aspect of the man, and felt a touch of reproach. "I hope," said I, hurriedly putting something into a glass for myself, and drawing a chair to the table, "that you will not think I spoke harshly to you just now. I had no intention of doing it, and I am sorry for it if I did. I wish you well, and happy!"

As I put my glass to my lips, he stretched out his hand. I gave him mine, and then he drank, and drew his sleeve across his eyes and forehead.

"How are you living?" I asked him.

"I've been a sheep farmer, stock breeder, other trades besides, away in the new world," said he.

"Many a thousand mile of stormy water off from this."

"I hope you have done well?"

"I've done wonderful well. There's others went out alonger me as has done well too, but no man has done nigh as well as me. I'm famous for it."

"I am glad to hear it."

"I hope to hear you say so, my dear boy."

Without stopping to try to understand those words or the tone in which they were spoken, I brought up a point that had just come into my mind.

"Have you ever seen a messenger you once sent to me," I inquired, "since he undertook that trust?"

"Never set eyes upon him. I warn't likely to it."

"He came faithfully, and he brought me the two one-pound notes. I was a poor boy then, as you know, and to a poor boy they were a little fortune. But, like you, I have done well since, and you must let me pay them back. You can put them to some other poor boy's use." I took out my wallet.

He watched me as I laid my wallet upon the table and opened it, and he watched me as I separated two one-pound notes from its contents. They were clean and new, and I spread them out and handed them over to him. Still watching me, he laid them one upon the other, folded them lengthwise, gave them a twist, set fire to them at the lamp, and dropped the ashes into the tray.

"May I make so bold," he said then, with a smile that was like a frown, and with a frown that was like a smile, "as ask you how you have done well, since you and me was out on them lone shivering marshes?"

"How?"

"Yes!"

He emptied his glass, got up, and stood at the side of the fire, with his heavy brown hand on the mantelshelf. He put a foot up to the bars, to dry and warm it, and the wet boot began to steam. But, he neither looked at it, nor at the fire, but steadily looked at me. It was only now that I began to tremble.

I forced myself to tell him (though I could not do it distinctly), that I had been chosen to succeed to some property.

"Might a mere warmint ask what property?" said he.

I faltered, "I don't know."

"Might a mere warmint ask whose property?" said he.

I faltered again, "I don't know."

"Could I make a guess, I wonder," said the convict, "at your income since you come of age! As to the first figure now. Five?"

With my heart beating like a heavy hammer, I rose out of my chair, and stood with my hand upon the back of it, looking wildly at him.

"Concerning a guardian," he went on. "There ought to have been some guardian, or such-like, whiles you was a minor. Some lawyer, maybe. As to the first letter of that lawyer's name now. Would it be J?"

All the truth of my position came flashing on me. Its disappointments, dangers, disgraces, consequences of all kinds, rushed in in such a multitude that I was borne down by them and had to struggle for every breath I drew.

"Put it," he resumed, "as the employer of that lawyer whose name begun with a J, and might be Jaggers—put it as he had come over sea to England, and had wanted to meet with you. 'However, did you find me out?' you says just now. Well! However did I find you out? Why, I wrote from Portsmouth to a person in London, for particulars of your address. That person's name? Why, Wemmick."

I could not have spoken one word, though it had been to save my life. I stood, with a hand on the chairback and a hand on my breast, where I seemed to be suffocating—I stood so, looking wildly at him, until I grasped at the chair, when the room began to surge and turn. He caught me, drew me to the sofa, put me up against the cushions, and knelt on one knee before me: bringing the face that I now well remembered, and that I shuddered at, very near to mine.

"Yes, Pip, dear boy, I've made a gentleman on you! It's me wot has done it! I swore that time, sure as ever I earned a guinea, that guinea should go to you. I swore afterward, sure as ever I spec'lated and got rich, you should get rich. I lived rough, that you should live smooth. I worked hard, that you should be above work. Do I tell it, fur you to feel an obligation? Not a bit. I tell it, fur you to know as that there hunted dunghill dog wot you kep' life in, got his head so high that he could make a gentleman—and, Pip, you're him!"

The abhorrence in which I held the man, the dread I had of him, the repugnance with which I shrank from him, could not have been exceeded if he had been some terrible beast.

"Look'ee here, Pip. I'm your second father. You're my son—more to me than any son. I've put away money, only for you to spend. When I was a hired-out shepherd in a solitary hut, all the way in Australia, not seeing no faces but faces of sheep till I half forgot wot men's and women's faces wos like, I see yourn. I see you there a many times, as plain as ever I see you on them misty marshes. And I done it. Why, look at you, dear boy! Look at these here lodgings o' yourn, fit for a lord! A lord? Ah! You shall show money with lords for wagers, and beat em!"

In his heat and triumph, he did not notice my reception of all this. It was the one grain of relief I had.

"Look'ee here!" he went on, taking my watch out of my pocket, and turning toward him a ring on my finger, while I recoiled from his touch as if he had been a snake. "Your watch—a gold 'un and a beauty: that's a gentleman's, I hope! Your ring—a diamond all set round with rubies; that's a gentleman's, I hope! Look at your clothes; better ain't to be got!"

Again he took both my hands and put them to his lips, while my blood ran cold within me.

"Didn't you never think it might be me?"

"O no, no, no," I returned. "Never, never!"

"Well, you see it wos me, and single-handed. Never a soul in it but my own self and Mr. Jaggers."

"Was there no one else?" I asked.

"No," said he, with a glance of surprise. "Who else should there be? And, dear boy, how good looking you have growed! There's bright eyes somewheres—eh? Isn't there bright eyes somewheres, a girl you be sweet on? eh?"

O Estella, Estella!

"Let me finish wot I was a-telling you, dear boy. From that there Australian hut and that there hiring-out, I got money left me by my master (which died, and had been the same as me), and got my liberty and went for myself. In every single thing I went for, I went for you. It all prospered wonderful. It was the money left me, and the gains of the first few year wot I sent home to Mr. Jaggers—all for you—when he first come arter you, agreeable to my letter."

O, that he had never come! That he had left me at the forge—far from contented, yet, by comparison, happy!

"And then, dear boy, it was a recompense to me, look'ee here, to know in secret that I was making a gentleman. The blood horses of them colonists might fling up the dust over me as I was walking. What do I say? I says to myself, 'I'm making a better gentleman nor ever you'll be!' When one of 'em says to another, 'He was a convict, a few year ago, and is a ignorant common fellow now,' what do I say? I says to myself, 'If I ain't a gentleman, nor yet ain't got no learning, I'm the owner of such. All on you owns stock and land. Which one you owns a brought-up London gentleman?' This way I kep' myself a-going. And this way I held steady afore my mind that I would for certain come one day and see my boy, and make myself known to him, on his own ground."

He laid his hand on my shoulder. I shuddered at the thought that for anything I knew, his hand might be stained with blood.

"It warn't easy, Pip, for me to leave them parts, nor yet it warn't safe. But I held to it, and the harder it was, the stronger I held, for I was determined, and my mind firm made up. At last I done it. Dear boy, I done it!"

I tried to collect my thoughts, but I was stunned.

"Where will you put me?" he asked, presently. "I must be put somewheres, dear boy."

"To sleep?" said I.

"Yes. And to sleep long and sound," he answered; "for I've been sea-tossed and sea-washed, months and months."

"My friend and companion," said I, rising from the sofa, "is absent. You must have his room."

"He won't come back tomorrow, will he?"

"No," said I.

"Because, look'ee here, dear boy," he said, dropping his voice, and laying a long finger on my chest in an urgent manner, "caution is necessary."

"How do you mean? Caution?"

"By God, it's Death!"

"What's death?"

"I was deported to Australia for life. It's death to come back. I should of a certainty be hanged if took."

The wretched man had risked his life to come to me, and I held it there in my keeping! If I had loved him instead of abhorring him; if I had been attracted to him by the strongest admiration and affection, instead of shrinking from him with the strongest repugnance; it could have been no worse. On the contrary, it would have been better, for his preservation would then have naturally and tenderly addressed my heart. But now my fondest hopes were dashed! It was not Miss Havisham who was bringing me up to be a gentleman, so I would be fit company for Estella. Estella seemed further out of reach than ever.

My first care was to close the shutters, so that no light might be seen from outside, and then to close and lock the doors. While I did so, he stood at the table drinking rum and eating biscuit. When I saw him thus engaged, I saw my convict on the marshes at his meal again. It almost seemed to me as if he must stoop down presently, to file at his leg. I went into Herbert's room and prepared it for my visitor. Before retiring, he asked me for some of my "gentleman's linen" to put on in the morning. I brought it out and laid it ready for him. My blood again ran cold when he again took me by both hands to wish me good night.

I got away from him, without knowing how I did it, and tended the fire in the room where we had been together, and sat down by it, afraid to go to bed. For an hour or more, I remained too stunned to think. But when I finally composed myself, I came to horrible conclusions.

Miss Havisham's intentions toward me—all a mere dream. Estella was not designed for me. But the sharpest and deepest pain of all was that I had deserted Joe for no better reason than that the convict could heap praise upon me. I could never, never, never, undo what I had done.

Gradually I slipped from the chair and lay on the floor. When I awoke, the clocks of the churches were striking five, the candles were wasted out, the fire was dead, and the wind and rain intensified the thick black darkness.

THIS IS THE END OF THE SECOND STAGE OF PIP'S EXPECTATIONS.

VOLUME 3

As I lay in a daze, I realized the impossibility of concealing my visitor in the rooms I shared with Herbert. This was especially the case, as I was looked after by an excitable old female, assisted by an animated rag-bag whom she called her niece. To keep a roomer secret from them was out of the question. Therefore, I resolved to announce in the morning that my uncle had unexpectedly come from the country.

This course I decided on while I was groping about in the darkness for the means of getting a light. Finding no means of doing so, I decided to go out to the adjacent building and get the watchman there to come with his lantern. Now, in groping my way down the dark staircase I fell over something, and that something was a man crouching in a corner.

The man made no answer when I asked him what he did there. I ran as quickly as I could to the watchman and begged him to come quickly. We examined the staircase from the bottom to the top and found no one there.

It troubled me that there should have been a lurker on the stairs, on that night of all nights in the year. I asked the watchman whether he had admitted at his gate any person other than my visitor. Yes, he said; there was a man who came with him.

"Person with him!" I inquired.

"I judged the person to be with him," returned the watchman. "The person stopped, when your visitor stopped to make inquiry of me. Then the person came this way when your visitor did so."

"What sort of person?"

The watchman had not particularly noticed. He said the other man looked like a working person and wore dust-colored clothes under a dark coat.

After the watchman left, I lighted my fire and fell asleep. When I awoke, the old woman and the niece came in. I explained that my uncle had come in the night and was then asleep, and how the breakfast preparations were to be modified accordingly. Then I washed and dressed while they knocked the furniture about and made some dust.

By-and-by, his door opened and he came out. I could not bring myself to bear the sight of him, and I thought he had a worse look by daylight.

"I do not even know," said I, speaking low as he took his seat at the table, "by what name to call you. I have given out that you are my uncle."

"That's it, dear boy! Call me uncle."

"You assumed some name, I suppose, on board ship?"

"Yes, dear boy. I took the name of Provis."

"Do you mean to keep that name?"

"Why, yes, dear boy, it's as good as another—unless you'd like another."

"What is your real name?" I asked him in a whisper.

"Magwitch," he answered, in the same tone; "chrisen'd Abel."

"What were you brought up to be?"

"A rogue, dear boy."

He answered quite seriously, and used the word as if it denoted some profession.

"When you came in at the gate and asked the watchman the way here, had you any one with you?"

"With me? No, dear boy."

"But there was some one there?"

"I didn't take particular notice," he said. "But I think there was a person, too, come in alonger me."

"Are you known in London?"

"I hope not!" said he, giving his neck a jerk with his forefinger that made me turn hot and sick.

"Were you—tried—in London?"

"Which time?" said he, with a sharp look.

"The last time."

He nodded. "First knowed Mr. Jaggers that way. Jaggers defended me. And what I done is worked out and paid for!" he said, with feeling.

He ate in a ravenous way that was very disagreeable. All his actions were uncouth, noisy, and greedy. Some of his teeth had failed him since I saw him eat on the marshes, and as he turned his food in his mouth, and turned his head sideways to bring his strongest fangs to bear upon it, he looked terribly like a hungry old dog. I was repelled by him.

When he got up from table, he put his hand into the breast of the peacoat he wore and brought out a short black pipe and a handful of loose tobacco. Having filled his pipe, he put the surplus tobacco back again. Then, he took a live coal from the fire with the tongs, and lighted his pipe with it. He then turned toward me and went through his favorite action of holding out both his hands for mine.

"And this," said he, dandling my hands up and down in his, as he puffed at his pipe; "and this is the gentleman what I made! The real genuine One! It does me good fur to look at you, Pip. All I ask, is, to stand by and look at you, dear boy!"

I released my hands as soon as I could. I was beginning slowly to realize what I was chained to, and how heavily. I heard his hoarse voice, and sat looking up at his furrowed bald head with its iron gray hair at the sides.

"I mustn't see my gentleman a footing it in the mire of the streets. There mustn't be no mud on his boots. My gentleman must have horses, Pip! Horses to ride, and horses to drive, and horses for his servant as well."

He took out of his pocket a great thick pocket-book, bursting with papers, and tossed it on the table.

"There's something worth spending in that there book, dear boy. It's yourn. All I've got ain't mine; it's yourn. There's more where that come from. I've come to the old country fur to see my gentleman spend his money like a gentleman. That'll be my pleasure."

"Stop!" said I, almost in a frenzy of fear and dislike. "I want to speak to you. I want to know what is to be done. I want to know how you are to be kept out of danger, how long you are going to stay, what projects you have."

"Well, dear boy, the danger ain't so great. There's Jaggers, and there's Wemmick, and there's you. Who else is there to inform against me?"

"Is there no chance person who might identify you in the street?" said I.

"Well," he returned, "there ain't many. Nor yet I don't intend to advertise myself in the newspapers."

"And how long do you remain?"

"How long?" said he, taking his black pipe from his mouth, and dropping his jaw as he stared at me. "I'm not a-going back. I've come for good."

"Where are you to live?" said I. "What is to be done with you? Where will you be safe?"

"Dear boy," he returned, "there's disguising wigs can be bought for money, and there's hair powder, and spectacles, and clothes."

It appeared to me that I could do no better

than secure him some quiet lodging close by. Of course, I must tell Herbert when he returned. Mr. Provis (I resolved to call him by that name) reserved his consent to Herbert's participation until he should have seen him.

As he was at present dressed in a seafaring outfit, in which he looked as if he had some parrots and cigars to dispose of, I next discussed with him what dress he should wear. After some discussion, we decided he should look like a prosperous farmer. After giving him strict instructions not to leave my lodging until my return, I set out to find him rooms.

I was aware of a boarding house almost within hail of my windows. I went to that house, and was so fortunate as to secure the second floor for my uncle, Mr. Provis. I then went from shop to shop, making such purchases as were necessary to the change in his appearance. This business transacted, I made my way directly to the office of Mr. Jaggers. Mr. Jaggers was at his desk, but, seeing me enter, got up immediately and stood before his fire.

"Now, Pip," said he, "be careful. Don't tell me anything."

Of course I saw that he knew the man was come.

"I merely want, Mr. Jaggers," said I, "to assure myself that what I have been told, is true. I have been informed by a person named Abel Magwitch that he is the benefactor so long unknown to me."

"That is the man," said Mr. Jaggers, "from Australia."

"And only he?" said I.

"And only he," said Mr. Jaggers.

"I always supposed it was Miss Havisham."

Mr. Jaggers turned his eyes upon me coolly, and taking a bite at his forefinger, said, "I am not at all responsible for that. Good day, Pip," said Mr. Jaggers, offering his hand. "Glad to have seen you."

We shook hands, and he looked hard at me as long as he could see me. I went straight back to my rooms, where I found the terrible Provis drinking rum-and-water and smoking.

Next day the clothes I had ordered arrived. Whatever he put on became him less than what he had worn before. To my thinking, there was something in him that made it hopeless to attempt to disguise him. The more I dressed him and the better I dressed him, the more he looked like the slouching fugitive on the marshes.

The influences of his solitary hut life in Australia were upon him besides, and gave him a savage air that no dress could tame. In all his ways of sitting and standing, and eating and drinking—of chopping a wedge off his bread, and soaking up with it the last fragments of gravy round and round his plate, as if to make the most of an allowance, and then drying his finger ends on it, and then swallowing it—in these ways and a thousand more, there was Prisoner, Felon, Bondsman, engraved upon him.

I doubt if a ghost could have been more terrible to me, up in those lonely rooms in the long

evenings and long nights, with the wind and the rain always rushing by. A ghost could not have been taken and hanged on my account. But the consideration that he could be, and the dread that he would be, added to my horrors.

This state of affairs lasted about five days. Expecting Herbert all the time, I dared not go out, except when I took Provis for an airing after dark. At length, one evening when dinner was over and I had dropped into a slumber quite worn out, I was roused by the welcome footstep on the staircase. Provis, who had been asleep too, staggered up at the noise I made, and in an instant I saw his jack-knife shining in his hand.

"Quiet! It's Herbert!" I said, and Herbert came bursting in.

"Handel, my dear fellow, how are you, and again how are you? I seem to have been gone a twelvemonth! Why, so I must have been, for you have grown quite thin and pale! Handel, my—Halloa! I beg your pardon."

He was stopped in his running on and in his shaking hands with me, by seeing Provis. Provis, regarding him with a fixed attention, was slowly putting up his jackknife, and groping in another pocket for something else.

"Herbert, my dear friend," said I, shutting the double doors, while Herbert stood staring and wondering, "something very strange has happened. This is—a visitor of mine."

In vain should I attempt to describe the astonishment and uneasiness of Herbert, when he and I and Provis sat down before the fire, and I told the entire story. I saw my own feelings reflected in Herbert's face, and, not least among them, my repugnance toward the man who had done so much for me.

Of course, Provis could have no idea that I might find any fault with my good fortune. We were eager for the time when he would go to his lodging, and leave us together, but he stayed until midnight. As had become our routine, I escorted him to his lodging and then returned home. I experienced the first moment of relief I had known since the night of his arrival.

Herbert received me with open arms. I had never felt before how fortunate it is to have such a friend. When he had spoken some sound words of sympathy and encouragement, we sat down to consider the question, What was to be done?

We decided that the first order of business must be to find out about Provis's past life, including his criminal life.

With this project formed, we went to bed. I had the wildest dreams concerning him, and woke unrefreshed. At breakfast time he came around. As he often did, he took out his jackknife and sat down to his meal. He was full of plans for me. He considered my chambers and his own lodging as temporary residences, and advised me to look out at once for a "fashionable crib" near Hyde Park. When he had made an end of his breakfast, and was wiping his knife on his leg, I said to him, without a word of preface: "After you were gone last night, I told my friend of the struggle that the soldiers found you engaged in on the marshes, when we came up. You remember?"

"Remember!" said he. "I think so!"

"We want to know something about that man—and about you."

"Look'ee here!" he said. "Wotever I done, is worked out and paid for."

"So be it."

He spread a hand on each knee and, after turning an angry eye on the fire for a few silent moments, looked round at us and said what follows.

"Dear boy and Pip's comrade. I am not a going fur to tell you my life, like a song or a story-book. But here it is short and handy: in jail and out of jail, in jail and out of jail, in jail and out of jail. That's my life pretty much, down to such times as I got shipped off to Australia, arter Pip stood my friend.

"I've been done everything to, pretty well—except hanged. I've been locked up as much as a silver teakettle. I've been carted here and carted there, and put out of this town and put out of that town, and stuck in the stocks, and whipped and worried and drove. I've no more notion where I was born, than you have—if so much. My first memory was stealing turnips for my living.

"I know'd my name to be Abel Magwitch. There warn't a soul that see young Abel Magwitch but wot was afraid of him, and either drove him off, or took him up.

"When I was a ragged little creetur as much to be pitied as ever I see, I got the name of being hardened. 'This is a terrible hardened one,' they says to prison wisitors, picking out me. 'May be said to live in jails, this boy.' They always went on about the Devil. But what the Devil was I to do? I must put something into my stomach, mustn't I?

"Tramping, begging, thieving, working sometimes when I could, a bit of most things that don't pay and lead to trouble, I got to be a man.

"Some twenty years ago, I got acquainted wi' a man whose skull I'd crack wi' this poker, like the claw of a lobster, if he were right here. His right name was Compeyson. That's the man, dear boy, what you see me a pounding in the ditch in the marshes.

"He set up fur a gentleman, this Compeyson, and he'd been to a boarding school and had learning. He was a smooth talker and knew the ways of gentlefolks. He was good-looking too. I met him at a tavern. Him and some more was a-sitting among the tables when I went in, and the landlord called him out, and said, 'I think this is a man that might suit you'—meaning I was.

"Compeyson looks at me. He has a watch and a chain and a ring and a breast-pin and a handsome suit of clothes.

"'To judge from appearances, you're out of luck,' says Compeyson to me.

"'Yes, master, and I've never been in it much.' (I had just come out of Kingston Jail on a vagrancy committal.)

"'What can you do?' says Compeyson.

"'Eat and drink,' I says; 'if you'll find the materials.'

"Compeyson laughed, looked at me again, giv' me five shillings, and told me to meet him next night, same place.

"I went to Compeyson next night, same place, and Compeyson took me on to be his man and pardner. And what was Compeyson's business? Compeyson's business was the swindling, forging, stolen banknote passing, and such-like. All sorts of traps as Compeyson could set with his head, and keep his own legs out of and get the profits from and let another man in for, was Compeyson's business. He'd no more heart than a iron file. He was as cold as death, and he had the head of the Devil aforementioned.

"Him and me was soon busy. I won't go into the things that Compeyson planned, and I done—that 'ud take a week. I'll simply say that that man made me his slave. I was always in debt to him, always under his thumb, always a-working, always a-getting into danger. He overmatched me five hundred times. My Missis as I had the hard time wi'—Wait, I ain't brought her in—"

He looked about him in a confused way, as if he had lost his place in the book of his remembrance. He turned his face to the fire, and spread his hands broader on his knees, and lifted them off and put them on again.

"There ain't no need to go into it," he said.

"The time wi' Compeyson was a'most as hard a time as ever I had. That said, all's said.

"At last, me and Compeyson was both committed for felony—on a charge of putting stolen notes in circulation—and there was other charges too. Compeyson says to me, 'Separate defenses, no communication,' and that was all. And I was so miserable poor, that I sold all the clothes I had, except what hung on my back, afore I could get Jaggers.

"When we was put in the dock, I noticed first of all what a gentleman Compeyson looked, and what a common sort of a wretch I looked. When the prosecution opened and the evidence was supplied, I noticed how heavy it all bore on me, and how light on him. It was always me that the money had been paid to. It was always me that had seemed to commit the crime and get the profit. When it was our turn to defend ourselves, Compeyson's wicked strategy became plain. Says the lawyer for Compeyson, 'My lord and gentlemen, here you has afore you, side by side, two persons. One, the younger, well brought up. The other (meaning me), the elder, ill brought up. The younger, seldom if ever accused of anything, and only suspected. The other, the elder, always in and out of jail.' And when the verdict come, warn't it Compeyson's lawyer that called for mercy on account of good character and bad company, and giving up evidence agen me? And when we're sentenced, ain't it him as gets seven year, and me fourteen?"

He had so heated himself that he took out his

handkerchief and wiped his face and head and neck and hands, before he could go on.

"I told Compeyson that I'd smash that face of his. We was in the same prison-ship, but I couldn't get at him for long, though I tried. At last I come behind him and hit him on the cheek to turn him round and get a smashing one at him, when I was seen and seized. The black-hole of that ship warn't a strong one. I escaped to the shore, and I was a-hiding among the graves there, envying them as was in 'em, when I first see my boy!"

He regarded me with a look of affection that made him almost revolting to me again, though I had felt great pity for him.

"By Pip's words, I was giv' to understand as Compeyson was out on them marshes too. I half believe he escaped in his terror, to get quit of me, not knowing it was me as had got ashore. I hunted him down. I smashed his face. Then the soldiers found us and dragged us back to the prison ship.

"Of course, his punishment was light. I was put in irons, brought to trial again, and sent away to the penal colony in Australia for life."

He wiped his face again. He then slowly took his tangle of tobacco from his pocket, plucked his pipe from his buttonhole, slowly filled it, and began to smoke.

"Is he dead?" I asked, after a silence.

"I never heerd no more of him."

Herbert had been writing with his pencil in the cover of a book. He softly pushed the book over to me, as Provis stood smoking with his eyes on the fire. I read these words:

"Compeyson is the man who pretended to love Miss Havisham and then abandoned her. He is the cause of her bitterness. The name of Miss Havisham's brother is Arthur."

I shut the book and nodded slightly to Herbert. We put the book aside. Neither of us said anything, and we both looked at Provis as he stood smoking by the fire.

A new fear entered my mind as a result of his narrative. If Compeyson were alive and should discover his return, Compeyson would inform the police. I also made up my mind to see Estella and Miss Havisham as soon as I could.

I learned that Estella was in fact visiting Miss Havisham at the present time. Next day, I set off for Miss Havisham's by the early morning coach before daylight. The carriage was out on the open country road when the day came creeping on, halting and whimpering and shivering, and wrapped in patches of clouds and rags of mist, like a beggar. When we drove up to the Blue Boar after a drizzly ride, whom should I see come out under the gateway, toothpick in hand, to look at the coach, but Bentley Drummle!

I had a strong recollection of our dispute at the meeting of the Finches of the Grove, and I had no desire to be civil toward him. Furthermore, I strongly suspected that he was in these parts for the same purpose as me, namely, to visit Estella.

I could not gain access to the Blue Boar without taking notice of Drummle. We exchanged a few words, neither of us speaking very civilly.

"Large tract of marshes about here, I believe?" said Drummle.

"Yes. What of that?" said I.

Mr. Drummle looked at me, and then at my boots, and then said, "Oh!" and laughed.

"Are you amused, Mr. Drummle?"

"No," said he, "not particularly. I am going out for a horse ride. I mean to explore those marshes for amusement. Out-of-the-way villages there, they tell me. Curious little public houses—and smithies—and that. Waiter!"

"Yes, sir."

"Is that horse of mine ready?"

"Brought round to the door, sir."

"I say. Look here, you sir. The lady won't ride today. The weather won't do."

"Very good, sir."

"And I don't dine here this evening, because I'm going to dine at the lady's."

"Very good, sir."

Then, Drummle glanced at me, with an insolent triumph on his great-jowled face that cut me to the heart. In an increased state of smoldering ferocity, I said:

"Mr. Drummle, I did not seek this conversation, and I don't think it an agreeable one."

"I am sure it's not," said he.

"And therefore," I went on, "with your leave, I will suggest that we hold no kind of communication in future."

"Quite my opinion," said Drummle. "But don't lose your temper. Haven't you lost enough without that?"

"What do you mean, sir?"

As if to emphasize his point, Drummle called to the waiter. "Look here, you sir. You quite understand that the young lady don't ride today, and that I dine at the young lady's?"

"Quite so, sir!"

Drummle went outside and seized his horse's mane. He mounted the steed in his blundering brutal manner, sidling and backing away. I thought he was gone, when he came back, calling for a light for the cigar in his mouth, which he had forgotten. A man in a dust-colored outfit appeared with what was wanted. As Drummle leaned down from the saddle and lighted his cigar and laughed, the slouching shoulders and ragged hair of this man, whose back was toward me, reminded me of Orlick.

I was too heavily out of sorts to care much at the time whether it were he or not. I washed the weather and the journey from my face and hands, and went out to the memorable old house that it would have been so much the better for me never to have entered, never to have seen.

In the room where the dressing table stood, and where the wax candles burnt on the wall, I found Miss Havisham and Estella. Miss Havisham was seated on a sofa near the fire, and Estella on a cushion at her feet. Estella was knitting, and Miss Havisham was looking on. They both raised their eyes as I went in, and both saw an alteration in me. I could tell that from the look they exchanged.

"And what wind," said Miss Havisham, "blows you here, Pip?"

Though she looked steadily at me, I saw that she was rather confused. Estella paused a moment in her knitting with her eyes upon me, and then went on. I fancied that I read in the action of her fingers, as plainly as if she had told me in words, that she perceived I had discovered my real benefactor.

"Miss Havisham," said I, "I learned that some wind had blown Estella here, and so I followed."

Miss Havisham motioned to me to sit down. I took the chair by the dressing table, which I had often seen her occupy. With all that ruin at my feet and about me, it seemed a natural place for me, that day.

"What I have to say to Estella, Miss Havisham, I will say before you. It will not surprise you, it will not displease you. I am as unhappy as you can ever have meant me to be."

Miss Havisham continued to look steadily at me. Estella's fingers continued to work, but she did not look up.

"I have found out who my patron is. It is not a fortunate discovery, and is not likely ever to enrich me in reputation, station, fortune, anything. There are reasons why I must say no more about that. It is not my secret, but another's."

As I was silent for a while, looking at Estella and considering how to go on, Miss Havisham repeated, "It is not your secret, but another's. Well?"

"When you first caused me to be brought here, Miss Havisham; when I belonged to the village over yonder, that I wish I had never left; I suppose I did really come here to gratify a want or a whim, and to be paid for it?"

"Ay, Pip," replied Miss Havisham, steadily nodding her head. "You did."

"And that Mr. Jaggers—"

"Mr. Jaggers," said Miss Havisham, speaking in a firm tone, "had nothing to do with it, and knew nothing of it. His being my lawyer, and his being the lawyer of your patron, is a coincidence."

"But when I fell into the delusion I have so

long remained in, at least you led me on?" said I.

"Yes," she returned, again nodding steadily. "I let you go on."

"Was that kind?"

"Who am I," cried Miss Havisham, striking her stick upon the floor and flashing into wrath so suddenly that Estella glanced up at her in surprise, "who am I, for God's sake, that I should be kind? What else?"

"In humoring my mistake, Miss Havisham, you punished—practiced on—your self-seeking relations?"

"I did."

Waiting until she was quiet again—for this, too, flashed out of her in a wild and sudden way—I went on.

"I have been thrown among one family of your relations, Miss Havisham, and have been constantly among them since I went to London. I know them to have been as honestly under my delusion as I myself. You deeply wrong both Mr. Matthew Pocket and his son Herbert, if you suppose them to be otherwise than generous, upright, open, and incapable of anything designing or mean."

"They are your friends," said Miss Havisham.

"They made themselves my friends," said I, "when they supposed me to have replaced them as the beneficiaries of your wealth."

"What do you want for them?"

"If you would spare the money to do my friend Herbert a great favor in life, but which from the nature of the case must be done without his knowledge, I could show you how."

"Why must it be done without his knowledge?" she asked, settling her hands upon her stick, that she might regard me the more attentively.

"Because," said I, "I began the service myself, more than two years ago, without his knowledge. Why I fail in my ability to finish it, I cannot explain. It is a part of the secret which is another person's and not mine."

She gradually withdrew her eyes from me, and turned them on the fire. After watching it for what appeared in the silence and by the light of the slowly wasting candles to be a long time, she was roused by the collapse of some of the red coals, and looked toward me again. All this time, Estella knitted on. When Miss Havisham had fixed her attention on me, she said, speaking as if there had been no lapse in our dialogue:

"What else?"

"Estella," said I, turning to her now, and trying to command my trembling voice, "you know I love you. You know that I have loved you long and dearly."

She raised her eyes to my face, on being thus addressed. Her fingers plied their work, and she looked at me with an unmoved expression. I saw that Miss Havisham glanced from me to her, and from her to me.

"I should have said this sooner, but for my long mistake. It induced me to hope that Miss Havisham meant us for one another. While I thought you could not help yourself, as it were, I refrained from saying it. But I must say it now."

Preserving her unmoved countenance, and with her fingers still going, Estella shook her head.

"I know," said I, in answer to that action; "I know. I have no hope that I shall ever call you mine, Estella. I am ignorant what may become of me very soon, how poor I may be, or where I may go. Still, I love you. I have loved you ever since I first saw you in this house."

Looking at me perfectly unmoved and with her fingers busy, she shook her head again.

"It would have been cruel in Miss Havisham, horribly cruel, to take advantage of the innocence of a poor boy, and to torture me through all these years with a vain hope, if she had reflected on the gravity of what she did. But I think she did not. I think that in the endurance of her own trial, she forgot mine, Estella."

I saw Miss Havisham put her hand to her heart and hold it there, as she sat looking by turns at Estella and at me.

"It seems," said Estella, very calmly, "that there are sentiments, fancies—I don't know how to call them—which I am not able to comprehend. When you say you love me, I know what the words mean, but nothing more. You arouse no feelings of love in me. I don't care for what you say at all. I have tried to warn you of this, have I not?"

I said in a miserable manner, "Yes."

"Yes. But you would not be warned, for you thought I did not mean it. Now, did you not think so?"

"I thought and hoped you could not mean it. You, so young, untried, and beautiful, Estella! Surely it is not natural."

"It is in my nature," she returned. And then she added, with a stress upon the words, "It is in the nature formed within me. I make a great difference between you and all other people when I say so much. I can do no more."

"Is it not true," said I, "that Bentley Drummle is in town here, and pursuing you?"

"It is quite true," she replied, referring to him with the indifference of utter contempt.

"That you encourage him, and ride out with him, and that he dines with you this very day?"

She seemed a little surprised that I should know it, but again replied, "Quite true."

"You cannot love him, Estella!"

Her fingers stopped for the first time, as she retorted rather angrily, "What have I told you? Do you still think, in spite of it, that I do not mean what I say?"

"You would never marry him, Estella?"

She looked toward Miss Havisham, and considered for a moment with her work in her hands. Then she said, "Why not tell you the truth? I am going to be married to him."

I dropped my face into my hands, but was able to control myself better than I could have expected, considering what agony it gave me to hear her say those words. When I raised my face again, there was such a ghastly look upon Miss Havisham's, that it impressed me, even in my passionate hurry and grief.

"Estella, dearest Estella, do not let Miss Havisham lead you into this fatal step. Put me aside for ever—you have done so, I well know—but bestow yourself on some worthier person than Drummle. Miss Havisham gives you to him, as the greatest slight and injury that could be done to the many far better men who admire you, and to the few who truly love you. Among those few, there may be one who loves you even as dearly, though he has not loved you as long, as I. Take him, and I can bear it better, for your sake!"

"I am going," she said again, in a gentler voice, "to be married to him. Why do you injuriously introduce the name of my mother by adoption? It is my own act."

"Your own act, Estella, to fling yourself away upon a brute?"

"It is done. I shall do well enough, and so will my husband. As to leading me into what you call this fatal step, Miss Havisham would have had me wait, and not marry yet. But I am tired of the life I have led, which has very few charms for me, and I am willing enough to change it. Say no more. We shall never understand each other."

"Such a mean brute, such a stupid brute!" I urged in despair.

"Don't be afraid of my being a blessing to

him," said Estella. "I shall not be that. Come! Here is my hand."

"O Estella!" I answered, as my bitter tears fell fast on her hand, do what I would to restrain them. "Even if I remained in England and could hold my head up with the rest, how could I see you as Drummle's wife?"

"Nonsense," she returned, "nonsense. This will pass in no time."

"Never, Estella!"

"You will get me out of your thoughts in a week."

"Out of my thoughts! You are part of my existence, part of myself. You have been in every line I have ever read, since I first came here, the rough common boy whose poor heart you wounded even then. You have been in every prospect I have ever seen since—on the river, on the sails of the ships, on the marshes, in the clouds, in the light, in the darkness, in the wind, in the woods, in the sea, in the streets. The stones which form the strongest London buildings are not more real than your presence and influence have been to me. Estella, to the last hour of my life, you cannot choose but remain part of my being. But, in this separation I associate you only with the good, and I will faithfully see you like that always. O God bless you, God forgive you!"

How this torrent of words gushed out of me, in my abject misery, I do not know. I held her hand to my lips some lingering moments, and so I left her.

But ever afterward, I remembered that while Estella looked at me merely with incredulous wonder, the spectral figure of Miss Havisham, her hand still covering her heart, was reduced to a ghastly stare of pity and remorse.

All done, all gone! So much was done and gone, that when I went out at the gate, the light of the day seemed of a darker color than when I went in. For a while, I hid myself among some lanes and by-paths. Then I headed off to walk all the way to London. I certainly could not bear to go back to the inn and see Drummle there. I did not even want to sit upon the coach and be spoken to. I resolved the best thing I could do was to tire myself out.

It was past midnight when I crossed London Bridge into the city. As I was very muddy and weary, I did not take it ill that the night porter examined me with much attention as he held the gate a little way open for me to pass in. To help his memory I mentioned my name.

"I was not quite sure, sir, but I thought so. Here's a note, sir. The messenger that brought it, said would you be so good as read it by my lantern?"

Much surprised by the request, I took the note. It was directed to Philip Pip, Esquire, and on the envelope were the words, PLEASE READ THIS, HERE. I opened it, the watchman holding up his light, and read inside, in Wemmick's writing:

DON'T GO HOME.

CHAPTER 42

I immediately turned away and headed for the Hummums in Covent Garden. In those days, one could always secure a room there with no questions asked. The night porter showed me to a nondescript room and left me with a candle. When I had got into bed, and lay there footsore, weary, and wretched, I found that sleep was impossible.

What a doleful night! How anxious, how dismal, how long! There was an inhospitable smell in the room, of cold soot and hot dust. When I had lain awake a little while, those extraordinary voices with which silence teems began to make themselves audible. The closet whispered, the fireplace sighed, the little washing stand ticked, and one guitar string played occasionally in the chest of drawers. And all about me I saw written, DON'T GO HOME.

Why I was not to go home, and what had happened at home, and when I should go home, and whether Provis was safe at home, were all I could think of.

I had left directions that I was to be called at seven. It was plain that I must see Wemmick before seeing any one else. Accordingly, I made my way to his residence.

"Halloa, Mr. Pip!" said Wemmick. "You did come home, then?"

"Yes," I returned, "but I didn't go home."

"Very good," said he, rubbing his hands. "Let us sit and talk a bit."

"I accidentally heard, yesterday morning," said Wemmick, "that a certain person of doubtful reputation and considerable wealth has disappeared from Australia. There are theories—theories, mind you, unproven—about where he might be at present. I also heard that you at your chambers had been watched, and might be watched again."

"By whom?" said I.

"I can't go into that," said Wemmick, evasively.

I saw that he was restrained by his professional obligations from saying as much as he could. But I told him, after a little meditation over the fire, that I would like to ask him a question. He, of course, could decide whether or not to answer it. He nodded to me once, to put my question.

"You have heard of a man of bad character, whose true name is Compeyson?"

He answered with one other nod.

"Is he living?"

One other nod.

"Is he in London?"

He gave me one other nod.

"No more questions," said Wemmick. "Instead, let me tell you what I did, after hearing what I heard. I went to your chambers in Garden Court to find you. Not finding you, I went to Clarriker's to find Mr. Herbert."

"And you found him?" said I, with great anxiety.

"And I found him. Without mentioning any names or going into any details, I made him understand that if he was aware of anybody being about the chambers, or about the immediate neighborhood, he had better get him out of the way while you were out of the way."

"He would be greatly puzzled what to do?"

"He was puzzled what to do."

I asked him what Herbert had done.

"Mr. Herbert," said Wemmick, "after much pondering, struck out a plan. He mentioned to me as a secret, that he is courting a young lady who has, as no doubt you are aware, a bedridden father. You are acquainted with the young lady, most probably?"

"Not personally," said I.

The truth was, that she had objected to me as an expensive companion who did Herbert no good. Furthermore, when Herbert had first proposed to present me to her, she had received the proposal with such very moderate warmth, that Herbert decided to put off our meeting.

"This house," said Wemmick, "where the lady's father resides, is kept by a very respectable widow who has a furnished upper floor to rent. Mr. Herbert put it to me, what did I think of that as a temporary residence for this person? I told Mr. Herbert I thought he had an excellent idea."

Much comforted by these considerations, I thanked Wemmick again and again, and begged him to proceed.

"Well, sir! Mr. Herbert threw himself into the business with a will. By nine o'clock last night he housed this person quite successfully."

With these words, Wemmick looked at his watch, and began to get his coat on.

"And now, Mr. Pip," said he, "I have probably done the most I can do. Here's the address. There can be no harm in your going there tonight before you go home. But after you have gone home, don't go back there. And let me finally impress one important point upon you." He laid his hands upon my shoulders, and added in a solemn whisper, "Use this evening to lay hold of his assets. You don't know what may happen to him."

Quite despairing of making my mind clear to Wemmick on this point, I didn't even try.

"Time's up," said Wemmick, "and I must be off. If you have nothing more pressing to do than to stay here till dark, that's what I should advise. You look very much worried, and it would do you good to have a perfectly quiet day right here."

I soon fell asleep before Wemmick's fire. His aged father and I enjoyed one another's society by falling asleep before it more or less all day. When it was quite dark, I left Wemmick's house and headed for the riverside, where my Mr. Provis was now housed.

My footsteps took me in the direction of the boat-builders as well as the mast, oar and block makers. The spot I wanted was called Mill Pond Bank, Chinks's Basin.

It matters not what stranded ships repairing in dry docks I lost myself among. I passed old hulls of ships in course of being knocked to pieces, ooze and slime and other dregs of tide, yards of shipbuilders and shipbreakers, rusty anchors blindly biting into the ground, and mountains of accumulated casks and timber. At last I came upon Mill Pond Bank. One house there boasted a wooden front, three stories and bow windows. I looked at the plate upon the door, and read there, Mrs. Whimple. That being the name I wanted, I knocked, and an elderly woman of a pleasant appearance responded. At that same exact moment, who should appear but Herbert. He silently led me into the parlor and shut the door.

"All is well, Handel," said Herbert, "and he is quite satisfied, though eager to see you. My dear girl is with her father. If you'll wait till she comes down, I'll introduce you to her, and then we'll go upstairs.—That's her father."

I had become aware of an alarming growling overhead, and had probably expressed the fact in the expression on my face.

"I am afraid he is a sad old rascal," said Herbert, smiling, "but I have never seen him. Don't you smell rum? He is always at it."

"At rum?" said I.

"Yes," returned Herbert. "To have Provis for an upper lodger is quite a godsend to Mrs. Whimple," said Herbert. "Most lodgers won't stand for that noise. A curious place, Handel, isn't it?"

It was a curious place, indeed, but remarkably well kept and clean.

"Mrs. Whimple," said Herbert, "is the best of housekeepers. I really do not know what my Clara would do without her motherly help. For, Clara has no mother of her own, Handel, and no relation in the world but old Gruffandgrim."

"Surely that's not his name, Herbert?"

"No, no," said Herbert, "that's my name for him. His name is Mr. Barley. But what a blessing it is for the son of my father and mother, to love a girl who has no other relations, and who can never bother herself, or anybody else, about her family!"

As we were thus conversing in a low tone, the room door opened. A very pretty, slight dark-eyed girl of twenty or so came in with a basket in her hand. Herbert tenderly relieved her of the basket and presented Clara to me. She really was a most charming girl.

I was looking at her with pleasure and admiration, when suddenly the growl swelled into a roar again. A frightful bumping noise was heard above, as if a giant with a wooden leg were trying to drive it through the ceiling to come at us. Upon this Clara said to Herbert, "Papa wants me, darling!" and ran away.

"What do you suppose he wants now, Handel?"

"I don't know," said I. "Something to drink?"

"That's it!" cried Herbert. "He keeps his rum in a little flask on the table. Wait a moment, and you'll hear Clara lift him up to take some.—There he goes!" Another roar, with a prolonged shake at the end. "Now," said Herbert, as it was succeeded by silence, "he's drinking. Now," said Herbert, as the growl resounded in the beam once more, "he's down again on his back!"

Clara returned soon afterward, and Herbert accompanied me upstairs to see our charge. As we passed Mr. Barley's door, he was heard hoarsely muttering within.

In his two rooms at the top of the house, I found Provis comfortably settled. I decided not to say anything to him about Compeyson. For anything I knew, his hatred of the man might drive him to seek him out and bring about his own destruction. Therefore, when Herbert and I sat down with him by his fire, I asked him first of all whether he relied on Wemmick's judgment and sources of information.

"Ay, ay, dear boy!" he answered, with a grave nod, "Jaggers knows."

"I have talked with Wemmick," said I, "and have come to tell you what caution he gave me and what advice."

This I did accurately, except for omitting mention of Compeyson. I told him how Wemmick had heard, in Newgate Prison, that he was under some suspicion, and that my chambers had been watched. I told him how Wemmick had recommended his lying low for a time, and my keeping away from him. The man was very reasonable throughout. His coming back was a risk, he said, and he had always known it to be a risk. He would do nothing to make it a desperate venture, and he had very little fear of his safety with such good help.

Herbert, who had been looking at the fire, here said something we thought had much merit. "We are both good rowers, Handel, and could take him down the river ourselves should he need to make an escape onto a sea-going boat. Don't you think it might be a good thing if you began at once to keep a small boat at the nearby wharf, and were in the habit of rowing up and down the river? You fall into that habit, and then who notices or minds? Do it twenty or fifty times, and there is nothing special in your doing it the twenty-first or fifty-first."

I liked this scheme, and Provis was quite elated

by it. We agreed that it should be carried into execution, and that Provis should never recognize us if we rowed past Mill Pond Bank. We further agreed that he should pull down his window blind whenever he saw us, to signal all was well.

Our meeting being now ended, and everything arranged, I rose to go. I remarked to Herbert that he and I had better not go home together, and that I would take half an hour's start of him. "I don't like to leave you here," I said to Provis, "though I cannot doubt your being safer here than near me. Goodbye!"

"Dear boy," he answered, clasping my hands, "I don't know when we may meet again, and I don't like goodbye. Say good night!"

"Good night! Herbert will go regularly between us, and when the time comes, you may be certain I shall be ready. Good night, good night!"

We thought it best that he should stay in his own rooms, and we left him on the landing outside his door, holding a light over the stair rail to light us downstairs. Looking back at him, I thought of the first night of his return when our positions were reversed, and when I little supposed my heart could ever be as heavy and anxious at parting from him as it was now.

Old Barley was growling and swearing when we passed his door. When we got to the foot of the stairs, I asked Herbert whether he had preserved the name of Provis. He replied, certainly not, and that the lodger was Mr. Campbell. He also explained that the utmost known of Mr. Campbell there, was, that he (Herbert) had Mr. Campbell consigned to him, and felt a strong personal interest in his being well cared for, and living a secluded life. So, when we went into the parlor where Mrs. Whimple and Clara were seated at work, I said nothing of my own interest in Mr. Campbell, but kept it to myself.

All things were as quiet around my residence as ever I had seen them. The windows of the rooms lately occupied by Provis were dark and still. There was no lounger in Garden Court. I walked past the fountain twice or thrice before I descended the steps that were between me and my rooms, but I was quite alone. When Herbert arrived, he also reported no one was observing us. Opening one of the windows after that, he looked out into the moonlight and told me that the pavement was totally empty.

Next day, I set myself to get the boat. It was soon done, and the boat was tied where I could reach her within a minute or two. Then, I began to go out as for training and practice, sometimes alone, sometimes with Herbert. I was often out in cold, rain, and sleet, but nobody took much note of me after I had been out a few times. The first time I passed Mill Pond Bank, Herbert and I were pulling a pair of oars. Both in going and returning, we saw the blind toward the east come down. Herbert was rarely there less than three times a week, and he never brought me news that was

alarming. Still, I knew that there was cause for alarm, and I could not get rid of the notion of being watched.

In short, I was always full of fears for the rash man who was in hiding. Herbert had sometimes said to me that he found it pleasant to stand at one of our windows after dark, when the tide was running down, and to think that it was flowing, with everything it bore, toward Clara. But I thought with dread that it was flowing toward Magwitch, and that any black mark on its surface might be his pursuers, going swiftly, silently, and surely, to take him.

Some weeks passed without bringing any change. My life settled into an unremarkable routine. I was pressed for money by more than one creditor. However, I had quite determined not to take more money from my patron in the midst of such uncertainty. Therefore, I had sent him the unopened pocketbook by Herbert. Condemned to inaction and a state of constant restlessness and suspense, I rowed about in my boat, and waited as best I could.

One evening, to help pass the time, I decided to go see a play. Who should I find in the cast but Mr. Wopsle! His role allowed him a good bit of time to sit and stare while on the stage. And I observed with great surprise that he stared in my direction as if he were lost in amazement.

There was something absolutely remarkable in the increasing glare of Mr. Wopsle's eye. At the play's conclusion, I decided I must ask him about it.

When I came out of the theatre, I found him waiting for me near the door.

"How do you do?" said I, shaking hands with him as we turned down the street together. "I saw that you noticed me."

"Saw you, Mr. Pip!" he returned. "Yes, of course I saw you. But who else was there?"

"Who else?"

"It is the strangest thing," said Mr. Wopsle, drifting into a lost look. "Yet I could swear I saw him."

Becoming alarmed, I asked Mr. Wopsle to explain his meaning. Involuntarily, I looked around, for these mysterious words gave me a chill.

"Oh! He can't be in sight," said Mr. Wopsle. "He went out before I went offstage. I saw him go. I had a ridiculous fancy that he must be with you, Mr. Pip, till I saw that you were quite unconscious of him, sitting behind you there, like a ghost."

My former chill crept over me again, but I resolved not to speak yet. I was perfectly sure that Provis had not been there.

"I dare say you wonder at me, Mr. Pip. Indeed I see you do. But it is so very strange! You'll hardly believe what I am going to tell you. I could hardly believe it myself, if you told me."

"Indeed?" said I.

"Mr. Pip, you remember in old times a certain Christmas Day, when you were quite a child, and I dined at Gargery's, and some soldiers came to the door to get a pair of handcuffs mended?"

"I remember it very well."

"And you remember that there was a chase after two convicts, and that we joined in it, and that Gargery took you on his back, and that I took the lead and you kept up with me as well as you could?"

"I remember it all very well."

"And you remember that we came up with the two in a ditch, and that there was a scuffle between them? And that one of them had been severely beat up, especially about the face, by the other?"

"I see it all before me."

"Then Mr. Pip, one of those two prisoners sat behind you tonight. I saw him over your shoulder."

"Steady!" I thought. I asked him then, "Which of the two do you suppose you saw?"

"The one who had been mauled," he answered readily, "and I'll swear I saw him! The more I think of him, the more certain I am of him."

"This is very curious!" said I, with the best tone I could put on, of its being of no importance to me. "Very curious indeed!"

I cannot exaggerate the anxiety into which this conversation threw me, or the terror I felt at Compeyson's having been behind me "like a ghost." For, if he had ever been out of my thoughts since the hiding had begun, it was in those very moments when he was closest to me. To think that I should be so unconscious and off my guard after all my care!

When Mr. Wopsle had imparted to me all that he could recall, I treated him to a little refreshment, and we parted. It was between midnight and one o'clock when I neared my chambers. The gates were shut. No one was near me when I went in and went home.

Herbert was there, and we held a very serious council by the fire. There was nothing to be done, saving to communicate to Wemmick what I had that night found out. As I thought that I might compromise him if I went too often to his home, I made this communication by letter. I wrote it before I went to bed, and went out and posted it. Again no one was near me. Herbert and I agreed that we could do nothing else but be more cautious than before, if that were possible.

About a week after this encounter, I went for a row on the river. After tying up my boat late in the afternoon, I went in search of a place to dine. As I was walking, I felt a large hand upon my shoulder. It was Mr. Jaggers's hand, and he passed it through my arm.

"As we are going in the same direction, Pip, we may walk together. Are you going to dine?" said Mr. Jaggers. When I nodded my head yes, he invited me to dine at home with him. "Wemmick's coming too," he stated.

We picked up Mr. Wemmick at the office and took a hackneycoach to Jaggers's house. And as soon as we got there, dinner was served.

"Did you send that note of Miss Havisham's to Mr. Pip, Wemmick?" Mr. Jaggers asked, soon after we began dinner.

"No, sir," returned Wemmick. "It was going by post, when you brought Mr. Pip into the office.

Here it is." He handed it to his principal, instead of to me.

"It's a note of two lines, Pip," said Mr. Jaggers, handing it on, "sent up to me by Miss Havisham, on account of her not being sure of your address. She tells me that she wants to see you on a little matter of business you mentioned to her. You'll go to see her?"

"Yes," said I, casting my eyes over the note, which was exactly in those terms.

"When do you think of going down?"

"I have an impending engagement," said I, glancing at Wemmick, who was putting a piece of fish in his mouth, "that renders me rather uncertain of my time. At once, I think."

"If Mr. Pip has the intention of going at once," said Wemmick to Mr. Jaggers, "he needn't write an answer, you know."

Receiving this as advice that it was best not to delay, I said that I would go tomorrow. Wemmick drank a glass of wine and looked with a grimly satisfied air at Mr. Jaggers, but not at me.

"Now, Molly, Molly, Molly, Molly, how slow you are today!" Jaggers said to his housekeeper. She was at his elbow when he addressed her, putting a dish upon the table. As she withdrew her hands from it, she fell back a step or two, nervously muttering some excuse. And a certain action of her fingers as she spoke arrested my attention.

The action of her fingers was like the action of knitting. She stood looking at her master, not understanding whether she was free to go, or whether he had more to say to her and would call her back if she did go. Her look was very intent. Surely, I had seen exactly such eyes and such hands, on a memorable occasion, very recently!

He dismissed her, and she glided out of the room. But she remained before me, as plainly as if she were still there. I looked at those hands, I looked at those eyes, I looked at that flowing hair; and I compared them with other hands, other eyes, other hair, that I knew of, and with what those might be after twenty years of a brutal husband and a stormy life. And I felt absolutely certain that this woman was Estella's mother.

Only twice more did the housekeeper reappear, and then her stay in the room was very short, and Mr. Jaggers was sharp with her. But her hands were Estella's hands, and her eyes were Estella's eyes.

Wemmick and I took our leave early and left together. We walked a short way along Gerrard Street, when I turned to my companion and said, "Wemmick, do you remember telling me before I first went to Mr. Jaggers's house, to notice that housekeeper?"

"Did I?" he replied. "Ah, I dare say I did. Deuce take me," he added, suddenly, "I know I did."

"A wild beast tamed, you called her."

"And what do you call her?"

"The same. How did Mr. Jaggers tame her, Wemmick?"

"That's his secret. She has been with him many a long year."

"I wish you would tell me her story. I feel a particular interest in being acquainted with it. You know that what is said between you and me goes no further."

"Well!" Wemmick replied, "I don't know her story—that is, I don't know all of it. But what I do know, I'll tell you, in confidence.

"A score or so of years ago, that woman was tried at the Old Bailey for murder, and was acquitted. She was a very handsome young woman, and I believe had some Gipsy blood in her. Anyhow, it was hot enough when it was up, as you may suppose."

"But she was acquitted."

"Mr. Jaggers defended her," pursued Wemmick. "It was one of his earliest cases, and it greatly helped build his reputation. The murdered person was a woman. She was a good ten years older, very much larger, and very much stronger. It was a case of jealousy. They both led tramping lives. Molly had been married very young to a tramping man, and had an extremely jealous nature. The murdered woman was found dead in a barn. There had been a violent struggle, perhaps a fight. She was bruised and scratched and torn, and had been held by the throat and choked to death. Now, there was no likely suspect except Molly, on account of her jealous ways. Mr. Jaggers rested his case on the improbability that Molly was strong enough to commit the murder. You may be sure," said

Wemmick, touching me on the sleeve, "that he never dwelt upon the strength of her hands then, though he sometimes does now."

I had told Wemmick of his showing us her wrists, that day of the dinner party.

"Well, sir!" Wemmick went on, "it happened that this woman was so artfully dressed from the time of her apprehension, that she looked much slighter than she really was. Her sleeves were so skilfully tailored that her arms had quite a delicate look. She had only a bruise or two about her—nothing for a tramp—but the backs of her hands were lacerated, and the question was, was it with fingernails? Now, Mr. Jaggers showed that she had struggled through a great lot of brambles which were not as high as her face. She could not have got through those brambles without using her hands. Bits of those brambles were actually found in her skin and put in evidence, as well as the fact that the brambles in question were found on examination to have been broken through, and to have little shreds of her dress and little spots of blood upon them here and there. But the boldest point he made was this. The prosecutor argued, as proof of her jealousy, that she was under strong suspicion of having, at about the time of the murder, frantically destroyed her child by this man—some three years old—to revenge herself upon him. Mr. Jaggers used that allegation in this way. 'We say these are not marks of fingernails, but marks of brambles, and we show you the brambles. You say they are marks of fingernails, and you say that she destroyed her child. For anything we know, she may have destroyed her child. Is it not possible that the child, in clinging to her, may have scratched her hands? But you are not trying her for the murder of her child.' Well, the jury bought it, and they set her free."

"Has she been in his service ever since?"

"Yes."

"Do you remember the sex of the child?"

"Said to have been a girl."

"You have nothing more to say to me tonight?"

"Nothing. I got your letter and destroyed it. Nothing."

We exchanged a cordial good night, and I went home, with new matter for my thoughts, though with no relief from the old.

The next day I took the coach to Miss Havisham's residence. However, I alighted at the Halfway House, and breakfasted there, and walked the rest of the distance. This way, I would get into the town quietly by little-used streets, and to leave it in the same manner.

As I passed through the outskirts of the town, I sensed the cathedral chimes had a sadder and a more remote sound to me than they had ever had before. The swell of the old organ was borne to my ears like funeral music. The crows, as they circled about the gray tower and swung in the bare high trees of the church garden, seemed to call to me that the place was changed, and that Estella was gone out of it for ever.

An elderly woman opened the gate to Satis House. The lighted candle stood in the dark passage within, as of old, and I took it up and ascended the staircase alone. Miss Havisham was not in her own room, but was in the larger room across the landing. Looking in at the door, after knocking in vain, I saw her sitting in a ragged chair lost in contemplation of the ashy fire.

Doing as I had often done, I went in, and stood, touching the old mantel, where she could see me when she raised her eyes. There was an air of utter loneliness upon her that moved me to pity, despite the injury she did me. As I stood there, I thought how I too had come to be a part of the wrecked fortunes of that house. She raised her eyes and said in a low voice, "Is it real?"

"It is I, Pip. Mr. Jaggers gave me your note yesterday, and I have lost no time."

"Thank you. Thank you."

As I brought another of the ragged chairs to the hearth and sat down, I remarked a new expression on her face, as if she were afraid of me.

"I want," she said, "to pursue that subject you mentioned to me when you were last here, and to show you that I am not all stone. But perhaps you can never believe, now, that there is anything human in my heart?"

When I said some reassuring words, she stretched out her trembling right hand, as though she was going to touch me. But then she recalled it.

"You said, speaking for your friend, that you could tell me how to do something useful and good. Something that you would like done, is it not?"

"Something that I would like done very much." This, of course, was for my friend Herbert.

"What is it?"

I began explaining to her that secret history of the relations between Herbert and his employer, which I was financing (unknown to Herbert). I then began to describe the possibility that Herbert could purchase a full partnership in the business, if he could obtain the money.

"So!" said she, nodding her head. "And how much money is wanting to complete the purchase?"

I was rather afraid of stating it, for it sounded a large sum. "Nine hundred pounds."

"If I give you the money for this purpose, will you keep my secret as you have kept your own?"

"Quite as faithfully."

"And your mind will be more at rest?"

"Much more at rest."

"Are you very unhappy now?"

She asked this question without looking at me, but in an unaccustomed tone of sympathy. I could not reply at the moment, for my voice failed me.

"I am far from happy, Miss Havisham. But I have other causes of unhappiness than any you know of."

After a little while, she raised her head and looked at the fire again.

"It is noble in you to tell me that you have other causes of unhappiness. Is it true?"

"Too true."

"Can I only serve you, Pip, by serving your friend? Regarding that as done, is there nothing I can do for you yourself?"

"Nothing. I thank you for the question. I thank you even more for the tone of the question. But there is nothing."

She presently rose from her seat and looked about the blighted room for the means of writing. There were none there, and she took from her pocket a yellow set of ivory tablets, mounted in tarnished gold, and wrote upon them with a pencil in a case of tarnished gold that hung from her neck.

"You are still on friendly terms with Mr. Jaggers?"

"Quite. I dined with him yesterday."

"This is an authority to him to pay you that money."

"Thank you, Miss Havisham."

She read me what she had written, and it was direct and clear. I took the tablets from her hand, and it trembled again, and it trembled more as she took off the chain to which the pencil was attached, and put it in mine. All this she did, without looking at me.

"My name is on the first leaf. If you can ever write under my name, 'I forgive her,' though ever so long after my broken heart is dust—pray do it!"

"O Miss Havisham," said I, "I can do it now. There have been sore mistakes, and my life has been a blind and thankless one. I want forgiveness and direction far too much, to be bitter with you."

She turned her face to me for the first time since she had averted it, and, to my amazement and terror, dropped on her knees at my feet. She raised her folded hands to me in the manner in which, when her poor heart was young and fresh and whole, they must often have been raised to heaven from her mother's side.

To see her with her white hair and her worn face kneeling at my feet gave me a shock through all my frame. I entreated her to rise, and got my arms about her to help her up. But she only pressed that hand of mine which was nearest to her grasp, and hung her head over it and wept. I had never seen her shed a tear before, and, in the hope that the relief might do her good, I bent over her without speaking. She was not kneeling now, but was down upon the ground.

"O!" she cried, despairingly. "What have I done! What have I done!"

"If you mean, Miss Havisham, what have you done to injure me, let me answer. Very little. I should have loved her under any circumstances.—Is she married?"

"Yes."

It was a needless question, for a new desolation in the desolate house had told me so.

"What have I done! What have I done!" She wrung her hands, and crushed her white hair, and returned to this cry over and over again. "What have I done!"

I did not know how to answer, or how to comfort her. She spoke on.

"Until you spoke to her the other day, and until I saw in you a looking glass that showed me what I once felt myself, I did not know what I had done. What have I done! What have I done!" And so again, twenty, fifty times over, What had she done!

"Miss Havisham," I said, when her cry had died away, "you may dismiss me from your mind and conscience. But Estella is a different case. If you can ever undo any scrap of what you have done to distort her ability to love another, it will be better to do that."

"Yes, yes, I know it. But, Pip—my Dear!" There was an earnest womanly compassion for me in her new affection. "My Dear! Believe this: when she first came to me, I meant to save her from misery like my own. At first I meant no more."

"Well, well!" said I. "I hope so."

"But as she grew, and promised to be very beautiful, I gradually did worse. With my praises, and with my jewels, and with my teachings, and with this figure of myself always before as an example of what love can do, I stole her heart away and put ice in its place."

"Better," I could not help saying, "to have left her a natural heart, even to be bruised or broken."

With that, Miss Havisham looked distractedly at me for a while, and then burst out again, What had she done!

"If you knew all my story," she pleaded, "you would have some compassion for me and a better understanding of me."

"Miss Havisham," I answered, as delicately as I could, "I believe I may say that I do know your story, and have known it ever since I first left this neighborhood. It has inspired me with great pity, and I hope I understand it and its influences. Does what has passed between us give me any excuse for asking you a question relative to Estella? Not as she is, but as she was when she first came here?"

She was seated on the ground, with her arms on the ragged chair, and her head leaning on them. She looked full at me when I said this, and replied, "Go on."

"Whose child was Estella?"

She shook her head.

"You don't know?"

She shook her head again.

"But Mr. Jaggers brought her here, or sent her here?"

"Brought her here."

"Will you tell me how that came about?"

She answered in a low whisper and with caution: "I had been shut up in these rooms a long time. I told Jaggers that I wanted a little girl to rear and love, and save from my fate. He told me that he would look about him for such an orphan child. One night he brought her here asleep, and I called her Estella."

"Might I ask her age then?"

"Two or three. She herself knows nothing, but that she was left an orphan and I adopted her."

So convinced I was of that woman's being her mother, that I needed no evidence to establish the fact in my own mind.

What more could I hope to do by prolonging the interview? I had succeeded on behalf of Herbert. Miss Havisham had told me all she knew of Estella. I had said and done what I could to ease her mind. And so we parted.

Twilight was closing in when I went downstairs into the natural air. I called to the woman who had opened the gate when I entered, that I would not trouble her just yet, but would walk round the place before leaving. For, I had a feeling that I should never be there again, and I felt that the dying light was suited to my last view of it.

I made my way to the ruined garden. I went all round it, round by the corner where Herbert and I first met, round by the paths where Estella and I had walked. So cold, so lonely, so dreary!

With a sad foreboding in my heart, I decided to look in one final time upon Miss Havisham. I journeyed back into the room where I had left her. There she was seated in the ragged chair upon the hearth close to the fire, with her back toward me. In the moment when I was withdrawing my head to go quietly away, I saw a great flaming light spring up. In the same moment, I saw her running at me, shrieking, with a whirl of fire blazing all about her, and soaring several feet above her head.

I had a double-caped greatcoat on, and over my arm another thick coat. I took them off, threw her down, and got them over her. I then dragged the great cloth from the table for the same purpose, and with it dragged down the heap of rottenness that lay upon it. We were on the ground struggling like desperate enemies. The closer I covered her, the more wildly she shrieked and tried to free herself. I spied patches of cloth yet alight floating in the smoky air, which, a moment ago, had been her faded bridal dress.

Then, I looked round and saw the disturbed beetles and spiders running away over the floor. The servants came in with breathless cries at the door. I still held her forcibly down with all my strength, like a prisoner who might escape.

She was unconscious, and I was afraid to have her moved, or even touched. Assistance was sent for, and I held her until it came. When I got up, on the doctor's coming to her with other aid, I was astonished to see that both my hands were burnt. I had no knowledge of it through the sense of feeling.

The doctor pronounced that she had received serious injuries, but that they of themselves were not fatal. The danger lay mainly in the nervous shock she had experienced. By the doctor's directions, her bed was carried into that room and laid upon the great table. When I saw her again, an hour afterward, she lay indeed where I had seen her strike her stick, and had heard her say that she would lie one day.

Though every vestige of her dress was burnt, she still had something of her old ghastly bridal appearance. They had covered her to the throat with white cotton-wool. And as she lay with a white sheet loosely overlying that, the phantom air of something that had been and was changed, was still upon her.

I found, on questioning the servants, that Estella was in Paris. I got a promise from the doctor that he would write to her by the next post. Miss Havisham's family I took upon myself. I arranged to communicate with Mr. Matthew Pocket only, and leave him to do as he liked about informing the rest.

That evening, she uttered unconnected words relating to what had happened that day. Toward midnight she began to wander in her speech. After that she said innumerable times in a low solemn voice, "What have I done!" And then, "When she first came, I meant to save her from misery like mine." And then,—"Take the pencil and write under my name, 'I forgive her!'" She never changed the order of these three sentences, but she sometimes left out a word in one or other of them.

I could do no service there. Furthermore, I had, nearer home, that pressing reason for anxiety and fear which even her wanderings could not drive out of my mind. Therefore, I decided in the course of the night that I would return to London by the early morning coach. At about six o'clock in the morning, therefore, I leaned over her and touched her lips with mine, just as they said, not stopping for being touched, "Take the pencil and write under my name—'I forgive her.'"

My hands had been dressed twice or thrice in the night, and again in the morning. My left arm was a good deal burned to the elbow, and, less severely, as high as the shoulder. It was very painful, but I felt thankful it was no worse. My right hand was not so badly burnt; I could move the fingers. It was bandaged, of course, but much less inconveniently than my left hand and arm. Those I carried in a sling. I could only wear my coat like a cloak, loose over my shoulders and fastened at the neck. My hair had been caught by the fire, but not my head or face.

Herbert came back to me at our chambers and devoted the day to attending on me. He was the kindest of nurses. At stated times, he took off the bandages and steeped them in the cooling liquid that was kept ready, and put them on again, with a patient tenderness that I was deeply grateful for.

At first, as I lay quiet on the sofa, I found it impossible to get rid of the sight of the glare of the flames, their hurry and noise, and the fierce burning smell. If I dozed for a minute, I was awakened by Miss Havisham's cries, and by her running at me with that crown of flames above her head. This pain of the mind was much harder to bear than any bodily pain I suffered.

Neither of us spoke of the rowboat, but we both thought of it. That was made apparent by our avoidance of the subject, and by our agreeing—without agreement—to make my recovery of the use of my hands, a question of so many hours, not of so many weeks.

My first question when I saw Herbert had been, of course, whether all was well with Provis down the river? As he replied in the affirmative, with perfect confidence and cheerfulness, we did not resume the subject until the day was wearing away. But then, as Herbert changed the bandages, more by the light of the fire than by the outer light, he went back to it spontaneously.

"I sat with Provis last night, Handel, two good hours."

"Where was Clara?"

"Dear little thing!" said Herbert. "She was up and down with Gruffandgrim all the evening. He was perpetually pegging at the floor, the moment she left his sight. I doubt if he can hold out long though. What with rum and pepper—and pepper and rum—I should think his pegging must be nearly over."

"And then you will be married, Herbert?"

"How can I take care of the dear child otherwise?—Lay your arm out upon the back of the sofa, my dear boy. I'll sit down here and get the bandage off so gradually that you shall not know when it comes. I was speaking of Provis. Do you know, Handel, he improves?"

"I said to you I thought he was softened when I last saw him."

"So you did. And so he is. He was very communicative last night, and told me more of his life. You remember his breaking off here about some woman that he had had great trouble with.—Did I hurt you?"

I had started, but not under his touch. His words had given me a start.

"I had forgotten that, Herbert, but I remember it now you speak of it."

"Well! He went into that part of his life, and a dark wild part it is. Shall I tell you? Or would it worry you just now?"

"Tell me by all means. Every word."

"It seems," said Herbert, "—there's a bandage off most charmingly, and now comes the cool one—makes you shrink at first, my poor dear fellow, don't it? but it will be comfortable presently—it seems that the woman was a young woman, and a jealous woman, and a revengeful woman; revengeful, Handel, to the last degree."

"To what last degree?"

"Murder.—Does it strike too cold on that sensitive place?"

"I don't feel it. How did she murder? Whom did she murder?"

"Why, the deed may not have merited quite so terrible a name," said Herbert. "But she was tried for it, and Mr. Jaggers defended her, and the reputation of that defense first made his name known to Provis. It was another and a stronger woman who was the victim, and there had been a struggle—in a barn. Who began it, or how fair it was, or how unfair, may be doubtful; but how it ended, is certainly not doubtful, for the victim was found strangled."

"Was the woman brought in guilty?"

"No; she was acquitted.—My poor Handel, I hurt you!"

"It is impossible to be gentler, Herbert. Yes? What else?"

"This acquitted young woman and Provis had a little child, a little child of whom Provis was exceedingly fond. On the evening of the killing, the young woman visited Provis and swore that she would destroy the child (which was in her possession), and he should never see it again. Then, she vanished.—There's the worst arm comfortably in the sling once more, and now there remains but the right hand, which is a far easier job. I can do it better by this light than by a stronger, for my hand is steadiest when I don't see the poor blistered patches too distinctly.—You don't think your breathing is affected, my dear boy? You seem to breathe quickly."

"Perhaps I do, Herbert. Did the woman keep her oath?"

"There comes the darkest part of Provis's life. She did."

"That is, he says she did."

"Why, of course, my dear boy," returned Herbert, in a tone of surprise, and again bending forward to get a nearer look at me.

"Now, whether," pursued Herbert, "he had treated the child's mother badly, or whether he had treated the child's mother well, Provis doesn't say. But she had shared some four or five years of the wretched life he described to us at this fireside, and he seems to have felt pity for her. Fearing he should be called upon to testify about this destroyed child, and so be the cause of the mother's death, he hid himself away. He was only vaguely talked of as a certain man called Abel, who was the subject of the accused woman's jealousy. After the acquittal she disappeared, and thus he lost the child and the child's mother."

"I want to ask—"

"A moment, my dear boy, and I have done. That evil genius, Compeyson, the worst of scoundrels, became aware of the details of the case. He used this information to keep Provis a poor man and to work him harder. It was clear last night that this sharpened the point of Provis's animosity."

"I want to know," said I, "whether he told you when this happened?"

"Let me remember, then, what he said as to that. His expression was, 'a round score o' year ago, and a'most directly after I took up wi' Compeyson.' How old were you when you came upon him in the little churchyard?"

"I think in my seventh year."

"Ay. It had happened some three or four years then, he said. You brought into his mind the little girl so tragically lost, who would have been about your age."

"Herbert," said I, after a short silence, "the man we have in hiding down the river is Estella's father."

The very next day, I resolved to visit Mr. Jaggers, to tell him about the fire and to confirm my suspicions regarding Estella's parentage.

I found Mr. Jaggers and Wemmick together. While I described the fire, Mr. Jaggers stood, as he often did, before the fire. Wemmick leaned back in his chair, staring at me, with his hands in the pockets of his trousers.

My narrative finished, and their questions answered, I then produced Miss Havisham's authority to receive the nine hundred pounds for Herbert. Mr. Jaggers's eyes retired a little deeper into his head when I handed him the tablets. He presently handed them over to Wemmick, who prepared a check for his signature.

"By the way," I said to Mr. Jaggers, "I did ask something of Miss Havisham. I asked her to give me some information relative to her adopted daughter, and she gave me all she possessed."

"Did she?" said Mr. Jaggers, bending forward to look at his boots and then straightening himself. "Hah! I don't think I should have done so, if I had been Miss Havisham. But she ought to know her own business best."

"I know more of the history of Miss Havisham's adopted child than Miss Havisham herself does, sir. I know her mother."

Mr. Jaggers looked at me inquiringly, and repeated, "Mother?"

"I have seen her mother within these three days."

"Yes?" said Mr. Jaggers.

"And so have you, sir. And you have seen her still more recently."

"Yes?" said Mr. Jaggers.

"Perhaps I know more of Estella's history than even you do," said I. "I know her father too."

A certain reaction on Mr. Jaggers's part assured me that he did not know who her father was.

"So! You know the young lady's father, Pip?" said Mr. Jaggers.

"Yes," I replied, "and his name is Provis—from New South Wales, Australia."

Mr. Jaggers looked startled when I said those words. "And on what evidence, Pip," asked Mr. Jaggers, very coolly, as he paused with his handkerchief halfway to his nose, "does Provis make this claim?"

"He does not make it," said I, "and has never made it, and has no knowledge or belief that his daughter exists."

My reply was so unexpected that Mr. Jaggers folded his arms and looked with stern attention at me, though with an immovable face.

Then I told him all I knew, and how I knew it; with one reservation. I allowed him to infer that I knew from Miss Havisham what I, in fact, had learned from Wemmick.

"Hah!" was all that Mr. Jaggers said before turning to Wemmick to resume their normal business. But I could not submit to be thrown off in that way. I made a passionate, almost an indignant, appeal to him to confirm or deny my suppositions. I represented myself as being surely worthy of some little confidence from him, in return for the confidence I had just now imparted. I said that I did not blame him, or suspect him, or mistrust him, but I only wanted assurance of the truth from him.

"Pip," said Jaggers, after a lengthy pause, "I'll put a hypothetical case to you. Mind! I admit nothing."

I nodded my agreement that he admitted nothing.

"Now, Pip," said Mr. Jaggers, "consider this. Suppose that a woman, under such circumstances as you have mentioned, kept her child concealed and communicated the fact to her legal adviser. Suppose that at the same time he held a trust to find a child for an eccentric rich lady to adopt and bring up."

"I follow you, sir."

"Consider that he lived in an atmosphere of evil, and that the children he encountered were invariably tried at a criminal court. Consider also that he habitually knew of their being imprisoned, whipped, neglected, cast out, and generally headed for the hangman."

"I follow you, sir."

"Put the case, Pip, that here was one pretty little child out of the heap, who could be saved. The father believed her dead. As for the mother, the legal adviser told her, 'I know that you murdered a woman, and I know how you did it. Give the child into my hands, and I will do my best to defend you in court. I know of a good home for the child.' Now, let us imagine that this was done, and that the woman was cleared."

"I understand you perfectly."

"Consider too, Pip, that the murder trial had shaken the woman out of her wits. Frightened by the ways of the world, she went to her legal adviser to be sheltered. Put the case that he took her in, and that he kept down her wild violent nature whenever he saw an inkling of its breaking out. Do you comprehend the imaginary case?"

"Quite."

"Put the case that the child grew up, and was married for money. That the mother was still living. That the father was still living. That the mother and father, unknown to one another, were dwelling within so many miles, yards if you like, of one another. That the secret was still a secret, except that you had got wind of it. Put that last case to yourself very carefully."

"I do."

"For whose sake would you reveal the secret? For the father's? I think he would not be much the better for it. For the mother's? I think if she had done such a deed, she would be safer where she was. For the daughter's? I think it would hardly serve her. Her husband and all of society would learn of her criminal parentage. That would lead to her ruin."

I looked at Wemmick, whose face was very grave. He gravely touched his lips with his forefinger, signaling that it would be better to keep the entire matter under wraps. I did the same. Mr. Jaggers did the same. So, we all agreed that the secret should be kept. "Now, Wemmick," said Mr. Jaggers, "what were you doing when Mr. Pip came in?"

After my visit to Mr. Jaggers's office, I arranged to present the nine hundred pounds provided by Miss Havisham to Herbert's employer, Mr. Clarriker. Herbert was now a full partner in the business. Clarriker informed me that the affairs of the House were steadily progressing. Indeed, he was planning to establish a small branch in the Middle East. Herbert, in his new partnership capacity, would go out and take charge of it.

We had now got into the month of March. My left arm took so long to heal that I was still unable to get a coat on. My right arm was tolerably restored—disfigured, but fairly serviceable. Since the fire at Miss Havisham's, however, I had to suspend my rowing.

On a Monday morning, when Herbert and I were at breakfast, I received the following letter from Wemmick by the post.

"Burn this as soon as read. Early in the week, say Wednesday, you might convey Provis down river and place him aboard a ship leaving the country. Now burn."

I showed the letter to Herbert before placing it on the fire. We then considered what to do. We had earlier planned to transfer Provis to a ship, by rowing him to a point down river and placing him aboard. This would get him safely out of the country. Herbert and I would do the rowing. My injured arms, however, made my participation as an oarsman impossible.

"I have a suggestion," said Herbert. "Why not enlist as a rower one of the Finches of the Grove? Our friend Startop would be a good candidate. He is a good fellow, a skilled hand, fond of us, and enthusiastic and honorable."

"But how much would you tell him, Herbert?"

"It is necessary to tell him very little. Are you planning to accompany Provis to help him get settled abroad?"

"To be sure."

"Where?"

In my earlier consideration of this scheme, I was almost indifferent to what port we made for. The place signified little, so long as he got out of England. Any foreign steamer that fell in our way and would take us up would do. We could consult the shipping tables in the newspapers to see which ships were heading for foreign ports any day of the week. Our plan was to get down the river and lay by until the ship came into view. We now needed to move quickly.

Herbert and I went out immediately after breakfast to pursue our investigations. We found that a steamer for Hamburg was likely to suit our purpose best, and we directed our thoughts chiefly to that vessel. But we noted down what other foreign steamers would leave London with the same tide, and we satisfied ourselves that we knew the build and color of each. We then separated for a few hours. I went to get such passports as were necessary. Herbert went to see Startop at his lodgings. At one o'clock, we met near the center of London. We joyfully reported that our efforts had met with success. Startop was more than ready to join our enterprise.

Herbert and Startop should pull a pair of oars, we agreed. I would steer. Provis would be our passenger. Herbert would alert Provis to pack his things and be ready to depart Wednesday.

These plans well understood by both of us, I went home.

On opening the outer door of our chambers with my key, I found a letter in the box, directed to me. The envelope was quite soiled, but the message was not ill-written. The letter said: "If you are not afraid to come to the old marshes tonight or tomorrow night at nine, and to come to the little sluice house by the limekiln, you had better come. If you want information regarding your Uncle Provis, you had much better come and tell no one and lose no time. You must come alone. Bring this with you."

I had had enough upon my mind before the

receipt of this strange letter. I puzzled what to do now. I had to decide quickly, or I should miss the afternoon coach, which would take me down in time for tonight. Tomorrow night I could not think of going, for it would be too close upon the time of the escape. And again, for anything I knew, the promised information might have some important bearing on the flight itself.

Having hardly any time for consideration—my watch showing me that the coach started within half an hour—I resolved to go. I left a note for Herbert, telling him that I wanted to pay one last visit to Miss Havisham before traveling to distant parts with Provis. I had then barely time to get my coat, lock up the chambers, and dash for the coach office. I caught the coach just as it came out of the yard.

It was dark before we reached the village. Avoiding the Blue Boar, I put up at an inn of minor reputation and ordered some dinner. While it was being prepared, I went to Satis House and inquired for Miss Havisham. I was told she was still very ill, though considered somewhat better than before.

Dinner completed, I fastened my coat around my neck and went out. I had previously sought in my pockets for the letter, that I might refer to it again, but I could not find it. I was a bit uneasy to think that I must have dropped it in the coach. I knew very well, however, that the appointed place was the little sluice house by the limekiln on the marshes, and the hour nine. Toward the marshes I now went, having no time to spare.

It was a dark night, though the full moon rose as I reached the edge of the marshes. Beyond their dark line there was a ribbon of clear sky, hardly broad enough to hold the large red moon. In a few minutes she had climbed into the piled mountains of cloud. There was a melancholy wind, and the marshes were very dismal.

It was another half-hour before I drew near to the kiln. The lime was burning with a sluggish stifling smell, but the fires were made up and unattended. No workmen were visible. Hard by was a small stone quarry. It lay directly in my way, and had been worked that day, as I saw by the tools and barrows that were lying about.

I saw a light in the old sluice house. I quickened my pace and knocked at the door. Waiting for some reply, I looked about me, noticing how the sluice was abandoned and broken, and how the house—of wood with a tiled roof—would not be proof against the weather much longer. The choking vapor of the kiln crept in a ghostly way toward me. Still there was no answer, and I knocked again. No answer still, and I tried the latch.

It rose under my hand, and the door yielded. Looking in, I saw a lighted candle on a table, a bench, and a mattress on a small bed. As there was a loft above, I called, "Is there any one here?" but no voice answered. Then, I looked at my watch, and, finding that it was past nine, called again, "Is there any one here?" There being still no answer, I went out at the door, uncertain what to do.

It was beginning to rain fast. Seeing nothing save what I had seen already, I turned back into the house. I stood just within the shelter of the doorway, looking out into the night. While I was considering that some one must have been there lately and must soon be coming back, or the candle would not be burning, it came into my head to look if the wick were long. I turned round to do so, and had taken up the candle in my hand, when it was extinguished by some violent shock. The next thing I knew, I had been caught in a noose, thrown over my head from behind.

"Now," said a suppressed voice with an oath, "I've got you!"

"What is this?" I cried, struggling. "Who is it? Help, help, help!"

Not only were my arms pulled close to my sides, but the pressure on my bad arm caused me exquisite pain. Sometimes, a strong man's hand, sometimes a strong man's chest, was set against my mouth to deaden my cries. I struggled ineffectually in the dark, while I was fastened tight to the wall. "And now," said the suppressed voice with another oath, "call out again, and I'll make short work of you!"

I was faint and sick with the pain of my injured arm and bewildered by the surprise. Yet, aware how easily this threat could be carried out, I remained silent.

The man busied himself in trying to get some loose tinder to catch fire. At length a flare of light flashed up, and showed me Orlick. Seeing him, I felt that I was in a dangerous situation indeed, and I kept my eyes upon him.

With great deliberation, he lighted the candle from the flaring tinder. He sat with his arms folded on the table and looked at me. I discovered that I was bound to a ladder a few inches from the wall, the ladder leading to a loft above.

"Now," said he, when we had surveyed one another for some time, "I've got you."

"Unbind me. Let me go!"

"Ah!" he returned, "I'll let you go. I'll let you go to the moon. I'll let you go to the stars. All in good time."

"Why have you lured me here?"

"Don't you know?" said he, with a deadly look.

"Why have you set upon me in the dark?"

"Because I mean to do it all myself. One keeps a secret better than two. Oh you fiend, you fiend!"

His enjoyment of the spectacle I furnished, as he sat with his arms folded on the table, shaking his head at me, caused me to tremble with fear. As I watched him in silence, he put his hand into the corner at his side, and took up a gun with a brass-bound stock.

"Do you know this?" said he, making as if he would take aim at me. "Do you know where you saw it afore? Speak, wolf!"

"Yes," I answered.

"You cost me my position as guard at Satis House. You did. Speak!"

"What else could I do?"

"You did that, and that would be enough, without more. How dared you to come between me and a young woman I liked?"

"When did I?"

"When didn't you? It was you as always give Old Orlick a bad name to her."

"You gave it to yourself. You earned it for yourself. I could have done you no harm, if you had done yourself none."

"You're a liar. And you'll take any pains, and spend any money, to drive me out of this country, will you?" said he, repeating my words to Biddy in the last interview I had with her. "Now, I'll tell you a piece of information. It was never so well worth your while to get me out of this country as it is tonight." As he shook his heavy hand at me, with his mouth snarling like a tiger's, I felt that it was true.

"What are you going to do to me?"

"I'm a-going," said he, bringing his fist down upon the table with a heavy blow, and rising as the blow fell, to give it greater force, "I'm a-going to have your life!"

He leaned forward staring at me, slowly unclenched his hand and drew it across his mouth as if his mouth watered for me, and sat down again.

"You was always in Old Orlick's way since ever you was a child. You goes out of his way, this present night. You're dead."

I felt that I had come to the brink of my grave. For a moment I looked wildly around my trap for any chance of escape. There was none.

"More than that," said he, folding his arms on the table again, "I won't have a rag of you, I won't have a bone of you, left on earth. I'll put your body in the kiln to disintegrate completely. Let people suppose what they may of you, they shall never discover your body."

My mind traced out all the consequences of such a death. Estella's father, Provis, would believe I had deserted him. He would be captured and would die accusing me. Even Herbert would doubt me. Joe and Biddy would never know how sorry I was. No one would ever know what I had suffered, how true I had meant to be, what an agony I had passed through. The death close before me was terrible, but far more terrible was the dread of being misremembered after death. And so quick were my thoughts, that I saw myself despised by unborn generations—Estella's children, and their children—while the wretch's words were yet on his lips.

"Now, wolf," said he, "afore I kill you like any other beast—which is wot I mean to do and wot I have tied you up for—I'll have a good look at you and a few torments for you. Oh, you devil!"

I thought about crying out for help again. But I realized no one could be near this solitary spot. Above all things, I resolved that I would not beg him, and that I would die making some last poor struggle against him.

He had been drinking, and his eyes were red and bloodshot. Around his neck was slung a tin bottle, as I had often seen his meat and drink slung about him in other days. He brought the bottle to his lips and took a fiery drink from it. I smelled the strong spirits that I saw flash into his face.

"Wolf!" said he, folding his arms again, "Old Orlick's a going to tell you somethink. It was you as caused the death of your shrew sister."

My mind flashed to the unsolved attack upon my sister, her illness, and her death.

"It was you, villain," said I.

"I tell you it was your doing—I tell you it was done through you," he retorted, catching up the gun, and making a blow with the stock at the vacant air between us. "I come upon her from behind, as I come upon you tonight. I whacked her mighty hard! I left her for dead. If there had been a limekiln as near her as there is now near you, she shouldn't have come to life again. But it warn't Old Orlick that killed her; it was you. You was always favored, and Orlick always bullied and beat. That's why I done it—for revenge agin you. Old Orlick bullied and beat, eh? Now you pays for it. You done it; now you pays for it."

He drank again and became more ferocious. I saw by his tilting of the bottle that there was no great quantity left in it. I distinctly understood that he was working himself up, with its contents, to make an end of me. I knew that every drop it held was a drop of my life. I knew that when I was changed into a part of the vapor that had crept toward me but a little while before, he would do as he had done in my sister's case—make all haste to the town, and be seen slouching about there, drinking at the ale houses. My rapid mind pursued him to the town, made a picture of the street with him in it, and contrasted its lights and life with the lonely marsh and the white vapor creeping over it, into which I was about to dissolve.

When he had drunk this second time, he rose from the bench on which he sat and pushed the table aside. Then, he took up the candle, and shading it with his murderous hand so as to throw its light on me, stood before me, looking at me and enjoying the sight.

"Wolf, I'll tell you something more. It was Old Orlick as you tumbled over on your stairs that night."

In my mind's eye, I saw the staircase with its extinguished lamps. I saw the shadows of the heavy stair rails, thrown by the watchman's lantern on the wall.

"And why was Old Orlick there? I'll tell you something more, wolf. You and Biddy have pretty well hunted me out of these parts, so far as being able to find any work goes. I've took up with new companions, and new masters. Some of 'em writes my letters when I wants 'em wrote. I've had a firm mind and a firm will to have your life, since you was down here at your sister's burying. I've looked arter you to know your ins and outs. For, says Old Orlick to himself, 'Somehow or another I'll have him!' What! When I looks for you, I finds your Uncle Provis, eh?

"You with a uncle too! Why, I know'd you at Gargery's when you was so small a wolf that I could have snuffed out your life real quick. You hadn't found no uncles then. No, not you! But when Old Orlick come for to hear that your Uncle Provis had mostlike wore the leg-iron wot Old Orlick had picked up, filed asunder, on these marshes ever so many year ago, and wot he kep by him till he dropped your sister with it, like a bullock, as he means to drop you—hey?—when he come for to hear that—hey?—"

In his savage taunting, he flared the candle so close at me, that I turned my face aside, to save it from the flame.

"Ah!" he cried, laughing, after doing it again, "the burnt child dreads the fire! Old Orlick knowed you was a-smuggling your Uncle Provis away. Old

Orlick's a match for you and know'd you'd come tonight! Now I'll tell you something more, wolf, and this ends it. There's them that's as good a match for your Uncle Provis as Old Orlick has been for you. There's them that can't and that won't have Magwitch—yes, I know the name!—alive in the same land with them. There's them that might have wrote the note that brought you here. And that person's name might be Compeyson!" He flared the candle at me again, singeing my face and hair, and for an instant blinding me.

There was a clear space of a few feet between the table and the opposite wall. Within this space, he now slouched backward and forward. His great strength seemed to sit stronger upon him than ever before, as he did this with his hands hanging loose and heavy at his sides, and with his eyes scowling at me. I had no grain of hope left.

Of a sudden, he stopped, took the cork out of his bottle, and tossed it away. He swallowed slowly, tilting up the bottle little by little, and now he looked at me no more. The last few drops of liquor he poured into the palm of his hand, and licked up. Then, with a sudden hurry of violence and swearing horribly, he threw the bottle from him, and stooped down. I saw in his hand a stone hammer with a long heavy handle.

Expecting my life to be hammered out, I shouted out with all my might. In the same instant I heard responsive shouts, and I saw figures and a gleam of light dash in at the door. I heard voices and tumult,

and saw Orlick emerge from a struggle of men, clear the table at a leap, and fly out into the night.

I must have passed out momentarily. When I came to, I found that I was lying unbound on the floor, with my head on someone's knee. My eyes were fixed on the ladder against the wall, when there came between me and it, a face. The face of Trabb's boy!

"I think he's all right!" said Trabb's boy, in a sober voice. "But ain't he just pale though!"

At these words, the face of him who supported me looked over into mine, and I saw my supporter to be—

"Herbert! Great Heaven!"

"Softly," said Herbert. "Gently, Handel. Don't be too eager."

"And our old comrade, Startop!" I cried, as he too bent over me.

"Remember what he is going to assist us in," said Herbert, "and be calm."

The reference to the journey down the river made me spring up, though I dropped again from the pain in my arm. "The time has not gone by, Herbert, has it? What night is tonight? How long have I been here?" I had a strange and strong misgiving that I had been lying there a long time—a day and a night—two days and nights—more.

"The time has not gone by. It is still Monday night."

"Thank God!"

"And you have all tomorrow, Tuesday, to rest in," said Herbert. "But you can't help groaning, my dear Handel. What hurt have you got? Can you stand?"

"Yes, yes," said I, "I can walk. I have no hurt but in this throbbing arm."

They laid it bare and did what they could. It was violently swollen and inflamed, and I could scarcely endure to have it touched. They tore up their handkerchiefs to make fresh bandages, and carefully replaced it in the sling, until we could get to the town and obtain some cooling lotion to put upon it. We left the dark and empty sluice house and headed through the quarry on our way back. Trabb's boy—Trabb's overgrown young man now—went before us with a lantern, which was the light I had seen come in at the door. But, the moon was a good two hours higher than when I had last seen the sky, and the night, though rainy, was much lighter. The white vapor of the kiln was passing from us as we went by. I uttered a prayer of thanksgiving as we left the sluice house behind.

During our procession out of the marshes, I entreated Herbert to tell me how he had come to my rescue. I learnt that I had in my hurry dropped the letter, open, in our chambers. Herbert read it when he returned to our chambers, bringing with him Startop. The letter made Herbert uneasy. So he set off for the coach office, with Startop, who volunteered his company. They took the next coach and reached the village, but they had no idea where I was. Who should they run into but Trabb's boy—true to his ancient habit of happening to be everywhere where he had no business. Trabb's boy had seen me passing from Miss Havisham's in the direction of my dining place. Thus, Trabb's boy became their guide, and with him they went out to the sluice house. Now, as they went along, Herbert reflected that I might have been brought there for some valid reason to protect Provis's safety. Therefore, he stole round the house two or three times, trying to find out whether all was right within. As he could hear nothing but indistinct sounds of one deep rough voice, he even began to doubt whether I was there, when suddenly I cried out loudly. He answered the cries, and rushed in, closely followed by the other two.

Wednesday being so close upon us, we determined to go back to London that night. Herbert got a large bottle of lotion for my arm. He applied it liberally, and I was just able to bear its pain on the journey. It was daylight when we reached our chambers. I went at once to bed and lay in bed all day.

We could not communicate with my uncle that day. No precaution was more obvious. Yet this caused me much anxiety. Every footstep and every sound startled me, making me think that he was discovered and taken, and this was the messenger to tell me so. As the day wore on and no ill news came, an overshadowing dread of being disabled by illness before tomorrow morning overcame me. My burning arm throbbed, and my burning head throbbed, and I imagined I was beginning to wander. I counted up to high numbers, to make sure of myself, and repeated passages that I knew in prose and verse.

They kept me very quiet all day, and kept my arm constantly dressed and gave me cooling drinks. Whenever I fell asleep, I awoke with the notion that a long time had elapsed, and the opportunity to save him was gone. About midnight I got out of bed and went to Herbert, with the conviction that I had been asleep for twenty-four hours, and that Wednesday was past. It was the last self-exhausting effort of my fretfulness, for after that, I slept soundly.

Wednesday morning was dawning when I looked out the window. The winking lights upon the bridges were already pale. The rising sun was like a marsh of fire on the horizon. The river, still dark and mysterious, was spanned by bridges that were turning coldly gray. As I looked along the clustered roofs, with church towers and spires shooting into the unusually clear air, the sun rose up, and a veil seemed to be drawn from the river. Millions of sparkles burst out upon its waters. From me too, a veil seemed to be drawn, and I felt strong and well.

Herbert lay asleep in his bed, and our old fellow-student lay asleep on the sofa. I could not dress myself without help, but I made up the fire, which was still burning, and got some coffee ready for them. In good time they too awoke, strong and well.

It was one of those March days when the sun shines hot and the wind blows cold: when it is summer in the light, and winter in the shade. We had our heavy coats with us, and I took a suitcase. Of all my worldly possessions, I took no more than the few necessaries that filled the suitcase. Where I might go, what I might do, or when I might return, were questions utterly unknown to me. Everything depended on what was best for Provis's safety. I only wondered, as I stopped at the door and looked back, under what circumstances I should next see those rooms, if ever.

Herbert, Startop, and I went down to our dock by the river, got on board and cast off. Herbert and Startop rowed, while I steered. It was then about half-past eight in the morning.

Our plan was this. We would row downriver past London, where the waterside inhabitants are very few, and where lone public houses are scattered here and there. One of these we could choose for a resting place. There we meant to remain all night. The steamer for Hamburg, and the steamer for Rotterdam, would start from London at about nine on Thursday morning. We should know at what time to expect them, according to where we were, and would hail the first. If by any accident we were not taken aboard, we should have another chance. We knew the distinguishing marks of each vessel.

The crisp air, the sunlight, the movement on the river, and the moving river itself freshened me with new hope. I felt ashamed to be of so little use in the boat. But there were few better oarsmen than my two friends, and they rowed with a steady stroke that was to last all day.

We picked up Provis at a pre-arranged point. Once he stepped on board, we were off again. He had a boat-cloak with him, and a black canvas bag, and he looked as much like a river pilot as I could have wished.

"Dear boy!" he said, putting his arm on my shoulder as he took his seat. "Faithful dear boy, well done. Thankye, thankye!"

At the landing where we had taken him aboard, and ever since, I had looked warily for any sign of our being suspected. I had seen none. We certainly had not been, and at that time we were not, followed by any boat.

"If all goes well," said I to my benefactor, "you will be perfectly free and safe again, within a few hours."

"Well," he returned, drawing a long breath, "I hope so."

"And think so?"

He dipped his hand in the water over the boat's side and said, "Ay, I s'pose I think so, dear boy. But, we can no more see to the bottom of the next few hours, than we can see to the bottom of this river. We can't no more hold their tide than I can hold this. And it's run through my fingers and gone, you see!" holding up his dripping hand.

He put his pipe back in his mouth with an undisturbed expression, and sat as composed and contented as if we were already out of England. The air felt cold upon the river, but it was a bright day, and the sunshine was very cheering. The tide ran strong, and we took every advantage of it. We decided to go ashore among some slippery stones while we ate and drank what we had with us, and looked about. It was like my own marsh country, flat and monotonous, and with a dim horizon.

We pushed off again, and made what progress we could. By now the tide had turned against us. However, Herbert and Startop kept rowing and rowing until the sun started to go down. There was the red sun, on the low level of the shore, in a purple haze, fast deepening into black. And there was the solitary flat marsh. And far away there were the rising grounds. Between them and us there seemed to be no life, save here and there in the foreground a melancholy gull.

The night was fast falling. We held a little council

and decided to stay at the first lonely inn we could find. So they plied their oars once more, and I looked out for anything like an inn. Thus we held on, speaking little, for four or five dull miles. It was very cold. The night was as dark by this time as it would be until morning. What faint light we had seemed to come more from the river than the sky, as the oars in their dipping struck at a few reflected stars.

We were all possessed by the idea that we were being followed. The river flapped at irregular intervals against the shore. Whenever such a sound came, one or other of us was sure to look in that direction. Here and there, the current had worn down the bank into a little creek, and we were all suspicious of such places, and eyed them nervously. Sometimes, one of us would say, "What was that ripple?" in a low voice, or, "Is that a boat yonder?" And afterward, we would fall into a dead silence, and I would sit impatiently thinking what an unusual amount of noise the oars made.

At length we spied a light and a roof. We pulled to the bank, and I stepped ashore to investigate. I found the light to be in a window of a public house. It was a dirty place enough, and I dare say not unknown to smugglers and adventurers. However, there was a good fire in the kitchen, and there were eggs and bacon to eat, and various liquors to drink. Also, there were two double-bedded rooms. No other travelers were staying the night. Only the landlord, his wife, and a grizzled helper were there.

With this assistant, I went down to the boat.

We all came ashore, and brought out the oars, and rudder, and boat-hook, and all else, and hauled her up for the night. We made a very good meal by the kitchen fire, and then assigned the bedrooms. Herbert and Startop were to occupy one; I and Provis the other. We considered ourselves fortunate, for we could not have found a more solitary place.

After our meal, we rested by the fire. The helper was sitting in a corner, toying with a bloated pair of shoes that he had taken a few days ago from the feet of a drowned seaman washed ashore. In his hoarse voice, he asked me if we had seen a four-oared galley going up with the tide. When I told him no, he said she must have gone down then.

"A four-oared galley, did you say?" said I.

"A four," said the man, "and two other men besides."

"Did they come ashore here?"

"They put in with a stone two-gallon jar, for some beer. I'd ha' been glad to put something nasty in their beer," he said.

The landlord explained that his helper believed the boat was a Customs vessel, or maybe a police craft, searching for something. The helper had no love for such folks, we were told.

This discussion made us all uneasy. Was there a search party about? Were they looking for Provis? The dismal wind was muttering round the house, the tide was flapping at the shore, and I had a feeling that we were caged and threatened.

Nevertheless, we were fatigued beyond measure and decided to go to bed.

I lay down with the greater part of my clothes on and slept well for a few hours. When I awoke, the wind had risen. The sign hanging by two chains outside the house was creaking and banging about. Rising softly, I looked out of the window. It overlooked the causeway where we had hauled up our boat. As my eyes adapted themselves to the light of the clouded moon, I saw two men looking into our little craft. They passed by under the window and struck across the marsh. I lay down to think of the matter and fell asleep again.

We were up early. As we walked to and fro, all four together, before breakfast, I told the others what I had seen. I proposed that Provis and I should walk away together to a distant point we could see, and that the boat should pick us up there at about noon. This being considered a good precaution, he and I set forth soon after breakfast.

He smoked his pipe as we went along, and sometimes stopped to clap me on the shoulder. One would have supposed that it was I who was in danger, not he, and that he was reassuring me. We spoke very little. As we approached the point, I begged him to remain in a sheltered place, while I went on to look about. I found no boat off the point, nor any boat drawn up anywhere near it, nor were there any signs of the men having passed there. I waved my hat to him to come up, and there we waited until we saw our boat coming round. We got aboard easily and rowed out into the track of the steamer. By that time it was ten minutes to one o'clock, and we began to look out for her smoke.

At half-past one we saw her smoke, and soon afterward we saw behind it the smoke of another steamer. As they were coming on at full speed, we got our two bags ready, and took that opportunity of saying goodbye to Herbert and Startop. We had all shaken hands cordially, and neither Herbert's eyes nor mine were quite dry, when I saw a four-oared galley shoot out from under the bank but a little way ahead of us. It rowed out in our direction.

The steamship was coming head on. I called to Herbert and Startop to keep before the tide, that she might see us preparing to climb aboard. I pleaded with Provis to sit quite still, wrapped in his cloak. He answered cheerily, "Trust to me, dear boy," and sat like a statue. Meantime the galley, which was very skillfully handled, had taken a position alongside us. Of the two sitters, one held the rudder lines, and looked at us attentively. The other sitter was wrapped up, much as Provis was, and seemed to shrink, and whisper some instruction to the steerer as he looked at us. Not a word was spoken in either boat.

Startop could make out, after a few minutes, which steamer was first, and gave me the word "Hamburg," in a low voice as we sat face to face. She was nearing us very fast, and the beating of her paddles grew louder and louder. I felt as if her shadow were absolutely upon us, when the galley hailed us.

"You have a returned prisoner there," said the

man who held the lines. "That's the man, wrapped in the cloak. His name is Abel Magwitch, otherwise Provis. I arrest that man, and call upon him to surrender, and you to assist."

At the same moment, the galley came alongside us. Two of its occupants grabbed onto the side of our boat. This caused great confusion on board the steamer. I heard them calling to us, and heard the order given to stop the paddle wheels. Nonetheless, the steamer continued to bear down upon us irresistibly. In the same moment, I saw the steersman of the galley lay his hand on Provis's shoulder. The steamer was almost upon us. Provis leaned across his captor and pulled the cloak from the neck of the shrinking sitter in the galley. The face revealed was the face of the other convict of long ago! I saw that face tilt backward with a white terror on it that I shall never forget. I heard a great cry on board the steamer as it collided with our boat. There was a loud splash in the water, and I felt our boat sink from under me.

For a fleeting moment, I struggled against a thousand paddle wheels and a thousand flashes of light. The next instant, I was fished out of the water and taken on board the galley. Herbert was there, and Startop was there. But our boat was gone, and the two convicts were gone.

Every man in the galley looked silently and eagerly at the water behind. Presently a dark object was seen in it, swimming with difficulty toward us. No man spoke. The steersman held up his hand, and the rowers softly backed water. As the shape came nearer, I saw it to be Magwitch. He was taken on board and instantly manacled at the wrists and ankles.

The galley was kept steady, and we scanned the water for the other convict. But, the Rotterdam steamer now came up, and we had to move out of the way. By the time both steamers were past us, we knew that the search was hopeless.

At length we gave it up and pulled into shore by the inn we had lately left. Here, I was able to get some dressings for Magwitch—Provis no longer—who had received a very severe injury in the chest and a deep cut in the head.

He told me that he believed himself to have gone under the keel of the steamer, and to have been struck on the head in rising. The injury to his chest (which rendered his breathing extremely painful) he thought he had received against the side of the galley. He did not say what he might or might not have done to Compeyson. They had both gone overboard together. He told me in a whisper that they had gone down, fiercely locked in each other's arms, and that there had been a struggle under water, and that he had disengaged himself, struck out, and swum away.

When I asked one of the officers for permission to change the prisoner's wet clothes by purchasing any spare garments I could get at the public house, he gave it readily. He hastened to add that he must take charge of everything his prisoner had about him. So the pocketbook which had once been in my hands passed into the officer's. He further gave me leave to accompany the prisoner to London, but declined to accord that grace to my two friends.

We remained at the public house until the tide turned, and then Magwitch was carried down to the galley and put on board. Herbert and Startop were to get to London by land, as soon as they could. When I took my place in the galley by Magwitch's side, I felt that that was my place as long as he lived.

My repugnance for him had all melted away. In the hunted, wounded, shackled creature who held my hand in his, I saw only a man who had meant to be my benefactor. He had behaved affectionately, gratefully, and generously toward me with great constancy through a series of years. I saw in him a much better man than I had been to Joe.

His breathing became more difficult and painful as the night drew on. Often he could not repress a groan. I tried to rest him on the arm I could use. That there were people enough who were able and willing to identify him, I could not doubt. That he would be leniently treated, I could not hope.

As we returned toward the setting sun we had yesterday left behind us, and as the stream of our hopes seemed all running back, I told him how grieved I was to think that he had come home for my sake.

"Dear boy," he answered, "I'm quite content to take my chance. I've seen my boy, and he can be a gentleman without me."

I had given that some thought while we were sitting there side by side. I realized that, being convicted, his possessions would be forfeited to the Crown. I would get nothing.

"Lookee here, dear boy," said he. "It's best as a gentleman should not be knowed to belong to me now. Only come to see me as if you come by chance along with Wemmick. Sit where I can see you when I am sworn in, for the last o' many times, and I don't ask no more."

"I will never stir from your side," said I, "when I am suffered to be near you. Please God, I will be as true to you, as you have been to me!"

I felt his hand tremble as it held mine, and he turned his face away as he lay in the bottom of the boat. I heard that old sound in his throat—softened now, like all the rest of him.

He was taken to the Police Court next day. Normally, he would have been committed for trial immediately. However, it was necessary to send for an officer of the prison-ship from which he had once escaped to formally identify him. Compeyson, who had meant to perform this duty, was tumbling on the tides, dead. I had gone direct to Mr. Jaggers at his private house, on my arrival in London. He explained that no power on earth could prevent the case from going against Magwitch.

I told Mr. Jaggers my design of keeping my benefactor in ignorance of the fate of his wealth. Mr. Jaggers was angry with me for having "let it slip through my fingers," and said we must try at all events for some of it. But, he was not at all optimistic on that score.

There appeared to be reason for supposing that the drowned informer had hoped for a reward, and had obtained some accurate knowledge of

Magwitch's affairs. When his body was found, many miles from the scene of his death, and so horribly disfigured that he was only recognizable by the contents of his pockets, notes were still legible, folded in a case he carried. Among these were the name of a banking house in New South Wales where a sum of money was, and the designation of certain lands of considerable value. Both these entries were in a list that Magwitch, while in prison, gave to Mr. Jaggers, of the possessions he supposed I should inherit.

After three days, the witness from the prison-ship arrived and identified Magwitch. He was to remain in jail until his trial, which would take place in a month.

It was at this dark time of my life that Herbert returned home one evening, a good deal cast down, and said:

"My dear Handel, I fear I shall soon have to leave you."

His business partner having prepared me for that, I was less surprised than he thought.

"We shall lose a fine opportunity if I put off going to Cairo, and I am very much afraid I must go, Handel, when you most need me."

"Herbert, I shall always need you, because I shall always love you. But my need is no greater now, than at another time."

"You will be so lonely."

"I have no leisure to think of that," said I. "You know that I am always with Magwitch to the full extent of the time allowed, and that I would be with him all day long, if I could. And when I come away from him, you know that my thoughts are with him."

The dreadful condition to which he was brought was so appalling to both of us, that we could not refer to it in plainer words.

"My dear fellow," said Herbert, "let the near prospect of our separation be my reason for troubling you about yourself. Have you thought of your future?"

"No, for I have been afraid to think of any future."

"But yours cannot be dismissed. I wish you would discuss it now, as far as a few friendly words go, with me."

"I will," said I.

"In this branch house of ours, Handel, we must have a—"

I saw that his delicacy was avoiding the right word, so I said, "A clerk."

"A clerk. And I hope it is not at all unlikely that he may advance into a partner. Now, Handel—in short, my dear boy, will you come with me? Clara and I have talked about it again and again. The dear little thing begged me only this evening to present this proposition to you. We should get on so well, Handel!"

I thanked her heartily, and I thanked him heartily, but said I could not yet plan on joining him as he so kindly offered. Firstly, my mind was too preoccupied to be able to think about the subject clearly. Secondly—Yes! Secondly, there was a vague something lingering in my thoughts that will come out very near the end of this narrative.

"But if you thought, Herbert, that you could, without doing any injury to your business, leave the question open for a little while—"

"For any while," cried Herbert. "Six months, a year!"

"Not so long as that," said I. "Two or three months at most."

Herbert was highly delighted when we shook hands on this arrangement, and said he could now take courage to tell me that he believed he must go away at the end of the week.

"And Clara?" said I.

"The dear little thing," returned Herbert, "holds dutifully to her father as long as he lasts. But he won't last long. He is certainly going."

"Not to say an insensitive thing," said I, "he cannot do better than go."

"I am afraid that must be admitted," said Herbert. "And then I shall come back for the dear little thing, and the dear little thing and I will walk quietly into the nearest church. Remember! The blessed darling comes of no family, my dear Handel, and hasn't a notion about her grandpapa. What a fortune for the son of my mother!"

On the Saturday in that same week, I took my leave of Herbert—full of bright hope, but sad and sorry to leave me—as he sat on one of the seaport mail coaches. I then went to my lonely home—if it deserved the name, for it was now no home to me, and I had no home anywhere.

At about the same time Herbert was separated from his beloved, Wemmick was joined with his. The following Monday, he wed his Miss Skiffins, and I was honored to be the best man.

Magwitch lay in prison very ill during the interval between his committal for trial and the trial itself. He had broken two ribs, and they had wounded one of his lungs. He breathed with great pain and difficulty, which increased daily. On account of his hurt, he spoke so low as to be scarcely audible. He spoke very little. But he was ever ready to listen to me, and it became the first duty of my life to say to him, and read to him, what I knew he ought to hear.

Being far too ill to remain in the common prison, he was removed to the infirmary. This gave me opportunities of being with him that I could not otherwise have had. Were it not for his illness, he would have been put in chains, for he was regarded as a determined prison breaker.

Every day he wasted away a little more and became slowly weaker. The kind of submission or resignation that he showed was that of a man who was utterly tired out.

It happened on two or three occasions in my presence, that his desperate reputation was referred to by one or other of the people in attendance on him. A smile crossed his face then, and he turned his eyes on me with a trustful look, as if he were confident that I had seen some small redeeming touch in him.

The time for his trial finally arrived. When the trial began, my benefactor was directed to sit in a chair. No objection was made to my sitting close to him and holding the hand that he stretched forth to me.

The trial was very direct. Such things as could be said for him, were said—how he had taken to industrious habits, and had prospered lawfully and reputably. But, nothing could negate the fact that he had returned. It was impossible to try him for that and find him not guilty.

At that time, it was the custom of the court to devote a concluding day to the passing of sentences. I could scarcely believe that on that day the judge sentenced thirty-two men and women to be executed. Foremost among them was he, seated, that he might get breath enough to keep life in him. Among the others, some were defiant; some were stricken with terror; some were sobbing and weeping; some covered their faces; and some stared gloomily about. There had been shrieks from among the women convicts, but they had been stilled, and a hush had ensued.

I began that night to write out a petition to the Home Secretary of State, setting forth my knowledge of him, and how it was that he had come back for my sake. I wrote it as fervently and pathetically as I could, and when I had finished it and sent it in, I wrote out other petitions to such men in authority as I hoped were the most merciful. I even drew up one to the Crown itself. For several days and nights after he was sentenced, I took no rest except when I fell asleep in my chair, but was wholly absorbed in these appeals. And after I had sent them in, I could not keep away from the places where they were, but felt as if they were more hopeful and less desperate when I was near them. In this unreasonable restlessness and pain of mind, I would roam the streets by evening, wandering by those offices and houses where I had left the petitions. To the present hour, the weary western streets of London on a cold dusty spring night, with their stern shut-up mansions and their long rows of lamps, are melancholy to me from this association.

The daily visits I could make him were shortened now, and he was more strictly kept. Nobody was hard with him, or with me. There was duty to be done, and it was done, but not harshly. The officer always gave me the assurance that he was worse, and some other sick prisoners confirmed this report.

As the days went on, I noticed more and more that he would lie placidly looking at the white ceiling. There was an absence of light in his face, until some word of mine brightened it for an instant. Then it would subside again. Sometimes he was unable to speak. Then, he would answer me with slight pressures on my hand, and I grew to understand his meaning very well.

On the tenth day, I saw a greater change in him than I had seen yet. His eyes were turned toward the door and lighted up as I entered.

"Dear boy," he said, as I sat down by his bed, "I thought you was late. But I knowed you couldn't be that."

"It is just the beginning of visiting hours," said I. "I waited for it at the gate."

"You always waits at the gate, don't you, dear boy?"

"Yes. Not to lose a moment of the time."

"Thank'ee dear boy, thank'ee. God bless you! You've never deserted me, dear boy."

He lay on his back, breathing with great difficulty. Do what he would, and love me though he did, the light left his face ever and again, and a film came over the placid look at the white ceiling.

"Are you in much pain today?"

"I don't complain of none, dear boy."

"You never do complain."

He had spoken his last words. He smiled, and I understood his touch to mean that he wished to lift my hand, and lay it on his breast. I laid it there, and he smiled again, and put both his hands upon it.

The visiting period ran out while we were thus. Looking round, I found the governor of the prison standing near me, and he whispered, "You needn't go yet." I thanked him gratefully, and asked, "Might I speak to him, if he can hear me?"

The governor stepped aside, and beckoned the officer away. Magwitch looked most affectionately at me.

"Dear Magwitch, I must tell you, now at last. You hear what I say?"

A gentle pressure on my hand told me he did.

"You had a child once, whom you loved and lost."

A stronger pressure on my hand.

"She lived and found powerful friends. She is living now. She is a lady and very beautiful. And I love her!"

With a last faint effort, which would have been powerless but for my yielding to it and assisting it, he raised my hand to his lips. Then, he gently let it sink upon his breast again, with his own hands lying on it. The placid look at the white ceiling came back, and passed away, and his head dropped quietly on his breast.

I knew there were no better words that I could say beside his bed, than "O Lord, be merciful to him, a sinner!"

Now that I was left wholly to myself, I decided to leave my chambers as soon as my lease expired. In the meanwhile, since I was seriously short of money, I planned to locate someone who might wish to occupy the rooms until the end of my lease. To this end, I posted notices all about. I was also feeling very ill. For a day or two, I lay on the sofa, or on the floor—anywhere, according as I happened to sink down—with a heavy head and aching limbs. I then slipped into a fevered delirium, imagining all sorts of events that never occurred. I alternated between inexplicable horror and complete calm, without knowing what brought on either of these states. My reason gave way, but then would suddenly return. I had visions of various people I know coming to visit me, but I was never certain whether I only imagined they were present. Then an even stranger notion possessed me. I began to see, in all the faces that attended me, the kindly face of Joe.

After I had passed the worst point of my illness, I began to notice that while all its other features changed, this one consistent feature did not change. I opened my eyes in the night, and I saw in the great chair at the bedside, Joe. I opened my eyes in the day, and, sitting on the window seat, smoking his pipe in the shaded open window, still I saw Joe. I asked for cooling drink, and the dear hand that gave it to me was Joe's. I sank back on my pillow after drinking, and the face that looked so hopefully and tenderly upon me was the face of Joe.

At last, one day, I took courage, and said, "Is it Joe?"

And the dear old home-voice answered, "Which it is, old chap."

"O Joe, you break my heart! Look angry at me, Joe. Strike me, Joe. Tell me of my ingratitude. Don't be so good to me!"

Joe had actually laid his head down on the pillow at my side and put his arm round my neck, in his joy that I knew him.

"Which dear old Pip, old chap," said Joe, "you and me was ever friends."

After which, Joe withdrew to the window, and stood with his back toward me, wiping his eyes. My extreme weakness prevented me from getting up and going to him. I lay there, guiltily whispering, "O God bless him! O God bless this gentle Christian man!"

Joe's eyes were red when I next found him

beside me. I was holding his hand, and we both felt happy.

"How long, dear Joe?"

"Which you meantersay, Pip, how long have your illness lasted, dear old chap?"

"Yes, Joe."

"It's the end of May, Pip. Tomorrow is the first of June."

"And have you been here all the time, dear Joe?"

"Pretty nigh, old chap. For, as I says to Biddy when the news of your being ill were brought by letter . . ."

"It is so delightful to hear you, Joe! But I interrupt you in what you said to Biddy."

"Which it were," said Joe, "that how you might be amongst strangers, and that how you and me having been ever friends, a wisit at such a moment might not prove unacceptabobble. And Biddy, her word were, 'Go to him, without loss of time.'"

There Joe cut himself short, and informed me that I was to be talked to in moderation. I was also to take a little nourishment at stated frequent times, whether I felt inclined for it or not. So I kissed his hand and lay quiet. Meanwhile, he proceeded to pen a note to Biddy, sending her my love. Evidently Biddy had taught Joe to write.

I postponed asking him about Miss Havisham until next day. He shook his head when I then asked him if she had recovered.

"Is she dead, Joe?"

"Why you see, old chap," said Joe, "I wouldn't go so far as to say that, for that's a deal to say; but she ain't—"

"Living, Joe?"

"That's nigher where it is," said Joe. "She ain't living. She's passed on."

"Dear Joe, have you heard what becomes of her property?"

"Well, old chap," said Joe, "it do appear that she had settled the most of it on Miss Estella. But she had wrote out a little coddleshell in her own hand a day or two afore the accident, leaving a cool four thousand to Mr. Matthew Pocket. And why, do you suppose, Pip, she left that cool four thousand to him?—'Because of Pip's account of him the said Matthew.'"

This account gave me great joy, as it confirmed the only good thing I had done. I asked Joe whether he had heard if any of the other relations had any legacies.

"Miss Sarah," said Joe, "she have twenty-five pound perannium fur to buy pills, on account of being sickly. Miss Georgiana, she have twenty pound down. Mrs.—what's the name of them wild beasts with humps, old chap?"

"Camels?" said I, wondering why he could possibly want to know.

Joe nodded. "Mrs. Camels," by which I presently understood he meant Camilla, "she have five pound fur to buy candles to put her in spirits when she wake up in the night."

"And now," said Joe, "you ain't that strong yet, old chap, that you can take in more nor one additional shovel-full today. Old Orlick he broke into someone's house."

"Whose?" said I.

"Pumblechook's house. And they took his cash box, and they drinked his wine, and they partook of his wittles, and they slapped his face, and they pulled his nose, and they tied him up to his bedpust, and they stuffed his mouth full of flowering annuals to prewent his crying out. But he recognized Orlick, and Orlick's in the county jail."

In this manner, we held many conversations. I was slow to gain strength, but I did slowly and surely become less weak. Joe stayed with me, and I fancied I was little Pip again.

The tenderness of Joe was so beautifully suited to my need that I was like a child in his hands. He would sit and talk to me in the old confidence, and with the old simplicity, and in the old unassertive protecting way.

We looked forward to the day when I should go out for a ride, as we had once looked forward to the day of my apprenticeship. Eventually the day came. An open carriage was got into the lane. Joe wrapped me up, took me in his arms, carried me down to it, and put me in, as if I were still the small helpless creature to whom he had so abundantly given of the wealth of his great nature.

Joe got in beside me, and we drove away together into the country. The rich summer growth was already on the trees and on the grass, and sweet summer scents filled the air. The day happened to be Sunday. We talked as we used to talk, lying on the grass at the old Battery. There was no change whatever in Joe. Exactly what he had been in my eyes then, he was in my eyes still; just as simply faithful, and as simply right.

When we got back to my chambers again, he lifted me out of the carriage and carried me up the stairs. I thought of that eventful Christmas Day when he had carried me over the marshes. We had not yet talked about my change of fortune. Nor did I know how much of my late history he was acquainted with.

"Have you heard, Joe," I asked him that evening, as he smoked his pipe at the window, "who my patron was?"

"I heerd," returned Joe, "as it were not Miss Havisham, old chap."

"Did you hear who it was, Joe?"

"Well! I heerd as it were a person what sent the person what giv' you the bank notes at the Jolly Bargemen, Pip."

"So it was."

"Astonishing!" said Joe, in the calmest way.

"Did you hear that he was dead, Joe?" I presently asked.

"Which? Him as sent the bank notes, Pip?"

"Yes."

"I think," said Joe, after meditating a long time, and looking rather evasively at the window seat, "as

I did hear that."

"Did you hear anything of his circumstances, Joe?"

"Not partickler, Pip."

"If you would like to hear, Joe—" I was beginning, when Joe got up and came to my sofa.

"Lookee here, old chap," said Joe, bending over me. "Ever the best of friends, ain't us, Pip?"

I was ashamed to answer him.

"Wery good, then," said Joe, as if I had answered. "That's agreed upon. Then why go into subjects, old chap, which as betwixt two sech must be forever onnecessary? There's subjects enough as betwixt two sech, without onnecessary ones. Lord! To think of your poor sister and her rampages!"

"I remember, Joe."

"Now, you mustn't go a-overdoing it, but you must have your supper and your wine-and-water, and you must be put betwixt the sheets."

But whether Joe knew how poor I was, and how my great expectations had all dissolved, like our own marsh mists before the sun, I did not know.

As the days passed, my condition gradually improved. With a little sorrow, I noticed that as I became stronger and better, Joe became a little less easy with me. In my weakness and entire dependence on him, the dear fellow had fallen into the old tone, and called me by the old names, the dear "old Pip, old chap," that now were music in my ears. I too had fallen into the old ways, only happy and thankful that he let me. But, imperceptibly, Joe's hold upon them began to weaken. I soon began to understand that the cause of it was in me, and that the fault of it was all mine.

Had I given Joe reason to think that in prosperity I should grow cold to him and cast him off? Had I given Joe's innocent heart cause to feel that as I got stronger, his connection with me would be weaker?

It was on the third or fourth occasion of my going out walking in the gardens, leaning on Joe's arm, that I saw this change in him very plainly. We had been sitting in the bright warm sunlight, looking at the river, and I chanced to say as we got up:

"See, Joe! I can walk quite strongly. Now, you shall see me walk back by myself."

"Which do not overdo it, Pip," said Joe. "But I shall be happy fur to see you able, sir."

That last word grated on me. I walked no further than the gate of the gardens, and then pretended to be weaker than I was, and asked Joe for his arm. Joe gave it to me, but was thoughtful.

I, for my part, was thoughtful too. How could I stop this growing change in Joe? I could tell him about my changed circumstances, and that I had almost no money. But then he would want to help me out with his little savings. I knew that he ought not to help me, and that I must not permit him to do it.

It was a thoughtful Saturday evening for both of us. But before we went to bed, I had resolved that I would wait until the day after tomorrow and then tell Joe about my situation. We had a quiet day on Sunday. We rode out into the country and then walked in the fields.

"I feel thankful that I have been ill, Joe," I said.

"Dear old Pip, old chap, you're a'most back to good health, sir."

"It has been a memorable time for me, Joe."

"Likeways for myself, sir," Joe returned.

"We have had a time together, Joe, that I can never forget. There were days once, I know, that I did for a while forget. But I never shall forget these."

"Pip," said Joe, appearing a little hurried and troubled, "what have been betwixt us—have been."

At night, when I had gone to bed, Joe came into my room, as he had done all through my recovery. He asked me if I felt sure that I was as well as in the morning.

"Yes, dear Joe, quite."

"And are always a getting stronger, old chap?"

"Yes, dear Joe, steadily."

Joe patted the coverlet on my shoulder with his great good hand, and said, in what I thought a husky voice, "Good night!"

When I got up in the morning, refreshed and stronger yet, I was full of my resolution to tell Joe all, without delay. I would tell him before breakfast. I would dress at once and go to his room and surprise him. It was the first day I had been up early. I went to his room, and he was not there. Not only was he not there, but all his belongings were gone.

I hurried then to the breakfast table, and on it found a letter. These were its brief contents.

"Not wishful to intrude I have departured fur you are well again dear Pip and will do better without Jo.

"p.s. Ever the best of friends."

I made up my mind that I would go to the dear old forge and tell Joe of the loss of my fortune. I also decided that I would seek out Biddy and say these words to her. "Biddy, I think you once liked me very well, before my wandering heart led me away from you. If you can like me only half as well once more, if you can take me with all my faults and disappointments, then I would like us to go through life as man and wife."

After three days more of recovery, I went down to the old place to carry out these resolutions.

News of my financial misfortune had arrived at the village before I did. The Blue Boar seemed quite aware of my situation. Whereas the Boar had sought greatly to please me when I was coming into property, the Boar was quite indifferent toward me now that I was going out of property.

It was evening when I arrived, much fatigued by the journey I had so often made so easily. The Boar could not put me into my usual bedroom, which was engaged (probably by someone who had expectations). They could only give me a very ordinary chamber among the pigeons facing the yard. But I had as sound a sleep in that lodging as in the most superior accommodation, and my dreams were the same.

Early in the morning while my breakfast was getting ready, I strolled by Satis House. There were printed bills on the gate, and on bits of carpet hanging out of the windows, announcing a sale by auction of the household furniture and effects, next week. The house itself was to be sold as old building materials and pulled down.

When I got back to my breakfast in the Boar's coffee-room, I found Mr. Pumblechook conversing with the landlord. Mr. Pumblechook was waiting for me, and addressed me in the following terms.

"Young man, I am sorry to see you brought low. But what else could be expected! What else could be expected!"

As he extended his hand with a magnificently forgiving air, and as I was broken by illness and unfit to quarrel, I took it.

"William," said Mr. Pumblechook to the waiter, "put a muffin on the table. And has it come to this! Has it come to this!"

I frowningly sat down to my breakfast. Mr. Pumblechook stood over me and poured out my tea—before I could touch the teapot—with the air of a benefactor who was resolved to be true to the last.

"William," said Mr. Pumblechook, mournfully, "put the salt on. In happier times," addressing me, "I think you took sugar. And did you take milk? You did. Sugar and milk, William."

I went on with my breakfast, and Mr. Pumblechook continued to stand over me, staring fishily and breathing noisily, as he always did.

"Little more than skin and bone!" mused Mr. Pumblechook, aloud. "And yet when he went away from here (I may say with my blessing), and I offered him all I had, he was as plump as a peach!"

I thought back to the way he had offered his hand in my former prosperity, saying, "May I?" Now, he lorded it over me as though I were his humble slave.

"And are you a-going to Joseph?"

I nodded my head in assent.

"I will tell you, young man, what to say to Joseph. Say, 'Joseph, I have this day seen my earliest benefactor and the founder of my fortun's.'"

"I swear I don't see him here," said I.

"Say you," Pumblechook went on, "'Joseph, I have seen that man. He knows your character, Joseph, and is well acquainted with your pig-headedness and ignorance. And he knows my total lack of common human gratitoode.'" With those words the pretender left the house, leaving me to finish my breakfast in peace.

This disagreeable conversation made it only the pleasanter to turn to Biddy and to Joe. I went toward them slowly, for my limbs were weak, but with a sense of increasing relief as I drew nearer to them.

The June weather was delicious. The sky was blue, and the larks were soaring high over the green corn. I thought all that countryside more beautiful and peaceful by far than I had ever known it to be. My heart was softened by my return. I felt like one who was toiling home barefoot from distant travel, and whose wanderings had lasted many years.

The forge was a very short distance off. I went toward it under the sweet green limes, listening for the clink of Joe's hammer. Long after I ought to have heard it, all was still. The limes were there, and the white thorns were there, and the chestnut trees were there. Their leaves rustled harmoniously when I stopped to listen. But the clink of Joe's hammer was not to be heard.

I came running toward the forge and saw that it was closed. No gleam of fire, no glittering shower of sparks, no roar of bellows; all shut up and still.

But the house was not deserted. There were white curtains fluttering in its window, and the window was open and gay with flowers. I went softly toward it, meaning to peep over the flowers, when Joe and Biddy stood before me, arm in arm.

At first Biddy gave a cry, as if she thought I were a ghost. But in another moment she was in my embrace. I wept to see her, and she wept to see me. I, because she looked so fresh and pleasant; she, because I looked so worn and white.

I looked at both of them, from one to the other, and then—

"It's my wedding day," cried Biddy, in a burst of happiness, "and I am married to Joe!"

They took me into the kitchen. Biddy held one of my hands to her lips, and Joe's restoring touch was on my shoulder. "Which he warn't strong enough, my dear, fur to be surprised," said Joe. And Biddy said, "I ought to have thought of it, dear Joe, but I was too happy." They were both so overjoyed to see me, so proud to see me, so touched by my coming to them, so delighted that I should have come by accident to make their day complete!

My first thought was one of great thankfulness that I had never told Joe of my intention to marry Biddy. How often, while he was with me in my illness, had it risen to my lips. How certain would have been his knowledge of it, if he had remained with me but another hour!

"Dear Biddy," said I, "you have the best husband in the whole world! And, dear Joe, you have the best wife in the whole world, and she will make you as happy as you deserve to be, you dear, good, noble Joe!"

Joe looked at me with a quivering lip, and fairly put his sleeve before his eyes.

"And Joe and Biddy both, receive my humble thanks for all you have done for me and all I have so ill repaid! I am leaving within the hour, for I am soon going abroad."

They were both affected by these words, and both entreated me to say no more.

"But I must say more. Dear Joe, I hope you will have children to love, and that some little fellow will sit in this chimney corner of a winter night, who may remind you of another little fellow gone out of it for ever. Don't tell him, Joe, that I was thankless. Don't tell him, Biddy, that I was ungenerous and unjust. Only tell him that I honored you both, because you were both so good and true. I know that he will grow up a much better man than I did."

"I ain't a-going," said Joe, from behind his sleeve, "to tell him nothink o' that natur, Pip. Nor Biddy ain't. Nor yet no one ain't."

"And now, pray tell me, both, that you forgive me! Pray let me hear you say the words, that I may carry the sound of them away with me. Then I shall be able to believe that you can trust me, and think better of me, in the time to come!"

"O dear old Pip, old chap," said Joe. "God knows as I forgive you, if I have anythink to forgive!"

"Amen! And God knows I do!" echoed Biddy.

"Now let me go up and look at my old little room and rest there a few minutes by myself. Then when I have eaten and drunk with you, go with me a little ways, dear Joe and Biddy, before we say goodbye!"

I sold everything I owned and paid small sums to my creditors. They gave me ample time to pay them in full. I went abroad and joined Herbert. Within two months I was clerk to Clarriker and Co. After four months I assumed directorship of the branch office. Herbert had gone away to marry Clara, and I was left in sole charge of the Eastern Branch until he brought her back.

Many a year went round, and then I became a partner in the firm. I lived happily with Herbert and his wife. I lived modestly, and paid my debts, and maintained a constant correspondence with Biddy and Joe. It was not until I became third in the firm that Clarriker revealed to Herbert how I had arranged for him to be taken on. He then declared that the secret of Herbert's partnership had troubled his conscience, and he must tell it. So he told it, and Herbert was as much moved as amazed. Happily, the end of the secret did not mean the end of our friendship. I cannot say that we were ever a huge company or that we made mints of money. But we had a good name, and worked for our profits, and did very well. We owed much to Herbert's ever cheerful industry and readiness. I often wondered how I could once have considered him less than competent. Then one day it occurred to me that perhaps it was not Herbert who lacked ability, but I myself.

For eleven years, I did not see Joe or Biddy—though they had both been often in my imagination while I was out of the country. Then, one evening in December, an hour or two after dark, I laid my hand softly on the latch of the old kitchen door. I touched it so softly that I was not heard, and I looked in unseen. There, smoking his pipe in the old place by the kitchen firelight, as hale and as strong as ever, though a little gray, sat Joe. And there, fenced into the corner with Joe's leg, and sitting on my own little stool looking at the fire, was—I again!

"We giv' him the name of Pip for your sake, dear old chap," said Joe. "And we hoped he might grow a little bit like you, and we think he do."

I thought so too, and I took him out for a walk next morning. We talked a lot, understanding one another to perfection. And I took him down to the churchyard, and set him on a certain tombstone there. He showed me which stone was sacred to the memory of Philip Pirrip, late of this parish, and also Georgiana, wife of the above.

"Biddy," said I, when I talked with her after dinner, as her little girl lay sleeping in her lap, "you must give Pip to me, one of these days; or lend him, at all events."

"No, no," said Biddy, gently. "You must marry."

"So Herbert and Clara say, but I don't think I shall, Biddy. I have so settled down in their home, that it's not at all likely. I am already quite an old bachelor."

Biddy looked down at her child, and put its little hand to her lips. She then put the same hand into mine.

"Dear Pip," said Biddy, "you are sure you don't fret for her?"

"O no—I think not, Biddy."

"Tell me as an old, old friend. Have you quite forgotten her?"

"My dear Biddy, I have forgotten nothing in my life that ever had a foremost place there, and little that ever had any place there. But that poor dream, as I once used to call it, has all gone by, Biddy, all gone by!"

Nevertheless, I knew, while I said those words, that I secretly intended to revisit the site of the old house that evening, alone, for her sake. Yes, for Estella's sake.

I had heard of her as leading a most unhappy

life, and as being separated from her husband, who had treated her with great cruelty. And I had heard of the death of her husband, from an accident due to his ill treatment of a horse. This incident had occurred two years ago. For all I knew, she was married again.

The early dinner hour at Joe's left me plenty of time to walk over to the site of Satis House before dark. There was no house now, no building whatever left, but the wall of the old garden. The cleared space had been enclosed with a rough fence. Examining it, I saw that some of the old ivy had struck root anew, and was growing green on low quiet mounds of ruin. I pushed open the unlocked gate in the fence and went in.

A cold silvery mist had veiled the afternoon, and the moon was not yet up to scatter it. The stars were shining beyond the mist, and the moon was coming, and the evening was not dark. I could trace out where every part of the old house had been, and where the brewery had been, and where the gates, and where the casks. I had done so, and was looking along the desolate garden walk, when I beheld a solitary figure in it.

The figure showed itself aware of me, as I advanced. It had been moving toward me, but it stood still. As I drew nearer, I saw it to be the figure of a woman. As I drew nearer yet, it was about to turn away, when it stopped, and let me approach it. Then, it faltered as if much surprised, and uttered my name, and I cried out: "Estella!"

"I am greatly changed. I wonder you know me."

The freshness of her beauty was indeed gone, but its indescribable majesty and its indescribable charm remained. Those I had seen before. What I had never seen before was the saddened, softened light of the once proud eyes. What I had never felt before was the friendly touch of the once unfeeling hand.

We sat down on a bench that was near, and I said, "After so many years, it is strange that we should thus meet again, Estella, here where our first meeting was! Do you often come back?"

"I have never been here since."

"Nor I."

Estella was the next to break the silence. "I have very often hoped and intended to come back, but have been prevented by many circumstances. Poor, poor old place!"

The silvery mist was touched with the first rays of the moonlight, and the same rays touched the tears that dropped from her eyes. Not knowing that I saw them, and setting herself to get the better of them, she said quietly, "Were you wondering, as you walked along, how it came to be left in this condition?"

"Yes, Estella."

"The ground belongs to me. It is the only possession I have not given up. Everything else has gone from me, little by little, but I have kept this."

"Is it to be built on?"

"At last it is. I came here to take leave of it before its change. And you," she said, in a voice of touching interest to a wanderer, "you live abroad still?"

"Still."

"And do well, I am sure?"

"I work pretty hard for a sufficient living, and therefore—Yes, I do well."

"I have often thought of you," said Estella.

"You have always held your place in my heart," I answered.

And we were silent again, until she spoke.

"I little thought," said Estella, "that I should take leave of you in taking leave of this spot. I am very glad to do so."

"Glad to part again, Estella? To me, parting is a painful thing. To me, the remembrance of our last parting has been ever mournful and painful."

"But you then said to me," returned Estella, very earnestly, 'God bless you, God forgive you!'

And if you could say that to me then, you will not hesitate to say that to me now. I have been bent and broken, but—I hope—into a better shape. Be as considerate and good to me as you were, and tell me we are friends."

"We are friends," said I, rising and bending over her, as she rose from the bench.

"And will continue friends apart," said Estella.

I took her hand in mine, and we went out of the ruined place. As the morning mists had risen long ago when I first left the forge, so the evening mists were rising now. And in the tranquil light that shone upon us, I knew there would never be another parting from her.

About the Author

Great Expectations is the story of Pip. We first meet him as a young boy visiting the graves of his family in the churchyard. The book then takes us through his teenage years into adulthood. During all this time, Pip's life is shaped by what other people direct him to do. Thus, the convict in the churchyard, Pip's older sister, Miss Havisham, Mr. Jaggers, and Provis, among others, mold Pip's life. Pip reacts to these characters but rarely initiates the key events in his life. To put it differently, Pip is much more acted upon than acting. Such a point of view is hardly surprising, for Charles Dickens himself, well into his young adulthood, was at the mercy of others.

Charles Dickens was born in 1812. He was the second of eight children; several other brothers and sisters died in infancy. His father, John Dickens, worked as a clerk in the Navy Pay Office. This was a good position, and his salary should have enabled the Dickens family to lead a comfortable middle-class life. However, John Dickens was poor at managing money. In addition, every time John was transferred to a new position—often along with a cut in pay—the family had to move. Life in the Dickens family was full of uncertainties, especially financial ones. Such uncertainty is mirrored in Pip's financial fortunes. Jaggers tells him he will come into a large sum of money, but Jaggers doesn't tell him how much. Jaggers also refuses to reveal, for a long interval, the name of Pip's benefactor.

Despite the moves and the financial problems, Charles's first ten years were relatively happy. He spent five of them in the seacoast town of Chatham, where he became involved with books at an early age. He loved reading adventure stories, such as *Robinson Crusoe* and *The Arabian Nights*, and pretending he was the hero. His father and uncle took him to see plays at the local theater. They also took him to taverns, where he would stand on the counter and sing funny songs. Even as a child, Charles was creative, enjoyed jokes, and loved to perform. He did well at school, which he also enjoyed; and he seemed destined for success.

But then disaster struck. In 1822, John Dickens was transferred to London, where the cost of living was much higher than in Chatham, and bill collectors were always at the door. His parents could no longer afford to keep Charles at school. So young Charles, just a few days after his twelfth birthday, was forced to take a job at a shoe polish factory on the Thames River. Here the sensitive, intelligent twelve-year-old spent from 8 a.m. to 8 p.m., six days a week, attaching labels to bottles of shoe polish—and breathing in the unhealthy fumes of the shuttered, rat-infested factory—for six shillings a week (about 60 cents today). At the end of each long workday, Charles walked three miles to a lonely rented room in a lodging house in North London. Charles felt as if he were in prison. Later Dickens wrote that he wondered "how I could have been so easily cast away at such an age."

Matters soon became worse. On February 20, John Dickens was arrested for debt and sent to the Marshalsea debtors' prison. In Dickens's time, debtors' prisons provided living quarters for the families of the inmates. The rest of the Dickens family (except for Charles and his older sister Fanny, who had a scholarship to study music at the Royal Academy) soon joined him there. Charles, already devastated by his own imprisonment at the factory, now had to endure the further humiliation of seeing his father (and his mother and brothers and sisters) in jail.

Three months later, John Dickens was declared a bankrupt and released from prison. Not long afterward, he rescued Charles from the shoe polish factory and placed him again in school. However, his mother, Elizabeth Dickens, had wanted Charles to remain at the factory. After all, he was earning money, and his earnings helped the family. Dickens, understandably, resented his mother's attitude. Many years later, Dickens wrote, "I never afterward forgot, I never can forget, that my mother was [eager to send] me back."

Charles Dickens eventually graduated from school at age fifteen and found a job as a clerk in a law firm. He soon became bored with the law and its endless details and delays (which he would later make fun of in his own writing). His creativity and sense of fun were very much out of place in a law firm. So he studied shorthand and became a court reporter, astonishing his colleagues with how fast and accurately he could reproduce what was said during a trial. Following this, he was a newspaper reporter—and then, finally, a very famous and successful author. But he never forgot the childhood injustices—the months of mindless work in the dreary factory, the betrayal by both parents, the stigma of his father's imprisonment. Abandoned children, lonely orphans (such as Estella), evil authority figures, and dismal prison scenes recur in all the novels he wrote.

While he was still a clerk, however, Dickens resumed a habit from his childhood. He took long, leisurely walks through London's streets, seeking out the more dangerous areas where poverty and crime were common. On these walks, Dickens, who was extremely observant, saw hundreds of interesting people whose facial expressions, speech, and habits would later appear in the characters he invented.

Also, while he was still a clerk, and before he became famous, Charles Dickens fell in love. The woman he adored, Maria Beadnell, was a flirtatious blonde beauty two years older than Dickens. She was very popular, and admirers were always visiting her home. Perhaps because she was so popular, or perhaps because her family assumed Dickens would be poor all his life and could never support her, she treated Dickens quite badly. During the four years that he courted Maria, she occasionally refused his gifts, did not answer his love letters, insulted him in public, and finally stopped writing to him altogether. Dickens was completely devastated by this experience. Perhaps Dickens had this woman in mind when he created Estella. When he finally did marry, he chose a quiet, submissive woman, someone as unlike Maria as possible.

Dickens's full-time writing career began when he was in his early twenties. In 1833, he began to contribute short stories and essays to magazines. A collection of these short pieces, *Sketches by Boz* (Boz was the family's nickname for his youngest brother) appeared in 1836 and was a great success. That same year, Dickens published the first installments of *The Pickwick Papers*, another collection of stories about London life and the fictional adventures of the members of the Pickwick Club. This was the book that made Dickens world-famous. Readers loved his vivid word-pictures, not realizing that the characters Dickens described were based on real people he had met on his wanderings.

You may have noticed the word installments in the previous paragraph. In Dickens's time, books were not published all at once, as they are today. Instead, like our soap operas, they appeared a little at a time, in short sections called installments. These sections were printed and sold either separately or as part of a monthly magazine. After the final installment appeared, the publisher collected all the parts and reprinted them as a complete book. This type of publication makes a great deal of sense. Authors had more time to finish their stories (although they had strict deadlines for each part). Publishers could see how well the installments sold before going to the extra expense of printing a hardcover book. The only people who might have objected were the readers. Once they were "hooked" on a story, they had to suffer in suspense for weeks while waiting for the next few chapters to appear.

By 1836, then, Dickens was internationally popular. In that year he married Catherine Hogarth, the eldest daughter of his editor. Although they had ten children, their marriage was not a happy one, and they finally separated in 1858. Perhaps contributing to their unhappiness was Dickens's obvious infatuation with Catherine's younger sister Mary, who had come to live with the couple shortly after their marriage. Dickens referred to her as "the grace and life of our home," and when she died suddenly a year later, he was devastated. Until his own death, he wore on his finger a ring that had belonged to her. Mary's place was taken by another of Catherine's sisters, Georgiana, and Dickens is thought to have loved her, as well. He also had a long relationship with a much younger actress, Ellen Ternan, which resulted in the final breakup of his marriage. Throughout Dickens's novels we can find examples of lovely, angelic women, whose gentle efforts make life delightful for those who love them, and who inspire men to do great things. In *Great Expectations,* Biddy fulfills this role. Were these characters based on Mary, or Georgiana, or Ellen, or all three? Only Dickens could have answered this question.

Dickens's fame and popularity continued to grow throughout his lifetime. He went on to write fifteen major novels. *Great Expectations* remains one of the most acclaimed. He also traveled; he first visited the United States in 1841, and more trips followed. On these tours, and others he made within Great Britain, Dickens gave paid readings of his works, an activity Dickens loved as much as his audience. His dramatic performances of scenes from his writings, some humorous and some hair-raising, thrilled everyone who came to see them. Although these readings always tired him, more so as he grew older, Dickens continued to perform onstage for the last fifteen years of his life. He had always wanted to be an actor since the days he stood on the counter as a child and sang funny songs. He loved the cheers of his audiences as much as he appreciated the income that they provided. In addition to writing novels and giving performances, Dickens founded various journals and wrote hundreds of essays, often on the social evils of the day.

The furious pace of Dickens's life eventually took a serious toll on his health. The work, particularly the dramatic readings, simply exhausted him, yet he would not even think of giving them up. In 1869 he collapsed after one of his public performances, and his doctors ordered him to stop performing. However, he ignored their advice. The following year, while only part way through writing his final novel, *The Mystery of Edwin Drood*, he suffered a massive stroke and died the next day.

Dickens is buried at Westminster Abbey in London—the greatest honor possible for a British author. The inscription on his tombstone reads: "He was a sympathiser to the poor, the suffering, and the oppressed; and by his death, one of England's greatest writers is lost to the world."

About the Book

Charles Dickens is arguably the greatest novelist in the English language. One of the reasons for Dickens's lofty status is his ability to include many human emotions and experiences within a single book. *Great Expectations* is an excellent case in point.

First and foremost, *Great Expectations* tells a wonderful and universal story: the adventures of a young boy who grows to manhood. We first meet Pip in the village churchyard where his parents and siblings are buried. Pip is a simple lad, symbolized by the very simplicity of his name. Dickens has named him well; the word pip means "seed"—and, like a seed, Pip will grow and flourish as the book goes on.

At the beginning of *Great Expectations*, Pip lives with two unworldly adults, his mean-spirited sister and her husband, the blacksmith Joe. Joe, by contrast to Pip's sister, is almost saintly in his kindness, but he too is a bit simple-minded. At this stage of his life, Pip knows very well what his future will be like. He will be apprenticed to Joe and will work in a forge.

Then, one day, the ever-meddlesome Mr. Pumblechook informs Pip that a mysterious and wealthy lady desires to amuse herself by watching a young boy play. Suddenly, Pip is thrust into the much more glamorous world of Miss Havisham and Estella. For the first time in his life, he feels inferior to someone else; for the first time in his life, he dreams of things he cannot have.

Pip's development proceeds further when he is informed that he is to come into "great expectations." At this point, he leaves Joe and the forge and moves to London, where he will become what he has dreamed of being—a gentleman. Pip's education in London is not limited to the schoolroom. He learns firsthand about fine clothes, fine dining, and debt; about the injustice of the justice system; about false appearances and true devotion—lessons often mastered painfully and at a great price. As the book continues, so does Pip's education, until he reaches full manhood and, sadder but wiser, goes abroad to seek his fortune. Pip's progress toward responsibility and self-awareness is, in one form or another, the journey that we all must take.

While Pip's development serves as the main plot of *Great Expectations*, the novel also includes other themes. *Great Expectations* is also a love story, or, in reality, several love stories. The central romantic plot involves Pip and Estella. Pip falls in love with the stony-cold Estella at first sight. Conditioned by the twisted mind of Miss Havisham to taunt and disdain all mankind, Estella both welcomes and repels Pip's attentions until the novel's very end. Indeed, Pip suffers unending torment from the time he first sees Estella until he meets her upon the ashen ruins of Satis House. Yet he cannot, and will not, forget her.

In *Great Expectations*, Dickens shows us several

forms of love—the most powerful of human emotions. There is devotion to an aged parent, as seen in Wemmick's and Clara Barley's treatment of their very different fathers. Another kind of familial love in *Great Expectations* is that of a father, or father-figure, for his son. The strongest example of this kind of love is Magwitch's love for Pip. This love is one-sided, as Pip feels gratitude, but little affection, for his benefactor and "second father." Magwitch, in contrast, has devoted much of his adult life to the young boy who brought him food and a file during his escape on the marsh, and intends to bestow upon Pip the riches he has accumulated, once released from jail in Australia. Still another example of paternal love can be seen in Joe Gargery's feelings for Pip. Joe is a warm-hearted individual to begin with. Only a forgiving soul could remain in the same house with such a dragon of a wife. Joe's love for Pip is virtually boundless. Even after Pip takes up his life in London and neglects to write to Joe, the blacksmith's affection for Pip does not recede. Joe even comes to London to tend to Pip during his illness and delirium. Finally, Dickens shows us other examples, happier ones, of romantic love. Wemmick feels romantic love for Miss Skiffins. Herbert Pocket has fallen in love with the faithful Clara. Both Herbert and Wemmick marry before the book ends. Joe, who certainly deserves a second chance at marital happiness, also finally finds it at the end of the novel.

Is Miss Havisham's story also one of love? We

do not learn much about her romance with Compeyson, who deserts her on their wedding day. The magnitude of her love can only be gauged by her behavior following that fateful day. Certainly, a moderate devotion would not have inspired her to stop the clocks, keep the wedding cake, shut out the light, and don the yellowing wedding dress. We can only assume that her love was extraordinarily intense. Only a monumental love can give rise to a monumental disappointment.

The desire for revenge is another emotion that Dickens explores in *Great Expectations.* After Compeyson deserts her, Miss Havisham seeks revenge against the entire male gender. Her instrument of revenge is Estella, her adopted daughter. Miss Havisham grooms Estella to win the hearts of countless suitors—including Pip—only to disappoint them. Miss Havisham hopes to plunge these suitors into the same grief she herself feels. Ironically, she herself suffers when Estella confesses that she feels no love for her. Another story of revenge involves Magwitch and Compeyson. Magwitch blames Compeyson for manipulating him and getting him to take the blame for illegal acts committed by both. Magwitch attacks Compeyson on the marshes at the beginning of the book. Near the end, Magwitch drowns Compeyson when Magwitch is on the point of escaping from England, but in the struggle, he is once again captured. Finally, Orlick's story is largely one of revenge. He blames Pip for the slights he feels while working at the forge. Orlick's anger is so great that he even tries to murder Pip by placing his body in the kiln on the marsh. Miss Havisham, Magwitch, and Orlick are equally single-minded in their determination to exact vengeance on their perceived persecutors. Perhaps appropriately, they suffer almost equally as a result.

Finally, *Great Expectations* is a mystery. Dickens presents the reader with an abundance of puzzles. Why does someone want to shower "great expectations" upon Pip? Who is this benefactor, and why must his or her identity remain a secret? Who is responsible for the savage attack on Mrs. Joe? Why does Miss Havisham preserve the trappings of the past? What is the true relationship between Miss Havisham and Estella? Will Pip manage to help Magwitch escape a second time? Will Pip and Estella ever find true love together?

A young boy's education and growth to manhood, several love stories, revenge, mystery—all of these are present in *Great Expectations.* It is a tribute to Dickens's artfulness that he weaves together all these themes and more within the pages of a single novel, one which is destined to remain a favorite for years to come.

If you liked
Great Expectations
you might be interested in other books in the Townsend Library.

continued on the following pages

JACK LONDON
White Fang
TP THE TOWNSEND LIBRARY

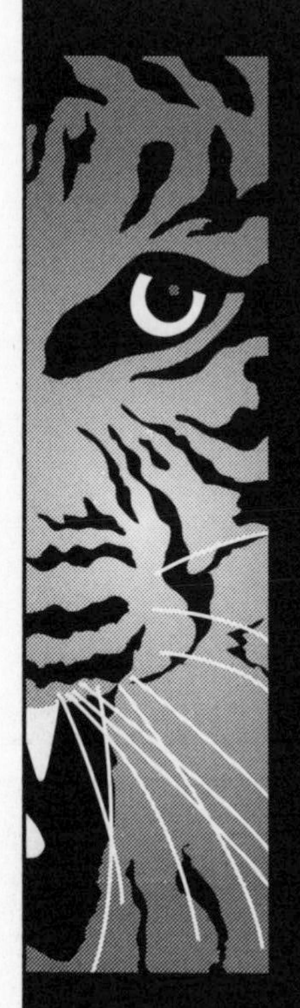

THE Jungle BOOK

RUDYARD KIPLING

THE TOWNSEND LIBRARY 

ANNA SEWELL

BLACK BEAUTY

The Autobiography of a Horse

TP THE TOWNSEND LIBRARY

THE ADVENTURES OF

TOM SAWYER

MARK TWAIN

TP THE TOWNSEND LIBRARY

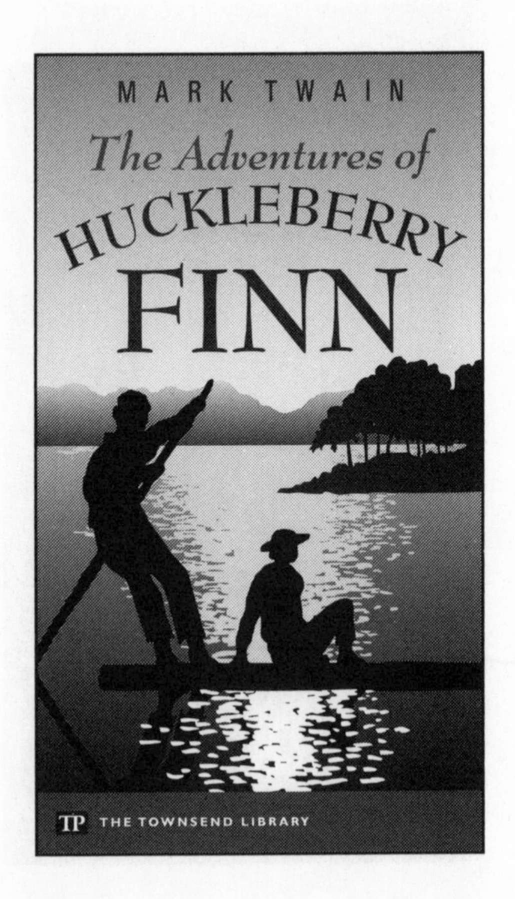
MARK TWAIN
The Adventures of
HUCKLEBERRY
FINN
TP THE TOWNSEND LIBRARY

LAUGHTER AND CHILLS

SEVEN GREAT STORIES

THE STORYTELLER

THE RANSOM OF RED CHIEF

THE OPEN WINDOW

THE CASK OF AMONTILLADO

THE TELL-TALE HEART

THE LEGEND OF SLEEPY HOLLOW

A CHRISTMAS CAROL

MARK TWAIN

The Prince and The Pauper

TP THE TOWNSEND LIBRARY

CHARLOTTE BRONTE

JANE EYRE

TP THE TOWNSEND LIBRARY

Charles Dickens

A TALE OF TWO CITIES

TP THE TOWNSEND LIBRARY